Published by Brett Pedersen writing under the pseudonym Conrad Bux

PO Box 318, Red Hill, Queensland, 4059, Australia

Visit the author's website at www.conradbux.com

ISBN: 978-0-9756554-0-5 (ebook)

ISBN: 978-0-9756554-1-2 (paperback)

Book cover design by 100 Covers

Interior design created in Atticus

Edited by 39 Toes

This first edition published in 2024

For my most beautiful wife

For always believing

Will you marry me again?

For we wrestle not against flesh and blood, but against principalities, against powers, against the rulers of the darkness of this world, against spiritual wickedness in high places.

Book of Ephesians 6:12

Prologue

P ersistent knocking jerked Jeremy out of his nightmare.

His elevated heart rate quickened in sync with the banging on the door. Disoriented, he struggled to remember what he'd been dreaming. Whatever it was, it had been disturbing enough to wake him up. Or had that been the relentless pounding after all?

He sat up, turned and let his legs slide down over the edge of the bed, then leaned forward and pried apart two metal slats of the Venetian blinds.

The sky was black. It was a typical Perth night: cloudless, freezing cold and so clear Jeremy felt he could reach up and grab one of the millions of stars glowing overhead. The blue glow from the nearly full moon illuminated his small front yard. The short, pebbled walkway leading up to the front door ended in a paved portico that, although small and narrow, was big enough to hide anyone standing behind one of its pillars. From this angle, the welcome mat and front door weren't visible. Jeremy scanned the yard.

The front gate was open.

Knock, knock, knock.

Jeremy let go of the slats and switched on the bedside table lamp. He turned to see his wife still sleeping. She was on her side, facing away from him. Her blonde hair was spilling over the pillow. The red digits of her bedside table clock displayed 3:26 AM.

Jeremy's unease grew. In boxers and a T-shirt, he walked around the bed and over to the mirrored wardrobe on his wife's side. Watching the mirror, he quietly slid one door open. His wife had one hand under her chin, eyes shut. Jeremy reached into the corner of the wardrobe and felt the reassuring rubber grip of his baseball bat. He retrieved it and was about to turn for the hallway when she began opening her eyes.

Her brows bounced up and down, and then her eyes grew wide. "What the hell, Jeremy?"

Jeremy raised an index finger and held it vertically in front of his pursed lips.

Knock, knock, knock, knock.

Bat tucked behind his back, he turned and tiptoed out of their small bedroom, into the narrow hallway and took three steps up to the front door. He was thinking about who it could possibly be when it banged on the door again.

"Who is it?" Jeremy said.

"It's Richard," a man said.

Jeremy tried to remember a Richard. He thought hard and gripped the bat even harder. It definitely wasn't a colleague. No one from his local boxing club was named Richard. Or from the scuba diving group. Most of his wife's girlfriends were married, but none of them to a Richard. Teachers from Sebastian's primary school? From Hannah's high school? Parents? Neighbors?

"Richard who?" Jeremy said. He'd been to the local pub in Butler last week, gotten drunk, spoken with a few people. No one came to mind.

"You know," the man said. Then, after a brief pause, "Richard."

The voice was gravelly. Slightly hoarse. And older. The man on the other side of the door would have to be someone in his fifties. Maybe sixties.

Jeremy relaxed his grip on the baseball bat. He went through possible connections again, starting with the people they knew best, all the way out to the bigger circle of acquaintances, people at the periphery of their lives. He even tried to remember name tags of all the employees they had become accustomed to greeting when doing their weekly grocery shopping. Amanda's colleagues. The family dentist. The woman selling tickets at the sports arena with the big pool they liked to frequent.

Then something triggered.

Jeremy felt a knot growing in the pit of his stomach. But that couldn't be. That was a different time. A different life.

"People call me Dick," the man said. "Sometimes 'Big Dick', as well as many other versions, I'm sure."

The baseball bat vibrated in Jeremy's hand. He was shaking. He turned and saw his wife had appeared in the doorway. Sebastian was in his room, still asleep. Hannah was camping in a small tent in the backyard. Everyone he loved was right here.

"And I'll admit," the voice on the other side of the door said, "you were damn difficult to find. Took some time too. Not to mention a lot of money."

Jeremy shook his head. "You've got the wrong house, mate!"

3

There was a low chuckle. "Oh, I don't think so. You were a star witness in the trial that put my brother away," the guy said. "For a very, very long time."

Jeremy tightened his grip on the baseball bat, held it with both hands and took up position as a professional batter. His whole body was shaking. "I've never been at a trial in my entire life," he said.

"Although, of course," the man said, "you were known under a different name back then."

Jeremy froze.

"You know you're going to have to let me in eventually. Better you and I talk rather than involve your wife," the man said. "Not to mention your beautiful children."

A patter of small feet sneaked up behind Jeremy, who turned and saw his son in his blue pajamas. Jeremy dropped the bat and picked him up. He hugged him tight and smelled soap and baby skin. Even though his son was growing into a big boy, Jeremy could sometimes still smell the newborn. The little blue trains on Sebastian's pajama top were smiling. So much time had passed, yet so very little.

Jeremy had done everything he possibly could to start fresh. To do good. To protect. He'd eventually managed to forget about the past, but the past clearly hadn't forgotten about him. This was something he could no longer run from. No need to even try—it would just make everything worse. That much he knew.

Sebastian's small fingers fiddled with Jeremy's left cheek.

"Why are you crying, Daddy?"

Jeremy looked his son in the eyes, forced a smile, then shrugged. He gave his son a kiss on the forehead, then turned and opened the front door wide.

A small, balding man stood outside, his cashmere coat buttoned up, a scarf shielding his neck from the chilly night. Behind him, on the other side of the street, a large, black four-by-four was idling, headlights off.

Richard took a quick peek left and right, then raised his gun. "You know you only have yourself to blame," he said.

Jeremy nodded, then hugged his son even tighter.

He didn't hear the shot, didn't feel the impact of the bullet. At 1,200 feet per second, the lead pierced Sebastian's heart just short of two milliseconds before it tore through his dad's.

Thirty seconds later, Jeremy's wife breathed her last while running through the house, her screams muted by the shot and the crunch of her head hitting the marble counter before she landed, face down, on the cold tiles of the kitchen floor.

Then Richard searched the rest of the house.

ONE

Frank was waiting for his first client.

He readjusted his seating position, trying to make himself comfortable on the wooden stool, then tugged at the front of his short-sleeved shirt. His huge teardrop gut stretched the cotton, making the shirt stick to his skin. Frank felt droplets running down his lower back and into his khaki Bermuda shorts. He was sweating in the fold underneath his belly, and the back of his thighs were burning due to heat and partially cut-off circulation.

Although the AC was cranked up all the way, the Brisbane heat and humidity still permeated the space. Late-afternoon traffic outside the window had slowed to a crawl in the subtropical downpour. Bemused, Frank watched a man in a suit running while holding an open magazine above his head, hopping and skipping to avoid the deep puddles. His light-blue suit was a darker shade from the middle of his tie, all the way down to his soaked shoes. A woman shrieked as a bus roared through its lane and hit a large pothole, spraying the entire sidewalk from curb to shopfronts.

Frank checked his wristwatch again, pulled at his damp shirt for the fifth time, then took another sip of his cappuccino. He eyed his plate and confirmed yet again that there really only were crumbs left.

He hated waiting. Couldn't stand it when people were late. His German genes often had to fight hard to fit into the relaxed—not to mention incredibly hot—Queensland lifestyle. Yet he loved the place. Over the past eighteen months, it had grown on him. It was completely different from his home country, but, Frank supposed, that was a big part of the attraction. He would have liked to stay for longer—a lot longer—but with his recent suspension from his sponsored workplace, time was running out fast. Frank would somehow have to get back on track and either get the suspension lifted or find another visa sponsor. And right now, neither option seemed plausible.

And it definitely wasn't a lack of skill that had earned him the suspension—without pay. It was an asshole of a boss who didn't understand that knowledge, experience and intelligence were far more important than a stupid fitness test. So what he was a few pounds overweight? Or that he wasn't a born runner? But Frank suspected there were other reasons why Australian Federal Police Commander Gregory Fordham had been busy getting Frank suspended from the AFP. For one, Gregory had always despised Frank; from the get-go, their relationship had been strained, greetings curt and opinions different. If it weren't for his gut feeling telling him otherwise, Frank would have simply put it down to cultural differences.

But Frank still had bills to pay. And as he didn't have the required credentials, he couldn't work as a private investigator officially; hence, his current and only payment arrangement—cash in hand. And

Frank supposed his PI career would be short-lived, which meant he couldn't commit to long-term leases, let alone invest in commercial real estate; hence, his current office—the local Mugs & Marmalade on Melbourne Street, South Brisbane.

Frank was savoring the smell of freshly baked donuts and pastry and melted cheese and freshly brewed coffee when, finally—and twelve minutes late—the small shopkeeper's bell tinkled. He lifted his gaze to a stunning woman standing in the doorway, surveying the room.

His first client.

Two

F rank's heart stopped.

She was wearing a simple cream dress with impossibly thin straps, the printed red flowers perfectly matching her red stiletto ankle-strap shoes. Somehow—and Frank really wasn't sure how she'd done it—she'd managed to stay completely dry. Not an umbrella in sight, just a tiny red purse hanging from one bare, tanned shoulder.

Had she been perhaps ten pounds heavier, and with freckles instead of a tan, she would have been the spitting image of Frank's dead wife.

Frank stood up, pulled at his shirt again, and waited for her gaze to fall on him. When it did, he raised a finger and smiled. The woman walked over and extended a freshly manicured hand.

"Frank Hofmann?" she asked.

Frank wiped his meaty hand on his shorts, then shook hers gently. Even her nails were red. "Pleased to meet you, Rebecca," he said.

The woman smiled. Her teeth were as white as German snow.

Frank plopped back on his stool while his client elegantly positioned herself across from him at the narrow table. As she eased herself onto a stool, Frank's eyes automatically sought her cleavage.

He forced himself to look up. Her warm blue eyes looked around the room. Her blonde, straight hair flowed down her back.

She leaned forward, her eyes settling on Frank's. "I was hoping for somewhere a bit more private?"

Frank shrugged. "Sorry," he said. "There're a couple of reasons why I asked you to meet me here, the number one most important being that they have great coffee. Can I get you one?"

Rebecca shook her head, keeping her voice down. "The ad said you can help with anything?"

Frank leaned in as well, nodded. "I began my career in Germany. Joined the army straight after school, spent a few years with a commando unit, then got a job with the state police, then the German Federal Police. I've worked in homicide, missing persons, organized crime, violent crimes, people smuggling, plus a bunch of other areas that were either mind-numbingly boring or shockingly horrific," he said, then scratched his red goatee. "Whatever you need help with, you don't have to worry. I'm qualified."

Rebecca looked impressed. "You don't seem that old."

"Forty-two."

"Do you work for the police here in Brisbane?"

Frank leaned back, crossed his arms and turned his face to the window. The shower had eased up and white clouds drifted past above the brown block that was the Queensland Performing Arts Centre. Time heals all wounds. After the rain, the sun will shine. Nothing is forever. All of it bullshit. Frank looked back at the woman. "What can I help you with?"

Rebecca blushed. "I think I'm being followed."

Frank uncrossed his arms and put his elbows on the table. "You think?"

"Actually," she said, "I'm sure. A few weeks ago, I literally bumped into a man at my local supermarket. I noticed him because . . . well, because he was good-looking. Tall, muscular, in his thirties, blond, styled hair. He wore a tight blue-checkered shirt and jeans that were stone-washed all the way back to the eighties."

Frank chuckled. "What makes you think he was following you?"

Rebecca leaned in further. "Two days later, I was having a mani-pedi at my local salon in the Valley. My regular nail technician—Nancy is her name—was giving me an exfoliating foot scrub when the doorbell went off as a customer entered. The sound must have caught my attention, because I looked up, and there he was, sitting on a bench just outside the shop window, pretending to read a newspaper."

Frank scratched his red goatee again. "Pretending?"

Rebecca shrugged. "Well, come on, Frank. Who reads the newspaper these days?"

"I do."

Rebecca was silent for a moment. "Well, you're over forty. That's probably different."

"It probably is," Frank said, nodding. "That it?"

Rebecca shook her head. "Over the past few weeks, I've seen him up the street when I leave my home. I've seen him sitting a few tables away when I'm out having a drink with friends. Just last week, I left my local hair salon, and I looked diagonally across the street, and guess what?"

Frank played along. "What?"

"There he was again, jumping into his car. He clearly didn't want me to spot him because he moved really quickly. But I did spot him. Same build, same hair, same jeans."

Frank nodded. "Secret admirer? Some kind of stalker?"

Rebecca shrugged. "I mean, I've had romances, brief relationships, but I've never had an issue with jealous guys or anything like that."

"And are you currently single?"

Rebecca lowered her gaze to the table between them, held it there for a while, her eyes seemingly unfocused. She shook her head, then looked up at Frank. "Technically, yes," she said. "Widowed."

Frank made big eyes. "I'm so sorry," he said.

Rebecca shrugged. "Just one of those things. My husband died five years ago and I've moved on."

Frank nodded. "Any direct threats from your stalker?"

Rebecca shook her head.

"Have you seen him near your workplace?"

"I don't work." Rebecca seemed to consider her words before continuing. "I don't have to. My husband left me a lot of money."

"Have you told the police any of this?"

Rebecca raised her perfectly plucked eyebrows, then lifted her hands and made air quotes. "'Ms. Wright, we can't pursue a case of a man who may or may not be following you,'" she said, then lowered her hands. "They're not interested in my story, Frank. It's probably the usual. He'd have to kill me before the police would want to get involved."

"Hmmm," Frank said. "And what would you like me to do?"

Rebecca looked surprised. "I need you to find out who this guy is, and, more importantly, why he's following me."

"Do you have any other information on him?"

Rebecca reached into her purse and took out a small square of folded paper, handed it to Frank. "I wrote down the license plate of the car I saw him leave in."

Frank nodded. He was impressed. He scratched around his belly button, then ran his fingers through his tousled, red hair that was stiff and poking out at the back due to a mix of dried sweat and AC. On one hand, he wasn't quite sure how to breach the subject, hadn't prepared for it either. On the other hand, Rebecca appeared to be a woman of means, so an opportunity was definitely there.

Finally, Frank said, "I can help, but it's going to be expensive, and I'll need payment upfront." He thought about his unregistered PI business, the fact that he was still technically employed by the AFP, as well as all the potential risks involving the Australian Taxation Office, so he added: "Cash."

"How much?" Rebecca asked, then took out a red wallet that matched her purse.

Frank then thought about rent, utilities, eateries he liked to frequent, and fuel for his big sedan. But even more importantly, he still hadn't bought any equipment for his little start-up. He'd need, at the very least, a good camera. More stuff if things turned out well, money to send his belongings back to Germany if they didn't.

"Ten thousand dollars. Five now," Frank said, "five when I find out who he is and what he wants."

Rebecca didn't flinch. "Fine," she said, then put her wallet back in her purse. "But I'll have to go to the bank."

Frank wriggled off the stool while carefully extending his lower limbs. He held onto the edge of the table as pins and needles spread in tune with his blood returning to his legs. His lower back was stiff and sore and a slight headache was building. "I'll come with you. Let's walk," he said, then checked his watch. "I could use a cigarette."

Rebecca stood up, clutching her purse with both hands. "You said there were a couple of reasons you wanted to meet here?"

Frank nodded.

"And you said the coffee is great, so what's the other reason?"

Frank smiled. This was a woman to watch. She was obviously both attentive and smart. Frank nodded to the plate with crumbs. "The bagels," he said. "The bagels are amazing."

THREE

F rank nosed his big sedan into a slot straight outside the door of his local family practice in Kelvin Grove. His rented flat was only a five-minute walk away, but he'd had to take the car to get to Mugs & Marmalade in Melbourne Street. It was true that he loved the coffee and bagels there, but a definite bonus was the distance he could put between his private home and work. An added precaution that was important, at least when it worked, which it didn't always, as Frank had learned a long time ago. The hard way. In Germany.

As soon as Frank entered the small reception, he introduced himself and was waved straight down the hall where, at the very end, a door was ajar. Frank approached it and knocked.

"Come in."

Dr. Lee was originally from Singapore. He was old, small, skinny and incredibly energetic. His white hair crowned smiling, all-seeing eyes that radiated compassion to a point that made Frank uncomfortable. He didn't think he deserved this man's goodwill and help. Definitely didn't feel ready to listen to what would undoubtedly turn out to be sound advice.

Dr. Lee pointed to a chair at the end of his small desk. "Have a seat, Frank," he said, then tapped away at his keyboard. It impressed Frank that a man his age could touch-type.

Frank sat down, wished that he were somewhere different.

Dr. Lee looked at his computer screen, mumbled something to himself, then nodded, clasped his hands in his lap and turned to Frank.

"Frank, the results from your tests have come back."

Frank sighed. "Okay Doc," he said. "Hit me with it."

Dr. Lee's smile disappeared. "Frank, you have developed type 2 diabetes. It's nothing to panic about," the doctor said, then raised one finger and smiled again, "if—and this is a big *if*, Frank—you do something about it now."

Frank nodded.

"Please," the doctor said, then gestured to the scales. "Hop on, let's see how you've been faring since your last visit."

Frank reluctantly stood up, took his phone out of one pocket, his wallet and keys out of the other, then removed his wristwatch and placed them all on the corner of the doctor's desk. Frank took off his shoes and stepped up. The digits flashed three times before steadily displaying a number.

The doctor craned his neck, noted Frank's weight and went back to his computer. "You can step down now."

Frank put everything back in his pockets, put his watch and shoes back on and sat back down.

The doctor placed a cuff on Frank's left arm, slid it up past his elbow and closed the velcro flap. Then he leaned over and pressed a button and the cuff began expanding and Frank felt his heart rate increase. He never knew if it was the constricting of the blood flow or his anticipation of another poor result. Then the machine beeped, the cuff deflated and Dr. Lee removed it again.

"Frank, the diabetes, combined with your high blood pressure and excessive weight, can cause significant, long-term damage if you don't take it seriously. Are you working with the dietitian I referred you to last time you were here?"

"Not yet," Frank said, then scratched his red goatee. "I've been extremely busy."

"Okay, how are you going on exercising? Are you at least doing some daily walks? What about the swimming you mentioned?"

Frank nodded. "I've walked a bit."

Dr. Lee sighed. "How's your mental health?" His smile had disappeared again and his voice had taken on a timbre that Frank hadn't heard before.

Frank didn't answer. Didn't know what to say.

"I only ask because you have gained weight again. You are now in the morbidly obese category."

Dr. Lee's eyes could penetrate the deepest, darkest corner of Frank's soul. He had the ability to tear down Frank's defenses by simply looking at him. Frank desperately needed to get out of that office, away from this man who could pinpoint the essence and truth in Frank's armor that was humor, deflection and—perhaps his favorite—denial.

"We're going to have to start you on some medication, Frank, unless you change your habits immediately. And by immediately, I mean today."

Frank tried not to choke on his words as he stood up. "I'll get right on it, Doc," he said, then tried on a smile and headed back out.

Four

F rank closed his eyes.

He didn't know what to choose. He was smoking and thinking. Thinking and smoking. One hand on the steering wheel and the other hand dangling his cigarette out the window, occasionally returning it to his lips for an inhale, then back out the window. He loved the feeling of hot smoke descending into his lungs, scratching the eternal itch and numbing his nerves, suppressing his appetite and buzzing his brain. Frank closed his eyes, puffed and contemplated. Contemplated and puffed. Choices, choices.

Finally, after a lengthy deliberation—and the car behind him honking twice—he opened his eyes, leaned out, spoke into the metal stand and ordered a double cheeseburger meal with a ginger beer, an extra hamburger and a caramel sundae. Then he rolled forward to the window and opened the glove compartment. Green one-hundred-dollar bills were floating around on top of a yellowed instruction manual from 1998 that had a faded cover photo of his car from when it had been brand new. Frank stuck a hand inside and grabbed one of the bills. He paid, threw the change back inside the glove compartment, snapped it shut, then rolled forward to the

19

next window and got his food. Then he drove around the restaurant, parked the car, flicked his cigarette butt into a nearby bush and dug in.

While eating, Frank thought about how to attack his first PI job. Perhaps he should get a still camera and a video camera. Maybe he could even get a gadget that did both, but it would have to be small enough to hide, and he'd need something plausible to hide it in. But, even more importantly, he'd need access to information. Information that could only be obtained through certain databases. Databases that only existed withing a few select law enforcement agencies. Such as the AFP.

Of course, he could try faking a call to the Department of Transport and Main Roads to see if he could get some information on the license plate details Rebecca had given him. But there was a good chance that it wouldn't work. And even if it did, the information he'd attain would most probably be limited, any details definitely sparse and so, ultimately, useless.

He desperately needed access.

It was time to find out if he'd made any real friends during his short stint with the AFP. And what better place to start than with his former and only partner?

Frank dug into the paper bag for a napkin, then eyed three runaway fries rattling around the bottom. He stuffed them into his mouth, then took out his phone and dialed a number he knew from memory.

Or, to be more Frank, by heart.

FIVE

Amy Lamborne spiraled downward, moving deeper into the underground car park until she hit the bottom level and screeched around the last corner where she stopped, then reversed her tiny, brand-new, cherry-red convertible into her corner slot. Her AFP federal agent salary hadn't been enough for her to buy the car cash, but she'd at least gathered a healthy down payment and had then negotiated a reasonable interest rate on the remaining chunk she'd had to finance.

Her black ankle boots clicked all the way from her car, across the parking expanse, past the elevators, through a fire escape door and onto the polished concrete of the stairs. She grabbed the metal banister and took two steps at a time, running up three parking levels, passed the ground floor and climbed one more level. Amy walked over to a red metal door that had a foot-long, white-painted *1* on it, pulled it open and stepped across the threshold into a different world: an air-conditioned haven of beige walls, artwork and plush hallway carpet. She inhaled deeply, savoring the smell of fresh paint, new carpet and what reminded her of glued, compressed wood. She was looking forward to putting her sore feet up and, with Jason doing evening shifts, enjoying the peacefulness of her own company, a cold beer in one hand and her recent online purchase in the other: a crisp crime novel by her favorite author.

She strolled down the hallway, found her apartment door, inserted a shiny key and felt the satisfying, minute vibration of well-oiled tumblers within a brand-new lock. Once inside, the door clicked shut behind her and Amy dropped her keys and wallet in the blue glass bowl she'd recently found at her local Saturday market in the adjacent park. She knew nothing about antiques—if that's indeed what it was—she'd simply found it pretty and, more importantly, cheap. Amy pulled off her boots and hung her black suit jacket—AFP credentials in the inside pocket—on a coat hanger inside her little hallway wardrobe.

As she entered the kitchen and open living area, a pleasant breeze met her. The ducted AC was still on and the bamboo ceiling fans were spinning silently. With utility prices soaring, she mentally swore at Jason for not switching everything off before heading to work, but simultaneously felt grateful for coming home to a cool apartment.

Having been able to secure such a beautiful, off-the-plan apartment in the posh West End of Brisbane filled Amy's heart with joy. With Jason's salary as a supermarket security guard and her Commonwealth Grade Six salary, they'd just managed to squeeze in by opting for the smallest of the two-bedroom properties at the bottom of the building. Fewer square feet, one bedroom windowless, as well as no view of the adjacent Brisbane River, all translated into huge discounts. And Amy loved every bit of it. To her, the deal didn't diminish the wonderful feeling of having secured a prime piece of property close to the city, in a beautiful building boasting amazing amenities.

Amy placed her phone on the kitchen countertop, then turned and grabbed a beer out of the fridge. She twisted off the cap and downed half. Then she took off her black trousers and blue shirt, threw them over the back of the couch and walked out onto her small balcony. Wearing panties and bra only, she sat down in a plush, faux-wicker chair and put her feet up onto the other.

Although the apartment was technically the lowest in the building, it was on top of the residents' gym, which was set above a high-ceilinged lobby. All in all, it was roughly as high up as a traditional flat on level three would have been. Amy took another swig of her beer. The street below was buzzing with the usual activity of locals; some were pulling wheeled shopping trolleys along the sidewalk while others were walking their dogs. People on orange and purple electric scooters were zooming about, most of them heading down in the direction of the river.

Amy relaxed, inhaled deeply and let her mind wander while humming along to Lalo Schifrin's "Burning Fuse". She loved the jazzy instrumental, and she took pride in knowing the name of the Argentine composer and title of the famous piece that most people simply knew as the *Mission: Impossible* theme song. Then she realized it was her phone ringing. She sighed, stood up and went back inside.

The display showed UNKNOWN CALLER.

Amy kept her eyes on the phone, took another swig, considered whether to pick up.

Six

F rank was about to hang up when the dial tone was replaced by static silence. He waited a beat, then decided to speak first.

"Amy?" he said. "It's me."

Even with the driver's side window open, Frank's big sedan was heating up rapidly.

"Frank?" Amy said. "Bloody hell, how are you? And why are you calling from a blocked number?"

"Old habits die hard," Frank said, then brought her up to speed on what amounted to roughly six weeks of limbo since his suspension; eateries he'd discovered, movies he'd watched, the latest crime fiction novel he was reading.

"Sounds like you're having a blast," Amy said.

"Hmmm," Frank said, wiping sweat off his forehead with the back of his hand. "The reason I'm calling is that I wanted to tell you I secured my first client today."

"Waw! Congratulations, Frank," Amy said. "So the ad I put in *The Brisbane Post* really worked?"

"Indeed," Frank said. "You did a great job, so I really only need one more thing from you."

"What's that?"

"It really isn't much," Frank said. Then, perhaps to convince himself more than Amy, "not much at all."

Silence filled the space between them, and Frank removed the phone from his ear as he realized the screen was wet with his sweat. He wiped it on his shorts, started the engine, cranked the AC up all the way, then rolled up his window.

"What's that noise?" Amy said.

"I'm in my car. Had to turn the AC on."

"No, that whining, chugging noise."

"Ah," Frank said. "I probably need a new timing belt."

Amy's electronically distorted laughter came through Frank's tiny phone speaker. He couldn't help but smile himself.

"Frank, you don't even know what a timing belt is, do you?"

Frank shrugged to no one. "Probably not, but I've heard people talk about these things, and for a moment there, I thought it sounded good."

Amy giggled.

"How's your new partner?" Frank asked.

"He's Scottish and, believe it or not, shorter than I am."

Frank feigned surprise in his voice, tried to do a Scottish accent. "You're working with Ewan McShortbread?"

Amy laughed again. "His name is Joe McAvoy, and he used to be with Major Crimes in Scotland."

"How long is he staying for?"

"As long as he wants, I guess."

"What sort of visa did *he* get?"

"His wife is Aussie."

"Yeah, that takes care of that," Frank said, nodding to the front windscreen. "Which makes me wonder, Amy, would you ever consider—"

"Shut up, Frank," Amy said.

Frank didn't say anything.

"What else is new?"

Frank sighed. "Just came back from the doctor's and, apart from being a few kilos overweight, all is good."

"I'm happy to hear that."

"Do you know what I've been thinking?" Frank said, not waiting for an answer. "Six months after I started with the AFP, while you and I were investigating those cold-case murders, I failed my first biannual fitness test, and Greg let it slide."

"Well, a year ago, it wasn't quite as, eh . . . bad, right?" Amy said. "I mean, it was a fail, but, as far as you told me, only just."

Frank's ear was getting hot, so he swapped the phone into his other hand and held it to his other ear. "Does it matter?" he said. "It's pass or fail, right? And then, as we dug deeper into those cases, we found patterns—"

"They were patterns to *you*, Frank."

"Okay, they were patterns to me, but do you remember how quickly Gregory got us doing different assignments once I began airing my theories and—"

"I remember all that, Frank. Where are you going with this?"

Frank shrugged again. "Same as always, I guess. I just want to get to the truth, catch the bad guys and sleep well at night."

"Anyway . . ." Amy said, drawing out the word.

Frank took the hint, thought about what to say next as an ibis walked past his driver's door and poked its long, curved, black beak at a few scattered fries soaking in a small puddle. "Anyway," he said. "Did you move yet?"

Amy told Frank about the final steps of the purchase and settlement, the days she'd been shopping for furniture, about the move itself and that she'd now been living there for all of two weeks. She was still exhausted from it all, close to broke because of purchases, bills and the fact that her former landlord had kept her deposit from her previous rental. But all in all, she was very happy.

When she was done filling him in, Frank hoped that he'd hit a sweet spot with his question about her new apartment. He let the silence work for him.

Finally, Amy spoke again. "Okay, Frank. What do you need?"

Frank told her what he needed.

SEVEN

A my put her phone down and left the rest of the beer.

She was thinking about what Frank had just suggested. If she was going to do it, her best option would be to go back to work straight away. This late in the afternoon, Gregory Fordham would have gone home for sure, meaning Amy could work undisturbed. If anyone else was hanging around the offices, she would just say that she was doing overtime.

Then a hand was on her shoulder.

Amy shrieked and spun on her heels at once. It took a moment for her nerves to realign, to take in the figure looming over her. "Jason? What the bloody hell!"

"Who was that?" Jason said, nodding to the phone on the kitchen countertop. He was wearing his favorite outfit: red sneakers, black basketball shorts and a matching jersey with huge red digits showing *13*.

"I thought you were at work," Amy said, looking him up and down. "Weren't you supposed to be at work now?"

"I asked you," Jason said, crossing his arms, his pecs and biceps and triceps bulging and flexing in front of her eyes. "Who was that?"

Jason had always been jealous, but this was different. Amy wondered if it had to do with him not enjoying his job, a job he'd had to stick with for them to obtain their mortgage, or perhaps he felt he could behave this way now that they had finally moved in together? She wasn't sure where it was coming from, but she certainly didn't like it. Not one bit.

"It was a colleague," she said.

"Joe?"

"No."

"It was your beloved Frank, wasn't it? Who isn't a colleague at all, is he? So what's he doing calling you?"

Amy frowned. She suddenly felt exposed and vulnerable in her underwear. "What the hell is your problem?"

"My problem is you sneaking around, laughing and having a ball with your hero. The oh-so-smart and amazing Frank. What was it you used to call him?" Jason said, then snapped his fingers. "That's right, your *mentor*. How sweet. And how lovely of him to call."

Amy made big eyes. "Are you seriously jealous of Frank?"

"Well, I don't hear you laughing like you just did when I say something around here."

Amy shook her head. "So what? Perhaps you're just not . . . the funny type."

"So now I'm not funny?"

"That's not what I mean, and you know it, Jason. Jesus! What is this?" Amy said, then looked around the open living area. "And where were you hiding, anyway?"

Jason bent over and picked up his gym bag. "I wasn't hiding, Amy. I was in the bathroom, getting ready."

"To go to the gym?"

Jason sighed, bowed his head, then put the bag back down. Amy caught the blur of a quick movement, then felt a sting on her left cheekbone. She lifted a hand to her face and noticed her skin was growing hot, her pulse pounding underneath the surface. It was then she realized that he'd struck her. He'd actually slapped her across the face. Amy was shocked. Didn't know what to say. She was still unsure if it had really happened.

Jason picked up his bag again, then took a few steps toward the front door and turned. "You know," he said, an unfamiliar tone of hurt in his voice, "my appearance used to matter to you. You actually used to appreciate the fact that I care about how I look."

Confusion fogged Amy's mind. This was not the Jason she had fallen in love with a little over two years ago. What was happening?

Jason made it to the front door and opened it.

Amy's shock was momentarily replaced by fear. "What about work?" she said.

Jason smiled at her. "I quit," he said, then the door clicked shut.

Amy stared at the front door for a moment, then picked up the beer bottle and pressed it gently against her cheekbone. As the bottle cooled her hot cheek, thousands of thoughts coursed through her head.

And once realization hit, Amy closed her eyes and let the tears flow.

EIGHT

A my powered up her computer, listened to it whir and hum while scanning the first-floor space. It was divided into roughly thirty institutional-blue padded cubicles. The chairs usually occupied by eager agents were all empty, their desks littered with paperwork, the dividers cluttered with internal memos, new procedures, computer logins and wall calendars.

The AFP building in Newstead operated as a satellite to headquarters in Canberra and, perhaps therefore, was small and only three stories high. It was located on a sharp corner—the acute angle of the intersecting streets forcing the building into a shape reminiscent of an enormous prehistoric hand axe made out of glass. Because of the AFP operating several public offices—as well as some hidden ones used for sting operations and surveillance—funding was stretched, which meant that the satellite office in Brisbane operated solely during standard office hours. Most of the work done here was background checks, dark web investigations, cold cases, operational procedure revisions, equipment purchasing decisions as well as administration topped with the usual red tape galore.

Amy looked over the padded divider at the desk where Frank used to sit and sighed. Due to his expertise, the AFP had recruited Frank to review and revise the procedures originally followed during previous investigations of murders that were now cold cases. They hoped that Frank's analysis would expose potential oversights, thereby opening avenues for fresh evidence to be considered, different angles to be explored and for improvements to be made to such a degree that it would enable the AFP to re-open those cases. And they had advised Frank to focus his efforts on revising staff behavior, their interactions with investigative procedures, and not to concern himself with the actual solving of the crimes themselves.

Initially, Amy hadn't been enthusiastic when she'd learned that she was going to be partnered with a chubby German fellow to perform boring administrative duties. But somehow—and almost immediately—Frank had managed to make it fascinating. His insight and experience from overseas contained elements that Amy had never heard of, let alone trained in. How much of it was actual knowledge that Frank had attained while working in Germany, lessons he'd learned with INTERPOL in France, or theory he'd picked up while completing a course on serial killers with the FBI in America—or how much of it was simply Frank—she didn't know. Didn't really care, either. He had a unique way of approaching cases, of attacking problems from impossible angles and of identifying patterns within apparent chaos. She felt she'd learned more during the eighteen months they'd spent together than she had during her decade-long career.

Amy's cubicle was next to the north-facing windows looking onto Commercial Street. Dusk was fast approaching, and Amy swiveled and faced the window. The overhead tube lights doubled in number as the windows reflected them, extending them through the glass so that they were hanging above the street. A ghostly copy of Amy was hovering on a chair just outside the building, looking in at her. She swiveled back and faced her old partner's desk, once again peeked over the divider and confirmed to herself that it was indeed true—Frank was no longer here and probably never would be again.

The PC stopped whirring and humming and a curser began blinking. Amy punched in her login and password, then accessed a Queensland database of vehicle license registrations.

The plate number Frank had passed on to her came up immediately. A brand new, blue BMW X5. The car was a lease, paid for by a company called JSG, located on the Gold Coast. A further search revealed that the acronym stood for Jacaranda Security Group and that they had an office in Brisbane city center as well.

Despite having over fifty employees, JSG had only leased three high-end cars. Amy found the names of the CEO, COO and CFO. After further searches, she discovered they operated a fleet of small hatchbacks as well, all of them white, all of them with round stickers on the doors with the company logo—a cartoon drawing of a jacaranda tree in full bloom. The vivid purple flowers matched the color of the font used for their acronym that spread across the bottom of the tree trunk—JSG. All the hatchbacks were identical, all were base models making them cheap, meaning they were for the minions, the luxury cars for management. She added everything to the print file, then eyed the enormous printer located across the room next to the double doors.

Then she moved on to Rebecca Wright. Frank had taught her that the better you know someone, the better you can serve them. A quick search revealed that Rebecca had a clean record. Amy was thorough, searching any and every database she could think of. It didn't take long until she found a death certificate; Rebecca had evidently lost her husband five years back and was now living alone in their house in Teneriffe. Amy noted the address. It was less than a mile away. Three minutes by car.

She wasn't sure how many laws she'd already broken by doing this for Frank, but one thing was for sure: She was putting more than just her job on the line. Huge fines. Never able to work for law enforcement again. Maybe even prison time. The list went on.

Amy panicked at the thought. Why the hell was she doing this? She didn't owe Frank anything.

Questions for later, she thought.

Satisfied that she had found everything she could, Amy collated it all and hit print.

A few moments later, the printer sprang to life.

Then the double doors opened.

NINE

Frank's chubby, sweaty fingers struggled to get the two-dollar coin into the tiny opening, but after three attempts and dropping it once, he finally managed to slot it in and wrestle out a shopping cart, then entered through the sliding glass doors.

The evening heat and humidity were immediately replaced by a cool breeze, bright lights, the low hum of cooling units and muffled bleeps of cash registers. The store was almost empty, so Frank whistled along and took a moment to savor the chill and the familiar atmosphere of his local German supermarket. He thought about what his doctor had told him while he strolled past the fruits and vegetables. There were Brussels sprouts, broccoli and beetroot, and he wondered what he could cook using carrots, cabbage and cauliflower. Frank kept walking and stopped wondering.

He found his favorite ground beef, spaghetti, jars of Bolognese, Parmesan, garlic bread. For dessert, he picked up a tray of ready-made tiramisu. Even remembered to get a new tub of chocolate chip ice cream. He piled up a selection of cookies, chocolates, candy, popcorn and ginger beer. Hummed to himself as he loaded up on breakfast favorites: buns, chocolate hazelnut spread, peanut butter, strawberry jam as well as a selection of Danish. With the essentials taken care of, Frank remembered he was almost out of toothpaste. He walked around for a bit, not sure where to find it. Eventually, he ended up in a far corner, staring down at a pallet of laundry detergent, sensing that he was getting closer.

Then Frank saw movement out of the corner of one eye. He glanced to his right and, just as he did so, noticed an elderly woman sliding something into a large side pocket of her raincoat. It had all happened fast and—Frank thought—deftly. Routinely, even. This was not her first time.

Frank closed his eyes, willing his brain to replay the vision. He'd seen her straighten up, which meant she'd just removed something from her cart. The reason for this, Frank thought, was that she'd been clever and initially placed the pack there, to mix it in with her other groceries. Then she'd waited until she thought no one was watching and had pulled the item back out of her cart and slid it into her pocket. Frank opened his eyes again.

She turned and headed in the direction of the cash registers.

This was not good. Frank had to act fast.

He half-jogged two parallel aisles away, which in Frank's case looked more like a limp turtle racing across a slippery floor. When he was sure that he'd moved far enough ahead, he turned and cut across, stopped right in front of the lady, blocking the aisle with himself and his cart. Frank reached into a metal basket and retrieved a barbecue tool, pretended to inspect it.

"Excuse me," the elderly lady said. Her voice had a slight quiver to it, her accent what Frank could only describe as perfect Australian.

Beautiful. Her hair was silver and her posture exuded pride and principles.

Frank put the tool back and lifted a hand in apology. "I'm the one who'll ask to be excused," he said.

The lady waited a moment, then looked puzzled as Frank still didn't move out of the way.

She began turning and pulling at her shopping cart when Frank once again raised his hand and took a step toward her. "Wait," he said. "Please."

Now the lady looked frightened. She cast her eyes downward, and Frank thought he saw her lip tremble.

He stepped closer, stopped when he was within whispering distance. "Listen," he said. "The steak packs have tiny, electric circuits embedded into them. Stuck onto the plastic, behind the label. Difficult to spot, unless you look closely. Leaving that pack in your pocket *will* set off the alarm. Not worth it. Just wanted to let you know," Frank said, then took a step back.

The lady looked at him in disbelief. "I haven't—"

"None of my business," Frank said, raising a hand. "But now you've been warned." With that, he turned and left.

He could hardly blame her. As he loaded the conveyor belt, Frank thought about his own mother, about all the poor souls like her on state pensions having paid taxes their whole lives, having always done the right thing. This lady had undoubtedly reached retirement, perhaps even a long time ago. Now was supposed to be her golden years, yet she still didn't have enough money to afford a piece of meat? Frank felt sick just thinking about it. Sure, the law was the law, but more importantly, right was right. And not looking after retirees was simply wrong.

As Frank paid, he noticed the lady down near the meat counter inspecting packages and swapping items.

Then, just as he left, she turned and sent him a smile and a friendly wave.

Frank returned both.

TEN

Joe McAvoy entered and turned to the printer and a look of surprise spread across his face as he watched page after page being spat out of the machine. He speedily scanned the room and lit up in a big smile as his gaze fell on Amy. He gave the printer another quick glance, then walked briskly across the worn, bright blue carpet.

Amy had never seen Joe stroll. His legs always pumped at double speed, regardless of where he was going. Amy wondered whether it was his personality or simply his overcompensating for having short legs. Either way, a few seconds later, he was standing at the end of her desk.

"Howdy, partner," he said, his poor attempt at an American cowboy accent made even worse when mixed with his Scottish. "What are you doing here at this unholy hour?"

Despite Joe still being in his thirties—Amy wasn't sure how far along—his petite face and delicate features were framed by dark brown hair that already had a good scattering of gray in it. His hair was voluminous, big and wavy, and the gray somehow made him look even younger.

Amy put on her best smile, shrugged. "Why sit at home when you can work, right? Also," she said, "I could ask you the same question."

Joe stuck out a slim finger, pointed it at Amy. "Fair play," he said, then tucked his finger away again. A somewhat smug smile spread across his lips. "I just had a performance review with a certain Mr. Gregory Fordham, and eh, it turns out he likes me. I'm doing a marvelous job—those were his words—and basically, a promotion could be on the cards soon."

Amy nodded in acknowledgement, craned her neck to look around Joe, who was blocking her view of the printer. "So," she said, then looked back up at Joe, "he's still here? In the building?"

Joe nodded, his hairdo flopping back and forth as he did so.

Amy found him a little too energetic and way too enthusiastic.

"He'll be right down," he said, then cocked both thumbs and pointed them down at his shoulders. "And taking me out for a beer."

Amy's eyes grew large. She didn't mean to look shocked, and she certainly didn't hope Joe would pick up on the fact that the thought repulsed her. She had to think fast. What the hell was she going to say if that idiot came down here?

"Congratulations," Amy said, hoping he couldn't hear the lack of conviction in her voice. "Well-deserved, you're a . . . smart fellow."

Joe began laughing. "Sorry, Amy, just pulling your leg," he said. "Would be nice though, could do with a raise, what with the inflation, grocery prices and post-COVID life in general."

Amy sighed in relief. "So he's not here?"

Joe's smile never faltered, but now he looked puzzled. "Oh, right. No, he's still here, still did the performance review, and he *is* happy. I was just joking about the promotion and raise," he said. "You're stuck with me for a while yet. Anyway, with your brain, chances are you'll get promoted before I do."

Amy didn't say anything.

"So," Joe said, "what *are* you doing here?"

The printer stopped humming. Amy stood up, took one step forward just as Joe stuck a hand in her face. She'd tolerated him since they'd been partnered up after Frank's suspension, but now she felt like punching him.

"Please, my lady, sit back down. I'll get it for you," he said, then turned and jogged across the room. Amy watched him reach the printer just as one side of the double doors was pulled open again, this time by the man himself: AFP Commander Gregory Fordham.

Amy held her breath. She suddenly felt hot and dizzy.

Through the open space and the quiet, she could hear Greg telling Joe that his workday was over, no need to print anything, tomorrow is another day, something to that effect. Very buddy-buddy. Then Joe shook his head, mumbled something, turned and pointed at Amy, then smiled and waved.

Fordham's head snapped around and his eyes bored into hers. He looked like a man who was thinking hard. Amy took in a deep breath, felt her left cheekbone throb. It was getting bloody sore.

Fordham finally nodded at her and tried on a small smile that vanished as quickly as it had emerged.

Joe was gathering the six-inch pile of papers when Fordham put a paternal hand on his shoulder. They exchanged a few hush words, then Joe handed the pile to Gregory, waved at Amy and left the room.

Fordham remained standing where he was, holding the stack, waiting for the doors to close. When they did, his gaze dropped to the pages and be began thumbing through them. He took his time, occasionally stopping at a page for several seconds. When he was finally done, he looked at Amy again, his menacing stare boring straight through her.

Then he walked toward her.

ELEVEN

W hile Frank unpacked his groceries and found pots and pans, late dusk brought with it the evening ritual of hundreds of rainbow lorikeets gathering in huge fig trees lining the street across from his rented, sixth-floor flat. Frank left the balcony door open, putting stuff away and cooking while listening to the harsh chattering of the colorful birds. To seasoned locals, they were simply a noisy nuisance, but to Frank, having parrots on your doorstep was strange, foreign and exotic, and definitely nothing that he had ever experienced before coming to Australia. It was, he realized, one of the many things that were growing on him; something that he'd come to cherish. As the days had gone by, his initial wish of going back to Germany had become increasingly distant and been slowly replaced by a love for this place that had sneaked up on him until he'd realized he never wanted to leave. Recently, he'd been considering how he could obtain a permanent visa, and in the end always reached the same conclusion: he couldn't.

Frank turned off the gas, drained the spaghetti, then loaded a plate and placed it on his bamboo tray, topped it with a generous amount of Bolognese, then flicked some powdery Parmesan out of a bag and onto the sauce. Then he took the garlic bread out of the oven and poured himself a large tumbler of ginger beer. Frank then gathered everything onto the tray and brought it out onto the balcony.

By the time he'd made himself comfortable in one of the two old couches he'd purchased from the Salvation Army, the sky above him had turned full dark. The lamps below lit up the street, leaving the fig trees and their enormous, dense crowns enveloped in darkness. The tops of the century-old trees were at Frank's eye level. The shadowy outline of a black flying-fox swooped across his field of vision; it turned, flapping its membranous skin between its long, spidery fingers, then it stalled and grabbed a twig, the weight of its heavy, inverted body swinging and bouncing nearby branches. While Frank ate, the mammals came and went, eating and screeching and flapping about. It occurred to Frank that he had a lot in common with the fruit bats: they roosted on the periphery of the crowns, allowed in—temporarily—at the permission of territorial parrots occupying the center. Just like Frank, they were granted a temporary visa. They even hung upside down, just as Frank did in relation to Germany. Upside Down Under. As he ate, the flapping and screeching eventually died down and was replaced by more standard city sounds: cars, people talking and music seeping through the open door of someone's balcony.

Frank enjoyed the balmy evenings, warm enough to sit outside yet cool enough to be enjoyable. He twirled spaghetti around his fork, held it against his spoon, waited for the loose ends to all spool up and create what Frank thought of as the perfect mouthful. In between, he munched on warm, buttery garlic bread and sipped on icy-cold ginger beer. There were few things in life that pleased Frank more than food. And few things that pleased him less than Gregory Fordham.

There had to be a reason for Frank's suspension other than his poor physical state. He had a wealth of experience and an abundance of knowledge gathered over two decades. But even more importantly, he'd used that experience to better himself by constantly seeking new approaches and applying different techniques to solve the crimes he'd been working on. And over the years, what had started out as logical, forensically sound, evidence-based approaches had warped into something akin to the opposite. The other side of logic. Emotions. The human factor. People's habits. Desires. Fears. Dreams. Love. Expectations. Values. Frank had discovered that whenever a human being was involved in a crime, his intuition became a tool as invaluable as a forensic lab. His hard work and strong instincts had resulted in expertise that no one else within the AFP had. And this, coupled with an insatiable drive for hunting down murderers, was what made Frank formidable.

But one case was at the forefront of Frank's mind, and always would be. The last three years before coming to Australia, he'd spent his days chasing a German serial killer considered responsible for over fifty killings. Frank eventually had enough leads to pursue a suspect operating under several aliases, one of which Frank was certain of: Garin Beygott. The media had dubbed him "The Cleaver". Frank had tracked the killer to the southern end of the country, to Munich, only to find the killer had moved on again. As it turned out, he'd been up north. In Hamburg. In Frank's home. With Frank's wife. By the time Frank got back, the killer had disappeared and Frank had found his wife slaughtered inside their bedroom.

Frank had broken down, shock had numbed his heart, denial had short-circuited his brain. A week later, he'd gone back to work, trying once again to track down Garin Beygott. In an explosion of fury, while racing to yet another address, Frank had lost control and slid the high-powered car sideways into a tree, seriously injuring a colleague.

Frank's boss and lifelong friend, Hans Richter, had called him into his office and asked him what had happened. Frank had shrugged and said, "I'm not going to stop until I catch him!" Garin Beygott had slipped between his fingers again. That was all that mattered.

Hans had Frank admitted to a local psychiatric unit. Frank had screamed and yelled, and in the end, it'd taken four colleagues to hold him down and place constraints on his arms and legs. They'd escorted him to the hospital where Frank's anger had slowly died down as he began speaking with Caroline in his room at night, asking her what he could do to get her back. They'd talked about their short time together, why she'd had to go, what would have happened if Frank hadn't been working for the police, wouldn't have had to leave her. And while Caroline's voice faded, Frank's depression deepened. With time, Frank had gone through his options as he saw them, which were three: slitting his wrists, hanging himself or overdosing on medication. In the end, the only thing preventing him from doing neither had been his desire to one day catch the man responsible, see him brought to justice.

After a few weeks, he'd finally mustered the energy to pretend that he'd reached what his psychiatrist had called "the acceptance stage". Pretended, because Frank would never reach the acceptance stage. Ever. He'd been discharged and had walked out of the hospital feeling anxious, still experiencing auditory and visual hallucinations that he'd thankfully managed to keep from the doctors until the end. They'd told him to be cautious, that he likely suffered from PTSD and that he would probably feel paranoid for a while. But, as Frank liked to think, how could it be paranoia if it really happened?

The chase had filled his days and food had filled his void until one day—not long after returning to work—Frank's new quirks had evolved into direct disobedience, stubbornness and unlawful behavior. The Human Resource Department of the German Federal Police had finally run out of patience and sacked him.

Although Hans could do nothing to prevent Frank from getting laid off, he also knew that working was what kept Frank alive. He'd once again called Frank into his office, explained that he had connections Down Under and that this would be Frank's only opportunity for a fresh start—his very last chance.

Soon after, Frank had gone to work for the Australian Federal Police on a two-year probationary work-visa. Hans's connections together with Frank's reputation had brought him to Australia, and it had provided him with a life-saving break from his obsessive, relentless pursuit of a deranged individual.

The AFP didn't know his medical background as it was kept confidential, only that Frank had taken a break from work after the "tragic death of his spouse". AFP Commander Gregory Fordham had made big eyes the first time they'd shaken hands at Brisbane Airport. Although he hadn't come right out and said it, Frank had a feeling that his reaction had to do with the hundred pounds Frank had gained since his last staff photo had been taken, the very photo that Gregory would have seen in the official application. The ride into

AFP's Newstead offices had been muted and awkward, and Frank had wondered if he'd taken the right decision in coming here.

He'd been partnered with Amy and together they had looked into cold cases of killings that had occurred within the past decade. The first few months they'd focused their energy on how and which police procedures had been followed, making recommendations for improvements to ensure future success of similar cases, but then Frank had noticed something connecting eight murders that had taken place more recently. Something that Amy said wasn't a pattern. Something that Gregory had made clear was not a lead, that Frank should forget about. But the cases had finally given Frank a lifeline, something to hold on to. He'd explored, examined and inquired, had relentlessly researched and investigated, and once he'd found that tiny thread, he'd held onto it wholeheartedly, then checked and double-checked.

Frank had always believed that, however faint, a whiff is a whiff, and whiffs exist for a reason. They don't suddenly cease to exist; they get carried around, camouflage themselves, hide behind solid materials or get mixed up and fade within more pungent surroundings. But the particles are always there, shifting and moving, constellations of molecules within a dark universe. And only a careless dog will stray from the trail. Despite how weak a scent is, if the nose is turned the right way and dug in at just the right moment—if the head is kept down and the focus up—that scent will eventually be replaced by a smell, a smell that'll slowly but surely be overpowered by a stench, a stench that will lead all the way to the rotten carcass of humanity.

And Frank had definitely gotten a whiff.

As a matter of fact, his nostrils were burning.

Twelve

G regory Fordham loomed large over Amy's desk. He looked down at her, clutching her pile of papers.

Amy stared into her monitor, closing programs, deleting names and replacing search details to better fit with what she was currently supposed to be working on: a case of alleged credit card fraud.

She could feel Fordham's intimidating presence: his older, wiry physique; his seemingly endless supply of testosterone; the way she knew he liked to furrow his brows before he spoke; the fact that he was several ranks above her in the hierarchy of the AFP. The only comfort right now was that he clearly wasn't perfect; his aftershave had been slathered on way too generously, way too many hours ago—the lingering, spicy-sweet smell probably worse than if he hadn't used any at all.

Fordham sat down on the corner of her desk, then placed the papers next to her keyboard. He was so close to her that Amy rolled her chair a few inches to the side. He was clearly invading her personal space and probably enjoying it too.

"Working late?" he said, not bothering to hide the condescending tone. At least he wasn't subtle.

Amy cleared her throat, forced herself to look him in the eyes. "Yes sir," she said. "I managed to trace the credit card to an individual right here in Brisbane—"

"My, my," he said, then leaned in and ran a finger slowly over her cheek. "Who did that?"

Amy was about to slap his hand away when Fordham quickly removed it himself. Her hand found her sore cheek. "I rented one of those electric scooters over the weekend," she said.

Gregory nodded, stared at her for a while. "It's turned bright red, Amy," he said, pointing at her cheek. "That means it happened more than a couple of hours ago but, since the color indicates that the blood gathering under your skin is still fresh, definitely less than twenty-four hours ago. There was nothing there this morning when I saw you. So that timeline tells me you're lying, probably because you're trying to hide the real reason behind the bruise, which makes me think that your current boyfriend slapped you a good one when you got back from work today," he said, nodding again, talking to himself as much as he was talking to Amy.

Amy didn't know what to say. This arrogant asshole was as perceptive as he was obnoxious.

"Reminds me of a joke. You have to hear this one, Amy. It's really good. And, I would even say, in this case, apt."

Amy swallowed. Nodded.

"What do you say to a woman boasting a huge shiner?"

Amy had never felt such hatred, intimidation and fear in the presence of this man before. Yet, given the circumstances, she had no choice but to play along. "What?" she said.

Fordham's eyes lit up. "Nothing," he said. "She's clearly been told already and it should be enough to say things once." Then he bent forward and cackled while theatrically holding onto his stomach.

Amy didn't laugh.

Fordham cackled a few more times before his forced laugh finally died out. He once more nodded to himself. "Okay, Amy, I'll let this one slide. But," he said, "three things." Fordham held up an index finger. "Number one: I'm warning you. If I ever find you here again, investigating people and companies outside your normal working hours for your own benefit, there will be severe consequences. No discussion. No further warnings. We clear?"

Amy nodded, equally relieved and puzzled that he would be willing to simply let it go.

Fordham added a middle finger next to his index finger. "Number two: If it gets out of hand with that bastard, you let me know," he said, then winked. "I'll personally pay him a visit and break both his arms. Would be my pleasure."

This made Amy smile.

The ring finger joined the other two. "Number three: And this should really go without saying." Fordham added, then smiled. As his nicotine-stained teeth were partially revealed, a scar from the left edge of his mouth up to his left ear pulsated pink behind his pockmarks. Amy had never noticed the scar before. Fordham lowered his voice just a notch. "You owe me one," he said, then stood up, turned and walked back toward the exit.

Amy was left speechless. Owed him one? What was this? A bad action movie about corrupt police officers? Did he expect her to break more laws now that he'd turned a blind eye to her unscheduled visit to the office?

Gregory had made it to the double doors.

Amy's voice was low when she spoke: "Sir, what do you mean by—"

"Anything I may need, Amy. Anything at all. Anytime," Fordham yelled over his shoulder as he pulled open both doors.

As Amy watched the doors close, she wondered if she was now in more trouble than if he'd simply turned her in.

Damage already done, with an asshole of a boyfriend probably lounging around at home, Amy decided to hang around a bit longer and get Frank what he really needed—what he'd been begging her for ever since his suspension.

Thirteen

F rank had moved back into the living room and was sprawled on
his couch.

He was watching Lieutenant Columbo puff on his
cigar—sometimes lit, sometimes not—smartly deducing, carefully
calculating, always asking one more thing. Frank had recently begun
rewatching the DVD box set and was now enjoying one of his favorite
episodes from a season produced in the early seventies.

Frank sat up, slid his butt along the couch, lay down on his other
side and propped a pillow under his head. Just as he got comfortable,
he realized that the empty plastic container of tiramisu sitting on the
coffee table was in his line of vision; the teaspoon was jutting up from
one corner, poking Lieutenant Columbo in the face. Frank sighed, sat
up again, grabbed the container and put it on the floor. He then fluffed
his pillow, flipped it over and lay back down.

He knew all the episodes, had seen them all dozens of times,
but that didn't diminish the experience. On the contrary. Knowing
the story, Frank could revel in Peter Falk's brilliant rendition of
the lieutenant. He found the familiarity comforting, the format
reliable and the predictive plotlines reassuring. To Frank, Lieutenant

Columbo represented a perfect world where the killer always got caught.

Frank was dozing off when the theme song from *The Love Boat* began playing. He reached out, and as his hand found the little plastic device, he realized that he'd grabbed the remote. He put it back down, got up on one elbow and spotted his phone. The display showed AFP NEWSTEAD.

Frank answered. Amy filled him in on what had happened at the office and asked to meet up. She had his papers.

Frank was intrigued. He checked his watch, realizing that his favorite Mugs & Marmalade had closed. Amy suggested another coffee place which Frank knew would be shut as well. Although Brisbane had the population to officially qualify as a city, it still, in many ways, felt and functioned like a small town. They discussed various bars, but they also wanted peace and privacy. Frank was contemplating other options when Amy spoke.

"I'll just come to yours," she said. "See you in fifteen."

Frank was about to object, but she'd already hung up.

For a moment, he stared at his phone, then promptly put it down. He quickly grabbed his remote, pressed pause and stopped Lieutenant Columbo just as he turned to ask one more question.

He gathered his rubbish, filled the dishwasher, sniffed his armpit, then walked back toward the bathroom for a quick shower. As he passed the couch, Columbo looked at Frank from behind the large screen, cigar in hand, a knowing smile on his face.

Frank could have sworn he winked.

FOURTEEN

J oe leaned over the old bar, looked down and tried to process what
Gregory had just said.

Tina Turner was blasting from a corner jukebox, telling people
that any old music would do. The bar had remnants of clear lacquer
around the edges, but on top, a plethora of pints and endless elbows
had rubbed it down to the wood. The room was dimly lit and smelled
of beer. The establishment had been around for decades, but the
beer taps must have been replaced, maybe several times and evidently
recently; a shiny copper base connected to a fat, horizontal, frosted
pipe held a dozen black handles hooked up to kegs of ales, stouts,
lagers, porters and pilsners. The wooden floor had the same purple
hue as the bar. Behind the bar, on top of the mirrored wall of shelves
bursting with alcohol bottles, fat wooden beams protruded back
across the room, hovering over tall tables and stools, as well as a single
pool table.

Joe turned and watched a guy lift a triangular rack away from the
table, place it on a shelf, then grab a cue and begin chalking it.

A new game was about to begin.

Joe turned back. He listened to the music above the discreet thumps of cue sticks and clacks of balls and shook his head.

"Is that a no?" Gregory asked.

"No, no, no," he said. "Just a lot to take in, that's all."

Gregory nodded. "Do you believe me?"

Joe made big eyes and pushed out his lower lip. "Of course," he said, then took another sip of his beer. "You're my boss. You have no reason to lie."

Gregory nodded. "That's right. As a matter of fact, I have a strong motive to tell the truth," he said, then downed the rest of his beer. "You see, every idiot knows that Amy's always been completely infatuated by the almighty Frank. She's young and naive and he's . . . well, old and fat. She's gullible, and he has all these wicked theories that should stay just that—theories. Do you think you're up for it?"

What choice did he have, really? He didn't know Frank that well, certainly didn't owe him anything, and—even more importantly—Joe had to look after his own career. This was a great opportunity to show Fordham that he was dependable, that he was willing to take risks when necessary, that he possessed grit and integrity.

"Are you sure this is a good idea?" Joe asked. "I mean, as far as I can tell, Frank is a smart fellow."

Fordham nodded. "How else are we going to know?"

"I have another idea, if you don't mind," Joe said, already holding up both hands in apology.

"Shoot," Gregory said.

"If you suspect Amy is helping Frank access classified material, why not get Internal Affairs to help? Isn't that their job?" Joe said.

Gregory nodded. "Absolutely," he said. "Only problem is, it's a serious offence, meaning it has to be investigated by a Professional Standards Team, what you call Internal Affairs. If it in any way involves corruption—which, I can tell you, it pretty much always does—the AFP Commissioner will get involved and he'll have to escalate it to the Australian Commission for Law Enforcement Integrity, an agency overseen by the Commonwealth Ombudsman. You see where I'm going with this?"

Joe shook his head.

"Well," Gregory continued, "my point is, it can take years to get to the bottom of these things, if it's all done using the official channels. And I don't have years. I need to stop this before it has a chance of escalating into a public embarrassment for our department. *Before* secret files are leaked to the public or a bloody journalist or—worst case—somebody gets killed."

Joe took a deep breath, then downed the rest of his beer. "Okay," he said. "I'll do it."

Gregory shook his head.

"What?" Joe asked.

Gregory leaned in, his face a few inches from Joe's. "I need you to say it. Say it to me now, out loud."

Joe didn't move. He spoke in a low volume. "I'll spy on Amy Lamborne, get all the info that I can and pass it onto you."

"And you'll pretend," Gregory prompted, then turned his index finger repeatedly around in a circular motion, indicating that Joe should keep going.

Joe was momentarily shocked, but quickly gathered himself. "And I'll pretend," he said, "to be Amy's friend and use that to get as close to her as possible."

Gregory smiled widely, slapped Joe on the shoulder, then turned and held up two fingers to the bartender, who promptly began pouring another couple of pints.

FIFTEEN

F rank had only just put away the vacuum cleaner when the intercom chirped.

He walked over to the unit and saw Amy's black-and-white face smile at the fisheye lens. He buzzed her in, then opened the front door and waited.

Moments later, the elevator dinged and Amy appeared. She was clutching a fat pile of papers. Her black suit jacket was wrinkled, as was her blue shirt underneath. Her short, dark hair had a greasy shine to it, yet Frank caught a scent of fresh flowers as she passed him and continued into his small living room. He closed the front door.

Amy stopped in the middle of the room, facing the open balcony doors. She turned and smiled at Frank, nodding to the balcony. "Candles?"

Frank shrugged. "I like it cozy."

He let Amy walk ahead onto the balcony, then waited for her to sit down on one couch before he chose the one opposite her.

"You like red?" he asked, lifting an already opened bottle.

"Yes, please." Amy put the papers on a seat next to her, then took a wineglass from the small table and held it out while Frank poured. She looked up at him. "Your hair is wet."

"Hmmm," Frank said, then poured himself a glass while nodding toward the pile of papers. "Did you bring me a whole ream?"

Glass in hand, Amy leaned back against a fat cushion and yawned. "Sorry," she said, "long day."

Frank took a sip of his wine.

Amy leaned forward again, shook her head. "I'm in trouble, Frank," she said, then put a finger to the inside corner of one eye.

It was dark, and Frank couldn't see whether she was crying. "What's up?" he said.

Amy told him about her encounter with Jason at home, her evening visit to the AFP, Joe's great results from his annual review, and Gregory nosing through her stuff.

Frank listened intently throughout, occasionally sipping his wine.

"So," Amy said, "I don't know what he means by 'you owe me one', but I suppose there's a good chance that I'll find out one day."

Frank shook his head. "He hit you?"

Amy looked confused for a second. "No . . . well, Jason, yes, but I'm talking about Gregory."

Frank emptied his glass, then poured himself another. "He actually hit you?"

Amy sat up straight. "It's not that big of a deal, Frank. Gregory is the problem here. My job is in jeopardy, my entire career is in the shits."

Frank once again nodded toward the pile of papers. "What have you got there?"

Amy sighed. "I printed out everything I could find on Rebecca, as well as everything and anything connected to that license plate you gave me. However, most of the pile," she said, then pointed, "meaning all the rest below the red piece of cardboard I stuffed in there, is something entirely different."

"What is it?" Frank asked.

Amy smiled. "It's a little something for you."

Frank's eyes grew big. He leaned forward, spread his meaty legs and placed his elbows on his knees. "Really?"

Amy nodded. "I've printed the eight cold-case files you said were connected, along with notes and everything else associated with those cases."

Frank felt his heart pound in his chest. "Amy, this is fantastic. Now I can finally continue working."

Amy took a sip of her wine, leaned back against a cushion. "And then what?"

"Well, if I manage to find something useful, I'll pass it on to the AFP and then they can do the arrest."

"You'd really do that?" Amy asked. "Even after how Gregory treated you?"

Frank grabbed the bottle and refilled both glasses. "Gregory is an ass, but this is not about him. It's about right and wrong, good and bad, legal and illegal, but even more importantly," Frank said, "it's about the outcome. To finally get to the bottom of all this. I get Gregory looking after himself and his unit and that he didn't share my theories. He clearly found it a waste of the department's money for me to pursue them. And in regard to my physique, if I have to be completely honest, in some imaginary situation where I'd have to—literally—run after a suspect, on one hand, I suppose there's a good chance that I wouldn't be able to catch him," Frank said, then shook his head. "Actually, better than a good chance. But on the other hand, what is this, Miami Vice?" Frank chuckled at his own comment. "No. Gregory is just doing his job, but of course that doesn't mean that I should let him prevent me from doing mine," he said, then raised his glass. "And now, thanks to you, I can put my talents to good use again."

"Cheers to that," Amy said, raising her glass and taking another sip. "You always were boastful about those talents. I remember when we were looking at the cases together, I didn't understand what you were on about. Even the small snippets I thought I understood still seemed far-fetched."

"You're young. You look up at the night sky and see shining stars," Frank said. "I see all the blackness between them."

Amy sighed. "Frank, please, just explain."

"Okay," Frank said. "In life, we're accustomed to certain norms, cultures, traditions and the reality of a human being differs greatly depending on who and where."

Amy's eyebrows shot up. "We have different realities?"

"Of course," Frank said. "Take you, for example. You live here in Brisbane, you're Australian, born and bread, so it's not unusual for you to hear a kookaburra laughing as you walk down the street here in Kelvin Grove. Your reality is lush vegetation, exotic animals, warm weather, kind people and a safe environment. And if I ask you to think back to when you were a young teenager, I'm sure your experience from then would be very similar to the one today, perhaps even better."

"Right."

"Now imagine the reality of a woman your age, perhaps even in the same job, but born, raised and living in London," Frank said. "Her life would be similar to yours, yet completely different. And, bear in mind, this is comparing two English-speaking countries," he said. "Now imagine that woman living in Rome. Or Cairo."

"The point?" Amy said.

"Picture yourself having to imitate that life," Frank said. "Let's say that you were a spy, working for the Australian government, and you had to go to London and pretend to be this woman, just for a week. Different accent, different use of the same language, different memories, culture, food, weather, traditions. The list goes on."

"Why would I have to imagine that?"

"Because the eight victims we looked at were out of place, as if they didn't belong. Maybe they weren't imitating anyone, but simply changed their lives dramatically at some stage. Enough to remove themselves from their previous identities to not know how to simply be."

"Are you saying they were all spies, Frank?" Amy said, then chuckled.

Frank sipped his wine, looked at the trees across the street.

Amy stopped chuckling. "Sorry," she said. "But I still don't get it. What exactly is the connection here?"

"That's what I need to find out," he said, then lifted his glass. "Amy, I can't thank you enough for what you've done. You're a real friend."

Frank thought he saw Amy blush. He sipped some more wine, leaned back, enjoying the buzz. Then, after a lengthy pause: "He really hit you?"

They both burst out laughing.

Sixteen

Frank's head was exploding.

From where he was sitting, facing southeast, squinting from his vantage point on Brisbane Square, The Brisbane Treasury Casino looked stately. The heritage-listed Italian Renaissance building's facade with its dozens of columns and arches faced the Brisbane River, which lay wide and flat, its brown surface occasionally rippled by passing catamarans.

Midday heat had cranked up the oven that was Frank's old sedan. The spacious cabin smelled of stale fries and muggy carpets. He leaned across and rolled down the passenger-side window as well, hoping to create a draft. But the air was stable, pressed low to the ground. Hot enough to be stifling, but still not hot enough to begin rising as it did in the afternoon, forming perfect cauliflower clouds that kept growing and intensifying until gentle breezes became strong gusts and then heavy rain from violent thunderstorms would dump a torrent of water, offering momentary relief from the oppressing heat.

But for now, it was quiet. And hot. The calm before the storm. There was no way Frank could turn on his noisy engine to crank up the AC. The small plaza was full of lunch-goers from the surrounding offices. He'd noticed lately that smoke from his exhaust was darker than usual, and to make matters worse, he'd also parked illegally. Besides, Frank had forgotten to fuel, and now the yellow warning light had come on.

Amy had stayed until midnight. They'd shared another bottle, then she'd insisted on leaving. She was going to go to her parents' house in The Valley, despite Frank offering her the couch. Several times. Probably too many.

Frank had waved to her from his balcony, then continued drinking while pouring through old files of cold cases, his brain making drunken, inexplicable connections. It wasn't until he had finally drunk himself into a stupor—and the booze had made the writing illegible—that he put down the papers. Instead, he began imagining ways to teach Amy's boyfriend a valuable lesson. Fantasized, even.

The next thing on his mind were open balcony doors, rainbow lorikeets screeching just before five am. With the sun streaming through his small, one-bedroom apartment, Frank had given in, downed two headache tablets and started the percolator. He'd then picked up the pages containing the information related to the car registration belonging to a blue BMW X5, driven by a guy allegedly following Frank's client, Rebecca Wright.

Amy had done amazing work, had gathered every bit of information that Frank could have imagined, including some that he couldn't. Waiting for his headache to subside, downing a liter of coffee with full-cream milk and sugar, Frank read, studied and memorized, attempting to get a rough overview. Mid-morning, he'd driven to Everything Electric where he'd bought himself a good camera with a serious lens. After the purchase he'd followed his phone GPS to Jacaranda Security Group's office at Brisbane Square, continued eastbound along North Quay, passed the access ramps of the parking garage, then coasted to the nearest corner. He'd crawled over the curb and onto the square, waved an apology to a couple of pedestrians and parked next to the bicycle racks and killed the engine.

It wasn't exactly an inconspicuous spot, but at least it provided a direct line-of-sight to JSG's underground garage and, Frank thought, whoever would drive that blue BMW X5 probably wouldn't expect to be followed, anyway.

Frank wiped sweat off his forehead with the back of his hand, reached into his cooler bag for a cold ginger beer and a chocolate bar, then leaned the seat back, tore off the wrapper and stuffed half a bar in his mouth. Sitting and waiting was something Frank was extremely good at. Didn't mind doing it for hours. Sometimes days.

He watched people crossing the Victoria Bridge, boats and barges flowing up and down the river, all while checking his mirrors for cars emerging from the depths of the Brisbane Square building.

His bursts of headache brought with them snippets of black-and-white film, of Frank feeling nauseous at the back of a rideshare. Of stepping out into fresh, nighttime air. Of standing down below, looking up at a shiny new building. Then a guy yelling from his window for Frank to shut up.

Frank opened the bottle of ginger beer and put it to his mouth. More strobe-like memories flashed before him, then his guts sank. He removed the bottle from his lips, tentatively turned his right hand and looked at two red, swollen knuckles.

"*Scheiße!*" he mumbled, just as a blue BMW X5 exited the underground car park, raced past him and accelerated across the intersection just as it turned red.

Frank threw the bottle out the window and scrambled for the key in the ignition.

Seventeen

A my stabbed at her salad while Joe finished up his meat pie.

The AFP canteen on the top floor was positioned at the pointy end of the glass building. Amy could just make out the Brisbane River to the east, watched it stretch toward the north before a right bend where it flowed into Moreton Bay and from there into the Coral Sea. The midday sun converted the surface to a sea of shimmering silver, the late-summer sky unusually blue, quiet and clear.

"So," Joe began. "You never did tell me what you were doing here last night."

"Didn't I?" Amy said, then turned her head, looked at the small buffet table. "You want coffee?"

"Sure," Joe said.

Amy stood up. "Milk? Sugar?"

"Black."

Amy walked over, grabbed two mugs, put a couple of teaspoons of instant coffee in each, then filled them with water from a boiler. She returned to the table, mugs in hand.

"So?" Joe said.

"You're welcome," Amy said.

"Sorry," he said. "Thank you."

Amy took a bit of time, considered if she should tell him. Then thought, what the heck, he was her partner after all.

"I had a fight with my boyfriend yesterday after work."

Joe's eyebrows shot up. "And?"

"Well, I got really upset and didn't want to be home anymore, so I came back in here and began digging up files for Frank."

Joe took a sip of his coffee. "Frank? I thought Gregory suspended him?"

"Of course he did, but Frank is obsessed with some old cases we were going over when we were partners."

"Oh," Joe said, holding his mug with both hands. "What cases are they?"

Amy was about to open her mouth when a male colleague she'd met only a handful of times passed their table, heading for the buffet. She waited until he was out of earshot, then leaned in and looked Joe in the eyes. "I'm not sure if you're aware," she whispered, "but Frank and I were looking into unsolved murders, and he believes that as much as eight killings, all committed within the past few years, may be connected."

"Eight?" Joe said. "Like a serial killer?"

Amy nodded. "Frank said he was finally seeing some patterns when his fitness test was due. And as you know, Frank failed that test and Gregory suspended him."

Joe put his mug down. "Well, I'm sorry for being blunt, but he is rather fat, don't you think?"

"Are you telling me that passing a treadmill test is more important than stopping a serial killer?"

Joe put his hands up in defense. "Whoa! All I'm saying is that agents working for the AFP must uphold a certain physical standard, that's all."

Amy sighed. "I guess you're right. It's just so damn frustrating. I don't even know if Frank is onto something or if he's just . . . being Frank, you know?"

"I think I know exactly what you mean," Joe said. "I did meet the guy, had to sit in on a few of his crash courses in . . . I'm not even sure anymore. Let's just call it criminal psychology, although that was only a small part of it, I guess."

Amy nodded.

Joe leaned in. "Between you and me, I think he was just talking mince."

Amy smiled. "I'm getting used to your Scottish accent, Joe, but your vocab? Mince?"

"Aye, you know, rubbish. Nonsense. I really didn't get it and I consider myself an intelligent man."

She pushed her coffee mug around, chuckled and took a moment. "Did you know, when profiling was first developed by the FBI, most people laughed at it, few understood it, and hardly anyone believed it would ever work?"

"I did not."

Amy took a sip of her coffee. "The really weird part is that the frontrunners, the innovators, the pioneers if you will, even they admitted that, despite all their work—constructing a sound framework, developing a step-by-step process—it simply wasn't enough. In addition to consulting this profiling manual of sorts, agents had to already possess skills that weren't taught—couldn't be taught."

"Right," Joe said. "What do you mean, exactly?"

"What I mean is, every law enforcement officer or agent who became truly good at profiling all shared a . . . certain talent," Amy said. "A hunch, an X-factor, something akin to them knowing that they had to use *both* the profiling manual *and* their own sixth sense to get results."

"That's fascinating," Joe said. "I never knew."

Amy nodded. "That's Frank. He's an intelligent man, knows his procedures, has the expertise, yet that all somehow fades compared to his gut feelings, his talent. Frankly, it's uncanny," Amy said. "Pun intended."

Joe's eyebrows shot up as he pushed out his lower lip. "Waw. He's really made an impression on you, hasn't he?"

"I suppose," Amy said. "Anyway, we better get going. Our exciting credit card case isn't going to solve itself, you know?"

Joe took another sip of his coffee. "Tell me about it," he said, then stood up.

Together, they began walking to the door leading to a corner staircase.

"Also," Joe whispered, leaning in while walking, "if your man lays a hand on you again, you let me know."

Amy looked and Joe and smiled. A few steps later, her smile disappeared. Then she stopped.

"What?" Joe said.

Amy cocked her head. "How do you know he hit me?"

Joe blushed, his eyes darting frantically around the canteen before they settled back on Amy. He pointed to her face. "Your makeup, it doesn't quite cover."

Amy put a hand to her cheek. She knew her bruise was small and hardly visible. All said and done, she supposed Jason hadn't hit her that hard. Besides, she'd made sure the foundation covered the faint, purple tinge that had developed. Then she remembered; the boys had gone out for beers.

"Gregory told you, didn't he?" she said.

"Amy, I—"

"Don't lie, Joe," Amy said, her finger in his face. "You're supposed to be my partner!"

Joe's head dropped. "Okay, yes. Yes, he did, Amy."

"Bastard!" she said, continuing toward the staircase.

"Wait! Who? Me?"

EIGHTEEN

T he blue BMW X5 was already getting small up ahead.

Frank was still idling at the red light when he decided he couldn't wait any longer and floored it. The old sedan shot out, then tore across the intersection at Victoria Bridge to the accompaniment of squealing brakes, screeching tires and honking horns. He was pushed back in his seat as he sped up past the old Treasury Brisbane Casino, where he swerved into the bus lane and spotted the BMW turning left around the building.

Frank kept the speed up for as long as he dared, then hit the brakes last moment, yanked on the steering wheel and held on as the car lurched and bounced around the corner into Elizabeth Street. He skidded across two lanes; the rear kicked out and Frank jerked the wheel in the opposite direction and once again floored it. The car momentarily sought its equilibrium, only to bounce in the opposite direction before he finally regained control as it settled in the third and outermost lane. Frank looked across all three lanes, then eyed the BMW in the middle one, six cars up.

Both sides of the one-way street were packed with parked cars, the sidewalks busy with buskers, beggars and browsers.

He kept pushing, swerving in and out of traffic to close the gap. Alternating between the outer and middle lane, Frank was closing in fast.

Just as he passed the Brisbane Department Store, the BMW changed to the inner lane while Frank was stuck in the outer. He swerved, almost hitting a guy on an electric scooter. His heart racing, he poked his arm out of the window and flipped him the bird. When his heart dislodged from his throat, he noticed he was now only one car back but still two lanes across.

Then the back of the BMW lit up red and hooked left, eased underneath the Brisbane Tower Hotel's porte cochère.

Frank craned his neck as he was forced to roll by, spotted a valet in a top hat open the back passenger door of the BMW, then caught a fleeting glimpse of a man with gray hair as he stepped out.

He desperately began looking for a place to dump his car, but the curbs were tightly packed and traffic around him kept flowing.

Frank punched the steering wheel and swore under his breath.

Nineteen

Frank slowed his awkward jog and walked as fast as he could. His teardrop belly bounced over his belt, and he was sweating under the folds of his man boobs. His throat was dry, and he felt dehydrated. His left knee was playing up again; it felt inflamed and the usual, light soreness had now turned into agonizing pain.

The good news was that he'd found an illegal parking spot two streets over, so he'd grabbed his newly acquired equipment and begun his frantic backtracking.

Frank adjusted the shoulder strap one more time, then turned and walked under the overhang to the Brisbane Tower Hotel entrance. The shade was an immediate relief. He slowed down even more as he approached the revolving doors, smiled at one of the bellboys, then pushed on the chrome handle and proceeded into the lobby.

Frank was met by a bright, grand interior with extremely high ceilings, an abundance of skylights and gentle classical music. The AC cooled every sweat-covered spot, which for Frank basically meant every square inch of his body. He took a few deep breaths, then casually walked up to the reception desk. A lady in a dark suit, with a small frame, delicate features and perfect makeup, came over. Her silver nametag read KAREN.

"Good afternoon, sir. How can I help?"

The guy Frank had glimpsed fifteen minutes earlier had looked like a man of stature. Someone up the top. Even from a distance, his clothes had appeared expensive and his chest had appeared puffed. Which told Frank that he was probably the most important of all. He mentally went through the names from the files he'd studied that morning, then decided to bet on the big cheese himself—the CEO.

He pointed to the square, insulated cooler bag slung over his shoulder. "Lunch for Mr. Brian Hearst from Jacaranda Security Group?"

The woman studied the bag for some time, then looked at Frank. "Mr. Hearst has already ordered food to be delivered to the conference room," she said. "From our own restaurant."

Frank cursed his luck. "What conference room is that?"

The woman smiled. "What food delivery service do you work for?"

Frank shook his head. "I don't. I'm the owner of Paul's Pizza, and I'm personally delivering this to Mr. Hearst. And, look, I'm not knocking your establishment here, Karen. I'm sure it's great. But no one—and I mean no one—makes cheesy garlic bread like we do. And Mr. Hearst knows that, 'cause he's had it before. Many times. So, whatever he's ordered from you, he wants to enjoy it with *my* garlic bread," Frank said, then leaned in and added: "Well, my mum's recipe, but also mine now." He put on his best smile, his heart pounding.

The woman looked perplexed. "Okay, my apologies," she said, then returned her attention to the monitor in front of her. "Conference room four."

"Which is?"

Karen stuck an arm out and pointed. "Down that way. You'll see signs to our Business Center."

"Thank you," Frank said.

As he began walking, he noticed Karen giving him a sidelong glance before rapidly typing away at her keyboard.

TWENTY

F rank didn't bother knocking.

He checked the contents of his bag, adjusted the shoulder strap, then resolutely opened the door.

The conference room was small. A table designed for a dozen people, chrome legs, black tabletop, black leather high-back chairs, half of which were empty. Two guys sitting with their backs against the floor-to-ceiling windows at the far end of the room looked straight across at Frank. Three on the near side with their backs to Frank turned their heads. On the right, at the head of the table, a guy in a fancy suit gave Frank a questioning look. He was tanned, with a gray slick of hair. The guy Frank had glimpsed. Up close he definitely looked like the headshot from the file. The guy he presumed was the CEO: Brian Hearst.

Frank took a step inside, stopped, then slowly turned his body left and right as he scanned the room.

"Help you, buddy?" the man in the fancy suit said.

Frank gave it a moment, did his best impersonation of a confused food-delivery guy. "Pizza for Giles and Mannheim?" he said.

The guy shook his head. "Wrong room, buddy. Move it along."

Frank put up a hand in apology. "Sorry," he said, then turned to go.

He zigzagged his way back and was halfway through the reception area when Karen came running across the expanse, her heels clicking rapidly.

"Excuse me," she said.

Frank stopped, waiting for her to catch up.

Karen stopped in front of him and crossed her arms. "I'm sorry, but there is no Paul's Pizza here in Brisbane."

Frank put on his confused look again. "And?" he said.

Karen's painted eyebrows dipped in a frown. "You said you're from Paul's Pizza."

Frank chuckled, shook his head. "Papa's Pizza, Karen, not Paul's."

Karen looked at him suspiciously.

"Listen," Frank said. "Why don't you go back to Brian Hearst, ask him yourself, and watch him pull strings of melted cheese out of his mouth so that he can answer your questions."

There was a glimmer of doubt in her eyes, but it disappeared as quickly as it'd emerged. "You know what, I think I will," she said, then pointed at Frank. "And you wait here!"

Frank gave her a mock salute. "Will do. Where can I get a coffee? I could use a break, anyway."

Karen lowered her arm, seemed to relax. "I'm really sorry, but Mr. Hearst is an important customer to us."

"No harm done. Just please point me in the direction of a place where I can get a coffee."

"Come with me," she said, then walked in front of Frank over to a bar area. Beside the bar, open double doors led to a green beer garden. For a moment, Frank wished he could just sit out there and down beers and eat fries and enjoy the sun that was illuminating the lush landscaping.

Karen got the attention of the man behind the bar, waved him over, then turned to Frank. "Order whatever you like. It's on the house, and I'll be back in a moment. Excuse me," she said.

Frank watched her disappear down toward the Business Center, then ordered a cappuccino, asked where the restrooms were and walked back toward reception.

When he was sure that he was out of sight, Frank exited the hotel and exploded into a sprint, which, for Frank—due to his weight and bad knee—resembled a half-sideways, limping jog.

Twenty-One

Frank rolled into Newstead and swore under his breath as he continued past the AFP building. He flipped the bird for the second time that day, hoping that Gregory Fordham would look out his window at the exact right time.

He checked his phone GPS and took a final right turn just before reaching the Brisbane River, then cruised south through Teneriffe, down a leafy blacktop with tasteful apartments on his right and expensive looking townhouses facing the river on his left. Passing the red-brick building of the old Wool Store, he began scanning house numbers on his left. Once he'd located the number, he slowed down, eyed a parking spot and parallel parked. He leaned over to the front passenger seat, accidentally squeezed his gut and let go of a burp. Note to self: Two hotdogs would have been enough. He shrugged, then unzipped his insulated food bag and retrieved the video camera.

Frank walked back. Somewhere above him, a couple of magpies began caroling. He stopped at a large stone pillar with an intricate bell and pressed the button. It was set in a solid brass plate, polished to a high shine and embellished with ornate edges. He didn't hear any static from the intercom but smiled up at the black glass globe anyway.

The gate clicked open.

Rebecca was standing in the doorway, different attire, equally stunning. She'd braided her blonde hair and her blue eyes matched her blue dress with white flowers. Frank's heart sunk.

"Frank," she said, then turned ninety degrees and held an arm out. "Come on in."

Frank nodded in greeting and cursed himself for not going home first to change and freshen up. After last night's drinking, the early morning studying and his adventures at the Brisbane Tower Hotel, Frank felt hot, sticky and tired.

Frank followed Rebecca into the house. The interior was grand and designed with an Aussie twist on the Hamptons style: bleached timber floors; creamy, raised panels; duck egg blue walls; furniture, cushions and artwork in different shades of soothing pastels. The style extended to the back porch.

Rebecca pointed to a wooden chair with plump, baby-blue cushions.

Frank sat down, placed his camera on the table and watched a city catamaran slide by, the wake gently spreading until the smooth, undulating water began lapping up against Rebecca's tastefully landscaped backyard. Lush foliage with broad, dark green leaves shaded flowers that Frank recognized as pink tulips, red roses and orange orchids, as well as some he didn't recognize that were round and yellow, some bell-shaped and purple, and others wide, waxy and white.

"Waw," Frank said.

Rebecca smiled. "Would you like some Kombucha?"

Frank shook his head. "I'm not hungry, but I'd love a coffee, please."

Rebecca looked puzzled for a moment, then chuckled. "How do you take it?"

Frank thought a woman in a house like this would probably also have a fancy coffee machine. "Can you make a cappuccino?"

"Full-cream, skim or soy?" she said. "I also have oat milk."

"Again," Frank said. "Waw."

Rebecca chuckled once more. "It's really not a big deal. Capsules, all automatic, no knowledge about the art of brewing necessary."

"In that case, full cream, please, three sugars."

Rebecca returned a few minutes later with his cappuccino and a tall glass of something that looked like apple juice for herself. She sat down across from Frank.

"Let me show you what I've got," Frank said, then switched on his new video camera. He lifted and turned the small LCD screen so that they could both see. "I filmed it earlier today. Let me know if you see the fellow who's been following you," he said, then pressed PLAY.

The footage bounced around and showed only a blur of walls and paintings.

"What are we watching?" Rebecca asked.

"Right here, I'm just walking to a conference room. It'll become clear in a moment."

The recording stabilized and a rustling sound came through the tiny loudspeaker as the camera was adjusted one last time. Then a door appeared and Frank's chubby hand could be seen grabbing the handle and opening the door.

The screen showed a small conference room. A table designed for a dozen people, chrome legs, black tabletop, black leather high-back chairs, half of which were empty. Two guys sitting with their backs against the floor-to-ceiling windows at the far end of the room looked straight across, their focus just above the camera. Three on the near side with their backs to the door turned their heads. On the right, at the head of the table, a guy in a fancy suit had a questioning look on his face. He was tanned, with a gray slick of hair.

The frame shook as Frank took a step inside, then bounced slightly as he turned left, then right, until the camera stopped moving and the entire conference room was captured on the wide lens.

Frank leaned over, pressed a button and froze the image, then pointed to the gentleman at the end of the table. "I think that's Brian Hearst, CEO of a company called Jacaranda Security Group," Frank said. "Not sure about the rest of them."

Rebecca leaned in closer, stared at the screen for a while. She didn't blink.

"Oh my God!" Rebecca put a hand in front of her mouth. Then she cocked her head, looked some more. She tentatively removed her hand and pointed at the man on the far left, from the row closest to the camera.

His face was clearly visible, his dark hair parted and styled.

"That's Bill," she said.

"Bill?"

Rebecca turned to Frank. "William Forrester. Best buddy and childhood friend of my husband."

Frank scratched his red goatee. "Your . . . deceased husband?"

Rebecca nodded. "They were inseparable, those two. Went to school together somewhere up north. Redcliffe, I think. Became best mates. Different university degrees, ended up in the same mining company. Carl, my husband, eventually became head of operations of a relatively minor outfit called FTGU Mining. Heard of it?"

Frank shook his head, looked back up at the house, then raised an eyebrow. "Relatively minor?"

Rebecca smiled. "Well, in the mining industry, it's considered a small company, but, of course, it provided plenty for us. Anyway, Bill became a tax accountant, got all the accreditations, and as soon as Carl got the top job in operations, he got Bill a job with FTGU."

"Good ol' nepotism," Frank said, then thought about the files he'd read that morning about JSG. "William Forrester, you say?"

Rebecca nodded.

Frank remembered. "He's now Chief Financial Officer with Jacaranda Security Group."

Rebecca shrugged. "I don't understand it. I haven't seen him since Carl's funeral five years ago. Why would he be following me?"

"I thought you said whoever's following you is a man in his thirties, with blond hair?"

"Yes, but surely he must be involved, right?"

"He?"

"Bill, I mean."

Frank leaned forward. "Who knows? Right now, we know that your husband's best friend is working for JSG, and that someone else who also works there has been following you," he said, then pointed at the small screen. "Can you see him anywhere here?"

"The guy who's been following me?"

Frank nodded.

Rebecca looked closer, pointed at a face against the far wall. "Could be him, but I can't be sure. Looks a lot like him, from what I can tell."

"Hmmm. Can I ask you a somewhat delicate question?"

"Yes, of course."

"How did your husband die?"

"I'll give you my version," Rebecca said.

"Your version?" Frank said.

Rebecca nodded. "And then I'll give you Bill's version."

Twenty-Two

Amy had decided to do something she'd never done in her entire career: She was going to malinger.

She slid the key into her front door, thought about what disease to come up with to get a week off. Hell, maybe even two. She'd left work straight after lunch with Joe. There were a few outstanding items she needed to sort in her life before she could once again fully engage and, besides, she hadn't been enjoying her job very much since being partnered with Joe. It felt like her workdays were consumed with unproductive administrative duties, superfluous meetings, futile phone calls and aimless emails. Only Frank had added a spark, but he was gone now.

The door opened before Amy could turn the key.

"I'm sorry," Jason said. He sounded like he was breathing through his mouth, as if his sinuses were stuffed. He had opened the door wide and was holding a bouquet of yellow flowers in his hand. He held it out to her. He was actually wearing nice slacks for a change, had even put on a shirt. Then she noticed his face.

"Jesus!" she said. "What happened to you?"

Jason shrugged, then stood aside to let her in.

Amy threw her keys in the blue glass bowl but kept her boots and jacket on. She nodded toward the living room and they both went and sat down—Jason in a chair, Amy on the end of the couch. He was still holding the flowers.

"What happened to you?" she said again.

Jason shrugged. "I don't know," he said. "Someone rang the security intercom late last night. I was sure it was you, so I stumbled out of bed, pretty much sleepwalked into the hallway and pressed the buzzer. Then I walked back into the kitchen to get a glass of water. After a few minutes, when you still hadn't entered, I went to have a look." Jason placed the flowers on the table, looked down. "I opened the door, registered a figure standing just outside, and the next thing I remember is waking up on the hallway floor."

"Waking up?"

Jason nodded. "The bastard punched my lights out."

Amy leaned forward to caress his face.

Jason pulled back. "Don't touch it! I think it's broken. It hurts like crazy."

Amy nodded. She felt sorry for him.

Just a hint of accusation had entered his voice when he spoke again: "You have any idea who could have done this?" he said, pointing at his nose.

In fact, Amy had a very good idea. When she'd shown up at her parents' with her bruised cheek, her brother—who was twenty and a Karate black belt—had been very clear about what he planned on doing to Jason if he "were to ever meet him in a dark alley". Amy smiled.

"I really don't know," she said. Again, she felt sorry for Jason. Sorry that he'd developed this needless jealousy. Sorry that he'd never managed to get an education. Sorry that he evidently felt inferior to Amy and now had to show it through childish behavior. But she also felt a little bit sorry for herself. Sorry that she'd let herself get swept off her feet by a white smile, good hair and bulging muscles. All of it surface stuff, yet Amy's dreams and desires ran much deeper than that. She put it down to a momentary lapse in judgement, something that she would never do again. Ever.

"You'll have to move out," she said. She felt as shocked at her own comment as Jason looked. She took a deep breath. Couldn't believe how good it felt to get it out. Hadn't even known that it was what she'd wanted, not until the moment the words had actually flown out of her mouth.

"I . . ." Jason began.

"I know. It's okay," Amy said. "But it's over, and that's okay, too."

"But," Jason said. It sounded like *ba* with his busted nose. "How will you pay the bills?"

Amy laughed. "Didn't you say you quit your job? Guess you didn't worry about bills when you did that," she said, then quickly and playfully tapped the tip of his nose with her finger. "Don't you worry about me."

Jason flinched, then began blinking rapidly. "Ow—bitch! Don't think you can—"

"I lied," Amy said, then stood up and held a finger in front of his face. "I do know who paid you a visit last night and if you ever—and I mean *ever*—touch me again, I'll make sure she pays you another visit."

Jason looked at her incredulously. "Very funny. *She?* It definitely wasn't a she. It was a *he* and—one thing is for sure—he was a chunky bastard!"

"I bet he was," Amy said under her breath. Then: "What? Chunky?"

Jason held a hand over his nose, making him even more difficult to understand. "Yes, chunky, as in big," he said. "Who the hell do you know that's so fat?"

Amy smiled and nodded, then walked back into the hallway and scooped up her keys. "You've got twenty-four hours. Then you and your shit will be out of here," Amy said, then slammed the door shut.

Damn, it felt good.

TWENTY-THREE

Rebecca took a sip of her brown water. "I'd been out shopping, let myself into the house and found . . ." Rebecca took a moment to gather herself. "And found him sitting in the chair you're sitting in now," she said, then looked down at Frank's feet. "He'd dropped his Irish coffee. There were shards of glass scattered on the deck. His head had plumped forward and his chin was resting on his chest. And that was that."

"Heart attack?"

Rebecca nodded.

"I'm very sorry."

"I've moved on. It's okay now."

"He died five years ago?"

"That's right."

"So, what's Bill's version?"

Rebecca shook her head and grunted. "Bill was always jealous. When I met Carl, I was nineteen and he was forty-seven," she said, a smile spreading across her face, her eyes seeking the river. "It was a whirlwind, a magical time of dinners, trips and hotels. Six months later, we got married in front of a hundred of Carl's friends and family at an outdoor venue in the Roma Street Parkland. During the wedding, most people kept a polite smile on their faces, but, of course, the traditional opinions quickly emerged and bombarded us from everywhere: she's too young; she only took him for his money; he's too old; he can't have chosen her for the conversations; it can't be true love. Blah, blah, blah."

"Hmmm."

"Anyway, soon after the wedding, we bought this house, and Bill and his wife began coming around a lot. He and Carl would be shooting pool in the games room or drinking brandy and smoking cigars out here, telling stories and bragging, whatever boys do. But," Rebecca said, "as time went on, Bill began showing an unhealthy interest in me, you know? I'd catch him checking me out, or I'd feel him staring at me. Not only did I pretend to not notice, but I also had to smile and chat to his wife to make sure that *she* didn't notice."

"Bill's married?"

Rebecca nodded. "I ignored his behavior completely, but that just seemed to make it worse. He'd show up unannounced—without his wife—and suggest we have a drink and this always at times when Carl wasn't home. And then his creepy texts: 'What are you doing now?' or 'Can't you sleep, either?' Stuff like that."

"Hmmm."

"Then, about three months before Carl died, we had a big party here and Bill once again showed up alone."

"Aha."

"After the guests had gone home, in the early hours as the sun was coming up, Carl went to bed, but Bill was still hanging around." Rebecca sighed. "I offered to call him a taxi, but he insisted on staying to help me tidy up. And . . . I don't know. There was something about him that morning. I didn't dare say no and ask him to go home, so I began tidying up out here, collecting glasses, fishing plastic cups out of the pool, putting chairs back, when he came up from behind and grabbed me and kissed my neck. I tried to break free, but he told me he couldn't ignore it anymore and neither should I. Some nonsense like that. Which is when I turned around and kneed him in the groin."

Frank made big eyes. "And did you tell Carl, then?"

Rebecca thought for a moment, then shook her head. "I couldn't get myself to do it."

"Why not?"

"This may sound stupid, but I was afraid of what Carl would say. After all, they were best friends, and I didn't want my husband to know that his friend was a jerk. I was also afraid that Bill's wife would find out. I didn't want to ruin their marriage. But, even more importantly, I didn't want Carl to think that I'd been leading Bill on."

"That doesn't sound so stupid," Frank said.

"He never tried anything after that," Rebecca said. "And apart from Carl's funeral, that was the last time I saw Bill."

Frank sensed Rebecca wanted to add something else. "What is it?"

"It's funny," she said. "I think that me rejecting him first and then Carl dying shortly after really changed Bill. He used to call and come here constantly, but now I never hear from him. Instead, he's having me followed? What's his deal?"

"Hmmm." Frank nodded. "Seems like it. But I still haven't heard Bill's version of why Carl died?"

"He verbally attacked me at the funeral," Rebecca said. "I'd just put my husband in the ground and as people were leaving, passing on their condolences, Bill comes over and tells me that Carl would still be alive if it weren't for me. Says that Carl had a heart attack because of me. That, rather than keep him young, I wore him out, spent all his money and expected him to be as fit as a twenty-five-year-old. Bill even stuck a finger in my face and said he was going to devote the rest of his life to making mine miserable."

Frank emptied his cappuccino. "Would you like me to talk to him?"

Rebecca shook her head. "He'd never admit anything. He's a creep. I remember Carl telling me once that Bill was involved in a bar brawl, and that the other party apparently got hurt really badly. I don't know the details, but I know in the pit of my soul that he's a bad man, Frank. Terrible. So if somehow you could figure out what's happening, that would be a great help," she said, then added: "I'm scared, Frank. Now that I don't have Carl around anymore, I feel exposed and vulnerable."

Frank nodded. "I understand," he said, then tapped his fingers on the table, looked at the river for a moment, then back at Rebecca.

"I need you to get me a list of all the people you know who are connected to Carl, Bill and yourself. Their names, numbers, addresses, workplaces, nature and extent of relationships. That's all colleagues, friends and family members that you can think of, as well as anyone in the periphery," he said, then stood up.

"Alright," Rebecca said. "I've got your email address."

Frank scratched his read goatee. "Is there an easier way?"

Rebecca looked puzzled.

"Email is good," Frank said. "And thank you for the coffee."

Rebecca stood up as well and when she spoke, Frank noticed an urgency in her voice, something just short of panic. "How will a list like that help you?"

Frank put a hand on her shoulder. "I'm not sure," he said. "But we have to start somewhere."

TWENTY-FOUR

Rattling noises bounced between concrete pillars and walls until Frank killed the engine of his old sedan. He trotted over to the elevator, which, through somewhat of a miracle, was already there waiting for him. He entered and was about to head up to his flat when he realized that he hadn't checked his mailbox in over a week. Frank pressed the button for the ground floor, then waited patiently as the doors closed and the elevator gently lifted him up one floor. He shuffled out through the small lobby, exited the building, then turned, crouched and found his mailbox on the bottom row. He inserted a key, turned it and pulled at the small flap, listening to the familiar squeak of tiny hinges desperately in need of oil. Frank peered into the darkness, saw a bunch of junk mail inside the aluminum slot. He delicately squeezed two fat fingers in there, retrieved the pile and locked the mailbox. He tightened whatever muscles were still left in his legs, grunted and pushed upward. Blood rushed to his face and Frank felt like it was on the verge of exploding. His knees clicked loudly and his lower back hurt as he slowly straightened. He walked back into the lobby, entered the elevator and pressed the button for the sixth floor.

Frank's belly was sore. On the way home, he'd remembered that he was out of coffee, so Frank had done a little detour and stopped in at his favorite shop. He'd watched with great satisfaction as the barista had poured beans into a hopper and ground them on the spot, then sealed the coffee in a fresh bag. Happy to have found his own fuel, he realized his car needed the same, so then Frank had begun looking for a gas station. He cursed himself for having ignored the yellow light for so long and was convinced that the old, big sedan would cough and die at any moment. But, surprisingly, he'd made it. While paying for his fuel, Frank had eyed a new range of chocolate bars. The guy behind the counter had explained that they were from some social media guru. Frank didn't understand what that had to do with chocolate, but out of sheer curiosity, he bought all eight flavors, then sat down on the curb in front of the shop and watched people come and go while demolishing them in quick succession. Now he felt nauseous and the worst part was that he hadn't even liked them. Apart from one that had been heavy on peanuts, caramel and nougat.

The elevator doors opened and Frank proceeded down a slightly musty hallway, then let himself into his small, one-bedroom apartment. He kicked off his sneakers and walked into the kitchen, where he threw the leaflets and flyers on the countertop and began scooping his freshly bought coffee into the filter of his percolator. Once he'd added water, he switched on the machine, went back into the bedroom and got his pile of papers. He brought them out to the balcony and began pouring through them as he waited for the coffee to brew.

Frank's phone chimed. Rebecca had emailed him a list with over fifty names. He scanned through it, top to bottom. Then again. The eleventh name from the top stirred something. Frank thought he'd seen it before, recognized it from somewhere. He closed his eyes and saw a dotted line with a hastily scrawled signature, the printed name below the dots. He opened his eyes and leafed through the pile until he found it: Matthew Clarkson from Clarkson Real Estate.

Matthew's company had managed the lease of a Brisbane apartment inside which a tenant had been murdered three years ago. The police had no leads. The only certainty was that the victim had been stabbed. The victim, Charles Grainer, had a clean record, worked as a local plumber and was known to keep to himself. Several theories were put forward: a jealous husband, assuming Grainer had had an affair with a married woman; a mistaken identity hit; a local dopehead looking for quick money. Mr. Grainer had no high standing in society, no connections and no other family in the country, so the police had put the case on the back burner.

Picking up the case, Frank had—against Gregory's orders—filled his days digging into the history of Charles Grainer. Wanting to examine Grainer's life from birth to the day he died, he'd requested Charles's papers from several authorities and closely studied all the documents in his file, including his original birth certificate from England. For a document supposedly just over forty years old, it was surprisingly crisp and in remarkably good shape. No coffee spills, no dog ears, no finger smudges or accidental folds or tears. Charles Grainer—a plumber who truly lived the life of the middle-class and whose hobby was watching and playing Australian rules football—apparently liked to take extreme care when handling his personal documents.

Frank didn't buy it, so he lowered his nose and dug further. Looked through every single line in the birth certificate. The way it had been filled out. The size of the margins. The color of the ink. The weight of the paper. Charles had been born in 1982 and his father's occupation was stated as train driver, his mother's as bookkeeper. On the surface, everything looked legitimate. But then Frank hit pay dirt. Upon further investigation, he's discovered that English birth certificates hadn't begun including the mother's occupation until 1984. Ergo, the birth certificate was a fake. Someone had messed up. Frank had, once again—and against orders—brought it to Gregory's attention. He'd dismissed it, told him that the world isn't perfect and even original documents can have mistakes in them, appear slightly different from one another, especially documents that are decades old. Frank had argued and pointed and raised his voice, Gregory had denied and thrown his hands around and screamed. Eventually, Frank had nodded and gone back to his desk, then added the name Charles Grainer to his growing list of people with seemingly fake backgrounds and clean records. And who'd all been killed.

Frank checked the email again. Rebecca had written that Matthew Clarkson, the real estate agent, was a friend of Bill's. In other words, Rebecca's deceased husband, Carl, had been best friends with William Forrester, or Bill. And Bill now worked for a company that was following Rebecca and he was also friends with the guy who'd rented out a flat to a man who was killed. Frank's guts turned. Rebecca was in trouble. Big trouble. Something didn't add up.

Or, to be more Frank, something did.

The coffee machine's hissing and crackling jolted Frank back to the present. He put the papers down and went into the kitchen, was about to grab the glass pot when something caught his attention. Poking out from under a pizza pamphlet, Frank noticed the corner of an envelope. It showed the familiar profile of a kangaroo on the left, an emu on the right, in the middle a shield depicting the six states of Australia, complete with a seven-pointed star up the top and golden wattle in the background: the Commonwealth Coat of Arms. Words were printed just next to it: AUSTRALIAN GOVERNMENT. DEPARTMENT OF HOME AFFAIRS. He put an index finger in the middle of a tiny pepperoni pizza, then gently slid the pamphlet aside, confirming that the envelope had his name on it. Frank opened a corner, then struggled to get a finger under the flap to tear it open. His hands were shaking as he retrieved the pages and unfolded them. Words stood out: WE HEREBY INFORM YOU . . . MUST BE TAKEN SERIOUSLY . . . UNDER NO CIRCUMSTANCES . . . ABSOLUTELY NO LATER THAN . . . FAILURE TO ACT WILL RESULT IN . . . DECISION IS FINAL AND CANNOT BE DISPUTED . . .

Frank had to leave Australia. In eight days.

He turned, relaxed his knees, then let himself slide down his cupboard doors until his butt hit the floor, his legs spread out before him.

And for the first time since coming to Australia, Frank cried.

TWENTY-FIVE

D on didn't turn on the lights.

    Something had woken him up and, within a few seconds, he realized it must have been his bladder, which was on the verge of bursting.

The moon was visible through the small, square window, dressing the bathroom in a faint glow. He pulled down his boxers, aimed for the center of the bowl, and listened to the splashing of his urine as it crashed through the surface of the water. There was a stench that Don couldn't quite place and it definitely wasn't piss.

Memories from yesterday flooded his hungover brain. The boys had arrived early and what Don thought was going to be a few beers had turned into a full-blown party. Brad had brought cocaine. Other guys had gotten beer and alcohol. Later in the night, there'd been a major surprise: a whole harem of girls. And not just any old corner bitches; these were some high-class ones, girls that properly dated and pretended and stuff. Girls that actually smelled good and looked the part. They'd danced and drunk and snorted and . . . Don tried to remember. Had he ended up with anyone? Oh, yes. Yes, he had. He cursed himself for drinking so much; he would have liked to savor that particular memory, but as it was, he could only recall fragments of what had probably been an awesome time. The alcohol had all but erased the memory and the drugs set him on edge.

As the splashing subsided, he shook twice, then pulled his boxers back up and flushed. He turned to the tiny sink; it was almost full of what—in the moonlight—looked like a shiny, brown substance with lumps in it. Another memory flashed of Brad holding onto the edges of the sink, bent over, gagging and retching until he turned red in the face. Don immediately turned away so that he wouldn't vomit himself.

Then he heard the clink of bottles somewhere. He leaned through the doorway and stuck his head out into the hallway.

A faint shadow moved across the hallway wall.

Don pulled his head back in. What the fuck? He tried to think clearly. There was a whole selection of knives in the kitchen. The baseball bat was under the bed.

Slowly, silently, he walked out of the bathroom and stayed snug up against the wall leading to the living room. His pulse pounded, and he looked for more shadows and listened for more sounds, but apart from the deep drumming of his own heart, all was quiet.

When he reached the door to the living room, he carefully poked one eye around the side jamb and held his breath. There was a dark figure sitting on the floor, facing away from the door. Don's brain was working overtime to understand who the hell was in his flat when the figure half-turned and knocked over another bottle.

"Don," Brad said. "Is that you, mate? Shit, here I go again," he said, then leaned sideways and vomited.

Don didn't have time to react. He simply breathed out and flicked the light switch and was horrified by what he saw: Brad sitting on the Turkish rug, one hand in a pool of puke, the other rubbing his face. He was in the middle of a sea of empty beer bottles and cans. The coffee table was overturned, the dining table was loaded with half-empty liquor bottles, overflowing ashtrays and discarded glasses, some of which were broken. Don's newly purchased leather couch had stains he didn't want to think about.

Brad stopped rubbing his face and gave Don a thumbs up. "Great party, bro!"

Don helped Brad get up and guided him back into the toilet, then exited and closed the door to the smell.

He continued into the kitchen to get some tea towels. He wouldn't be able to go back to sleep now and was dreading the work ahead. He took a bucket from under the sink, placed it under the tap, squirted in some dishwashing liquid and watched the soap bubbles grow as the warm water rose.

"You better clean up that sink, Brad," Don said, then turned off the tap, unaware that those would be his last words.

He didn't have the time or the ability to think about whether the excruciating agony in his stomach had been preceded by another shadow crawling across the wall. Nor did he have the awareness to register that the numbing pain originated somewhere inside his lower back, on the right, just below the ribcage.

He really didn't have anything anymore. His kidney froze and his intestines exploded and purple pulp sprayed out his ass, into his boxers and ran down his leg onto the kitchen floor while bright red juice hosed out through his mouth, the cupboards splattered in various shades of crimson even before his body hit the floor.

TWENTY-SIX

F rank sipped his cappuccino. "Hmmm."

He wiggled to get comfortable on the wooden stool. Mugs & Marmalade was full of people eating breakfast and Frank had been lucky to get a spot while waiting for Amy.

The top shelf in the glass display was bursting with bagels, hot buns, chocolate croissants, Danish, oversized cinnamon scrolls, rolls with bacon and eggs, baguettes with salads and sandwiches with ham and cheese. Below that, a shelf was stuffed full of cheesecakes, iced donuts, chocolate chip cookies, multi-colored macaroons and brownies. The bottom shelf was loaded with paninis, sausage rolls and meat pies. Frank's belly rumbled.

Amy snapped her fingers in front of his face. "Earth to Frank, come in!" she said.

Frank turned back toward Amy. "Sorry," he said. "I'm starving. I haven't had breakfast."

"No worries. Anyway—"

"How long do you think it takes to make a grilled cheese?" Frank said.

"Frank, seriously? Could you not think about food for one second?"

"Sorry."

"I asked you, what's the big deal here? Why do you want me to work for you?"

"No, no," Frank said. "If we do this, you work *with* me, not *for* me, okay?"

Amy's smile lit up her face. "Fine, *with* you. Now, can you answer my question, please?"

"Remember how I told you that the eight victims we looked at were out of place, as if they didn't belong?"

Amy nodded. "Your spy theory," she said. "How could I forget?"

"I think I figured out what connects them," Frank said.

"You mean, other than their—what did you call it—foggy and cardboardy backgrounds?"

Frank smiled. "Exactly right!"

"I'm all ears," Amy said.

"Well," Frank said. "Who has foggy and cardboardy, made-up lives?"

"Spies," Amy said.

Frank nodded. "And?"

Amy took a moment. "Con artists and people who steal other people's identities?"

Frank nodded again. "Sure, but these eight people all have squeaky-clean criminal records."

Amy thought for a bit, then shrugged. "Tell me."

"People who've seen something they shouldn't have," Frank said.

Amy crossed her arms. "Seen something . . ."

"Witnessed, if you will."

Amy uncrossed her arms, leaned forward. "People in a witness protection program?"

"Bingo!" Frank said. "The National Witness Protection Program."

Amy nodded. "They witness something, testify in court, or not, but they're in danger. They enter the program, get new identities and their past officially gets erased, a new one made up by a few select government officials."

"Whom we all know," Frank said, "are not always exceptional at what they do, hence the little red flags, such as the mistake I found with the English birth certificate belonging to Charles Grainer."

Amy nodded again. "That could be it, but how would that connect people inside our witness protection program?"

"Simple," Frank said. "I think all eight victims we found were in that program."

"And all of them killed by the same person?"

Frank nodded.

"But it's not as though there's a list floating around of people in the program. How would the killer know who to target?"

Frank shrugged. "He must be connected to a corrupt official," he said, then snapped his fingers. "Maybe it's even the official himself doing the deed."

"But why? What would the motive be?"

"I haven't figured that one out yet, but someone is out there, targeting people in witness protection."

"Come on, Frank! What are the odds of something like that happening?"

"I think low," Frank said.

"That's exactly what I mean."

"I don't think so."

"What?"

"I think what you mean is that the chances are slim."

Amy turned red in the face. "That's what I just said."

Frank shook his head. "No. You agreed with me that the odds are low, and low odds equals something is likely. It's a common misconception, this whole odds thing, not unusual at all to confuse high odds with low odds, but—just to be clear—low odds means likely, high odds means unlikely."

An elderly lady with gray hair and kind eyes and a loud voice exited the kitchen and put a plate on the counter. "Order for Frank!" she yelled.

Frank shot up and walked over, grabbed his large plate with grilled cheese, a blueberry muffin and a pain au chocolat, then came back and sat down.

Amy reached over and grabbed the blueberry muffin, tore off a piece from the top and stuffed it in her mouth. She spoke while chewing. "Jesus, Frank! Sometimes I really wish you could formulate just one clear sentence, make some sense for the rest of us not living in Frankland."

"Sorry," he said. Then: "Watch out!"

TWENTY-SEVEN

F rank had never had to explain "watch out" to Amy; she knew it was one of his rare, quirky translations and that what he really meant was "pay attention". He filled Amy in on what he'd studied, everything he'd noticed in the cases Amy had given him, his theories and suspicions, not stopping until he'd emptied both his brain and his plate. When he was finally done talking, Amy went to the restroom and Frank once again eyed the food under the counter, began considering. Choices, choices.

When Amy came back five minutes later, she stopped next to Frank. "So, the connection between the eight victims, according to you, is that they were all in witness protection, but you can't say for sure?"

Frank turned his head to face her. "No one can," he said. "The witness protection program was designed to protect sensitive information from being spread among numerous state and local organizations. So now the information is streamlined. Say a local AFP agent recommends a witness join the program, that is then immediately routed to an unknown contact within the system and a decision is made. If it's decided the person is to enter the program, necessary commands are distributed sporadically, fragments of need-to-know carefully assigned to only a handful of people, such as the Commissioner, Deputy Commissioner, maybe even the Assistant Commissioner. The commissioners, in turn, delegate further, but this time with any program specifics filtered out."

"How do you mean?"

"Only the very top of the hierarchy will know if a person is part of the program. That information will never be passed on because it would never be needed, plus it would also add extra risk for absolutely no gain. Say, for instance, if a person in the program needs a new passport for a new identity, someone within the AFP would simply lodge a request with the Department of Foreign Affairs and Trade, automatically omitting any information related to the program."

"But wouldn't the department ask questions?"

"Sure, they could ask questions. Then they'd be told that an undercover AFP agent needs a new passport, or whatever they could come up with."

"But wouldn't the department see that a previous passport under that name had never been issued?"

"Perhaps, but it's not unusual for people to have their first passport issued later in life. But regardless, there would always be a cover story to match the request."

"And with all this . . . smokes and mirrors, how on earth would a killer go about obtaining all that information? And where would he get it from?"

Frank shrugged. "I don't know how he would do it, but he would have to get it straight from the Commissioner. I'm pretty sure about that."

Amy looked at Frank.

"The AFP Commissioner," he said. "He'd be the one who knows the identities of everyone in the program."

"The *only* one?" Amy said.

"Who knows them *all*. These are top-secret files, inaccessible to regular AFP agents," he said. "But what I found for sure is that every single one of the eight victims has either generic, foggy backgrounds, or at least histories that are impossible to dig into. Amy, with this relatively new program, Australia's trying to learn from the only really successful witness protection program in the world."

"Being?"

"WITSEC, the Witness Security Program, run by the United States Marshall Service. Since they started in the late sixties, they've helped around twenty thousand people and they boast an incredible success rate. The rest of the world looks enviously at America when it comes to witness protection. In comparison, Australia helps maybe fifty a year and they're not very good at it."

"And this is important, how?"

Frank took a moment. "Hence the signs, the red flags. The dicey background stories put together by amateurs. The papers with flaws. The perfect condition of some seemingly decades old documents. The flatness and straight-forward, one-dimensional presentation of lives that should have been a lot more intricate and gnarly. But look, I agree. To have eight unrelated victims whose only common denominator is that their histories are somewhat stereotypical wouldn't necessarily get my attention—not on its own. But there's another thing."

Twenty-Eight

"You mean the fact that they were all stabbed?" Amy said.

"Yes, but from behind," Frank said, "right below the rib cage. And that, combined with their backgrounds, connects them. A hundred percent."

"So why hasn't that been discovered yet?"

"For two reasons," Frank said. "The number one being that state police would never know if a victim was in the program. It simply wouldn't be flagged. The second being that the murders I've uncovered took place in Victoria, Queensland and New South Wales, and unless it's clear that a crime has been committed against the Commonwealth, the case stays within the state."

Amy lowered her voice, leaned in. "Are you saying this is the work of a serial killer?"

Frank nodded. "I'll bet that these victims all saw something they were not supposed to see, so they had to be silenced. Like I said, the National Witness Protection Program, unfortunately, has never been known for its efficiency, so those eight witnesses must have been found again."

"But," Amy said, "isn't there a very good chance they witnessed different things, meaning that they're not necessarily related to the same criminal organizations? Why would they be targeted by one killer? That makes no sense, Frank."

Frank shrugged. "Could be a principle for this guy. Maybe he kills to make a statement, maybe he doesn't care which organization he's protecting and which he's attacking, as long as they're former criminals. Don't forget, many of these people get offered a spot in the program in return for information that they gathered from the inside while they were criminals themselves."

Amy blew air threw her lips, walked over and sat down. "I don't know, Frank. It seems far-fetched."

"I'll admit, my theory isn't foolproof and definitely hasn't matured yet, but the scent is getting stronger, Amy," he said. "I can smell it."

"So, where to from here?"

"I need more access. I need all of your login credentials to all the databases that we . . . that you have access to at work," he said. Then added: "Please."

"Are you out of your mind, Frank?" Amy shook her head. "I can't do that, and even if I did, they'd easily be able to track every single keystroke."

"I'll use an advanced VPN setup," Frank said. "By the time they find out, you can tell them that someone must have stolen your access codes."

Amy shook her head. "I can't—"

"I received a letter in the mail last week. My suspension has resulted in my work-visa being canceled," Frank said, then looked down at the table. "I need to leave this country soon and I need to get to the bottom of Rebecca's case, because no one else will. Or can." Frank looked back up, put his hands on the table and looked Amy in the eyes.

"You're being kicked out of the country?"

Frank nodded.

Amy's eyes darted around the café before finally settling back on Frank. When she spoke, there was a tenderness in her voice. "How long have you got?"

Frank paused. "A week."

"Seven days?" Amy said. "You've got seven days? That's ridiculous! I'm sure they need to give you a bit more warning than that."

Frank shook his head. "I probably received the letter over a week ago. I just didn't check my mailbox until recently."

"Oh."

"Listen. Rebecca's got a world of trouble coming her way and no one's looking into it. I just know it, in the deepest of my gut, that I need to get involved here. And now time is running out."

Amy reached out and held Frank's hand in hers. "I believe you," she said. "That you feel you have to help this woman. I understand. And printing all the files was perhaps a step too far. But giving you free access, that would be ten steps too far—" she said, when the *Mission: Impossible* theme song came from inside her jacket perched on the low backrest of her stool.

She turned and took out her phone, spoke in single syllables, nodded and agreed, then toward the end said "certainly" and "absolutely" and "no problem" and "on my way" before hanging up.

She looked Frank in the eyes. "I have to go to Beenleigh," she said.

"What happened there?"

"Frank, please. You know I can't share this with you!"

Frank stared at her, watched her eyes and body language as she swung on her jacket and reached for her bag.

"Who got killed?" Frank said. "Tell me, Amy, please?"

Amy sighed, kept her voice low. "Someone called to say he found a guy. Dead. Gave the police the address, refused to give his own details, said he'd be gone by the time we get there, then hung up."

Frank nodded. "He strikes again."

Amy shrugged. "We don't know that yet."

"Gregory call you?"

"Well, yes," Amy said.

"Stabbing?"

Amy shrugged. "I don't know, but I was warned there's a lot of blood there."

"Just like I told you, this murder would have initially gone to the Queensland Police, who would have attended and found some breach of the Commonwealth, something bigger than the state police can handle, so the case got passed on to the AFP, hence Gregory's call to you."

Amy looked at Frank. "And how the hell would they know that so quickly?"

"That should become clear soon, but I bet you this guy was in witness protection—victim number nine."

An elderly lady with gray hair and kind eyes and a loud voice exited the kitchen and put a plate on the counter. "Order for Frank!" she yelled.

Frank shot up and grabbed Amy's arm. "I'm running out of time, Amy, please. Take plenty of pictures. For me. Of every square inch of the place. And get me access to the systems," he said.

Amy opened her mouth to speak, but then seemed to change her mind, turned and ran for the door.

Frank watched her leave, then walked over to get his second order: warm pecan pie with sour cream.

Twenty-Nine

A my held a finger under her nose to quell the acrid smell; it was a pungent mix of bodily fluids, feces, stomach contents and blood.

"Did he swallow a whole watermelon?" Amy said.

Two forensics in full protective suits, complete with gloves, hoods and boot covers, kneeled either side of the victim, their white knees turning purple and brown.

Joe nodded to the body lying on the kitchen floor, legs curled underneath a distended stomach, vacant eyes staring up at a blood-stained ceiling.

"Putrefaction," Joe said. "Decomposition of organic matter, causing a release of gases internally, inflating the stomach like a balloon."

The forensic on the left looked up. She was rather plump, her white suit stretched to its limits and her voice was filtered through a heavy-duty mask. "It can't be putrefaction, not yet. He only died a couple of hours ago and there's no green sheen to his skin. In other words, there's simply no way that the decomposition has reached that stage yet."

Joe pushed out his lower lip. "My apologies."

Amy wiggled her nose. "What's that smell?"

The other forensic sounded like an elderly man when he spoke. "Well, for one," he said, then pointed toward the hallway, "the toilet sink is full of vomit and who knows what else is floating around this place. It's a bloody drug den."

Amy removed her finger for a moment, sniffed the air and gagged. She immediately put it back, then looked at the female forensic. "How did he die?" she asked.

The woman pushed on the victim's hip and lifted the body slightly, then pointed to a red slit an inch and a half wide on his back, below his ribcage, around the man's right kidney. "He was stabbed," she said.

A chill went down Amy's spine. She looked at the blood splatter on the ceiling and cupboards. "Why all the blood?"

The man spoke. "He projectile vomited just before he died. That could easily be due to drugs or alcohol, but we'll know for sure when we get him back into the lab and run all the tests. Maybe we'll also be able to explain the rectal bleeding."

Amy nodded. "Sorry to ask, but are you forensic technicians or pathologists or . . . what do you call yourselves?"

The man nodded to the woman. "Maggie calls me whatever she feels like, depending on her mood."

Maggie waved a hand. "Ron is a joker," she said. "But regarding job titles, let's just say it's fluent. We go where we're needed and do what needs doing, which is a bit of everything."

Amy chuckled, then turned to Joe. "Grab your notepad and go into the living room. Write down all the brands of beer, liquor, cigarettes, along with anything else that you may find. Bag the cigarette butts individually and lift fingerprints from the bottles. Take photos of it all."

Joe looked surprised. "Are you my boss now?" he said.

Amy put on her best smile. "I believe I am," she said, then took out her phone, ensuring it was on silent.

"And what are you going to do?"

"I'll call Gregory to give him an update."

Joe reached into the crime scene bag, retrieved the camera and proceeded into the living room.

With Joe gone, Amy took out her phone, opened the camera app and hit RECORD. She kept her phone pointed at the kitchen while pretending to look for a number. Then walked around the flat, listening out for Joe as she made her way from room to room. When she was back in the living room, Amy took twenty dollars out of her wallet.

"This is a mess and we're going to be here for a while. Why don't you go downstairs and get us a couple of bottles of cold water?" she said, then nodded toward the kitchen. "Buy some for the forensics team as well."

Joe looked perplexed, but took the money. "Go downstairs? We're in a flat in Beenleigh. There aren't any shops downstairs."

Amy shrugged, reached into her pocket and came out with a key. "Take the car. There are a few supermarkets just up the road."

Joe seemed stunned. He remained standing for a moment, then eventually took the key and disappeared without another word.

When he was gone, Amy began recording the living room.

THIRTY

Frank stopped right behind and perpendicular to a new Ford Falcon parked in one of the wide spots of the AFP underground staff car park. He pushed the gear selector up in park, then killed the engine, opened his door and grabbed the doorframe and door, half lifting and half pushing himself up and out of his car. The Falcon was parked nose-in, right up against a cinderblock wall. Two feet above the hood, attached to the concrete bricks with four brass screws, a white sign with blue letters confirmed to Frank that he'd found the right spot: AFP COMMANDER GREGORY FORDHAM.

Frank left his car where it was and, while walking to the elevator, took out his phone.

Here

It didn't take more than five seconds before his phone chimed.

Be right down

A minute later the elevator pinged and the doors opened. Inside the car stood an Asian man who could easily have passed for a college student. Smiling eyes, not a wrinkle on his youthful face or his impeccable shirt, with hair as black and shiny as a raven's feathers: Andrew Koh, Technical Specialist—Cybercrime.

Andrew lit up in a huge smile. Dangling his car remote from his left middle finger, he took a step forward and blocked the elevator doors, offering Frank his other hand. "Frank, buddy," he said. "I'll be damned."

Frank shook his hand, smiled back, then nodded. "Now you probably will be, Andrew," he said. "Thank you very much for your help."

"They didn't let you keep anything when they suspended you?" Andrew said. "Not even your security pass?"

Frank shook his head. "It's like I was never here."

Andrew slapped Frank on his shoulder as he exited, then turned just outside. "You know, sometimes I envy you, Frank."

"How so?"

"Amy told me you've started up your own PI gig? Sometimes I feel like breaking free and doing my own thing, you know? No limits, no company regulations, no square-minded colleagues, just go for it. I really don't know why I stay here. I mean, you know me, it's not like I need the money."

Frank stepped forward and put a hand on the sensor so the doors wouldn't close. "Sure, I hear you. But you can do so much good by staying, Andrew. Here you can really make a difference. You have access, authority, an entire police force to back you and you can arrest real criminals—make a difference."

Andrew nodded. "It's just, there's so much red tape, so many procedures and rigid rules that impede the job at hand. I feel so restricted here and, to some extent, unappreciated. But worst of all, sometimes I feel like I could contribute more to the world if I could really spread my wings. No red tape, no bureaucracy, no standard procedures. You know what I mean?"

"I do," Frank said. "But your help and input while I worked here were invaluable. You're a real asset to the AFP, so you should be proud of that. Where are you going, anyway?"

Andrew winked. "As soon as I got your text, I told a colleague that I decided to go out for lunch, so now I better go and actually get something," he said, then nodded. "I really miss you, Frank. You let me know if you ever need my help again."

Frank felt his cheeks grow hot. Andrew had always been a top professional, courteous and helpful, but he'd never opened up like this before. Frank wasn't sure how to answer, what the correct thing to say was. In the end, he removed his hand from the sensor and stepped back into the car, smiled and nodded. "I'll call you," he said, then watched Andrew grow narrower as the doors closed.

Thirty-One

J oe cradled his phone between chin and shoulder, listened to it ring as he inserted a twenty-dollar bill into the slot, then watched it being spat out again. The red polymer bill had a stubborn fold that Joe bent the opposite way, then tried again. High-pitch whirring was replaced by faint clacking as coins were dispensed. Joe pocketed the change, took his phone in one hand while lifting the cold six-pack of bottled water with his other. He turned and strolled toward the exit just as the call was answered.

"Did Amy call you yet?" Joe said.

"No," Gregory said. "Should she have?"

"She said so. Listen, I caught her using her private phone to record some of the crime scene."

"What?"

"Yeah. I'm not sure how much she's recorded, but she definitely had her phone out."

Gregory was silent for a while. When he spoke, he sounded deflated. "Frank again?"

Joe nodded. "I think so. All she does is talk about him and how amazing he is. You were right, Greg. I work with Amy every day, and even though it's just the two of us, it constantly feels like Frank is here as well, interfering, even calling the shots. And now I'm pretty sure she's recording the crime scene for him, so that he can help her with the investigation."

"Plus, we know she's giving him copies of files from the office," Gregory said.

"Yeah, exactly."

"Okay, this needs to stop. Now! When you get back, I want you to confiscate her phone. As soon as you find a video or a photo of anything inside that flat, or even just a text from her with any related info on it, you tell her to contact me immediately. I have the power to suspend her, and I will."

Joe walked through the sliding doors, spotted the car. "Consider it done. Is there anything else you need me to do?"

"Just make sure you get that damn footage," Gregory said, then hung up.

THIRTY-TWO

F rank walked down the carpeted hallway, spotted a sign that matched the one hanging in the downstairs parking lot. He considered knocking, then changed his mind and opened the door.

Gregory looked up from one of the dozens of papers scattered around his desk. Behind him in the distance, the Brisbane River slithered through a lush landscape like a fat brown snake slowly zoning in on its prey. Gregory opened his mouth to speak, and for a moment, Frank thought he saw the flipping of a forked tongue.

"What the hell are you doing here?" Gregory Fordham said.

Frank closed the door, walked over and sat down, folded his hands on top of his belly and looked around the office. "I've been thinking."

Gregory leaned back in his chair, crossed his arms and stuck his hands into his armpits. "You've got two minutes."

Frank scratched his red goatee, then looked at Gregory's left wrist, nodded. "How much did you pay for that watch?"

Gregory pushed his chin in and looked down as if he was looking at it for the first time himself, then shrugged. "Don't remember, Frank."

Frank nodded. "Roughly?"

Gregory spread his arms out and looked like a question mark. "Two hundred dollars?"

Frank shook his head.

Gregory crossed his arms again. "Why are you shaking your head, Frank?"

Frank pointed to the black face of the plain-looking analogue watch. "That there is a Kaitak Andromeda," Frank said. "Handmade, Swiss, exclusive, limited edition."

Gregory arched an eyebrow, rolled his chair forward and made a show of looking at his watch. "And according to my Kaitak, you have one minute left."

"How come you wear a watch that costs as much as you make in a year? Before tax."

A shadow crossed Gregory's face. "If you must know," he said, then put his arms on top of his desk, pointed to the watch, "this watch cost nowhere near that much. It cost me ten thousand dollars, and I saved up for it because I like watches. It's a little hobby of mine. Anything else?"

Frank sighed. "What about your Francois Jacquot shoes? Or your Raphael Donahue suits?" he said, then scanned the office once more. When Gregory didn't say anything, Frank pointed to a silver pen holder sitting at the edge of the desk. "Or what about that there? The discreet, yet stupidly expensive pen from Gabriel Matheo?"

Gregory placed his hands flat on his desk, took a deep breath. "If you have something to say, this is your last chance before I throw you out of my office. And how the hell did you get into this building in the first place?"

126

"I'm just wondering where it's all coming from," Frank said. "Making a bit of dirty money on the side to support your expensive habits?"

Gregory chuckled. "Come on, Frank! A watch and a pair of shoes. Really?"

Frank shook his head. "You're spending money you shouldn't have," he said. "What is it? You a betting man?"

"Hallelujah," Gregory said, then raised his hands. "You got me, Frank. I'll have to stop hitting on sixteen next time I play blackjack; it's simply too risky. Or maybe I should bet on red instead of black," he said, then slapped himself on the forehead. "Wait! I know. I'll include Gallop Girl next time for my trifecta."

Frank nodded. "You suddenly wanted me out in a hurry. And now I know why. You're somehow involved in all of this, aren't you? You're selling information to criminals, playing them out against each other. And I got too close, didn't I?"

Gregory smiled, then reached down and opened a desk drawer, produced a pair of handcuffs. "You tell yourself whatever you want, Frank," he said, then opened the cuffs with a key. "Now, would you like to spend some time in a cell, or would you like to get the hell out of my office and never return?"

Frank stood up, walked to the door, opened it and turned. "Gregory, tell me something."

Gregory threw the cuffs on the desk, spread his arms. "Shoot," he said.

"Be it criminals or not, what do people shop with?" Frank said.

"We all know the answer to that one," Gregory said. "Money."

Frank shook his head. "Wrong, Gregory. People shop with their emotions," he said, then looked down at the carpet for a moment. When Frank looked back up, the shadow on Gregory's face was back. "Whatever you're selling, it's clearly valuable to whoever's buying and I've got a pretty good idea what it is. The only thing I have to do now is prove it," he said, then exited and let the door shut behind him.

Frank was already trotting down the hallway when he heard Gregory shouting. "Piece of advice, Frank. Lose some fucking weight, you piece of lard!" he said, his voice muffled through the already closed door.

THIRTY-THREE

Amy lowered her phone, held it at her side and walked back toward the kitchen. She was thinking about what Frank had said about the Queensland Police, that they would normally be first on scene. "Has the Queensland Police already been here?"

Ron nodded. "Left ten minutes before you arrived. We told them to give you a call as soon as we got a good look at the guy."

"Why?"

Maggie nodded toward the victim. "He has a tattoo on his right biceps. It's a prison tattoo, effectively connecting him to a gang that we know operates nationwide."

"Oh," Amy said. "What gang?"

"Satan's Sharks," Maggie said. "They mostly dabble in drug smuggling."

"Could they be connected to this?"

Ron shrugged, then stepped into the hallway and stopped in front of Amy, removed his hood and mask. "I've never seen anything like this before," he said. "Whoever killed this poor fellow must be a vicious bastard, that's for sure."

"The blood splatter?" Amy said.

Ron nodded. "Whether drugs are involved, we don't know yet, but one thing is certain: Not only did his body eject his stomach contents, but it did so with what appears to be superhuman power."

Amy pointed to an overhead cupboard. "Are you referring to all the spray?"

"Not only that," Ron said, shaking his head. "There's also evidence of feculent vomiting."

"What does that mean?" Amy said.

"The victim basically vomited so violently that he threw up fecal matter."

"Wait," Amy said. "He puked poo?"

Maggie joined them in the hallway, but unlike her colleague, she didn't remove her hood or mask. "That's right," she said.

Amy looked at both of them in turn. "How's that even possible?"

Ron shrugged. "Only cases I know of are associated with cancer to the stomach, aggressive tumors eating up intestines."

Maggie nodded. "Or pressure," she said. "Extreme pressure can theoretically push fecal matter up through the mouth."

"But what could create such a pressure?" Amy said.

The forensic examiners looked at each other, then back at Amy, shrugged synchronously.

"Soon as we get the body up on the slab, we'll know more," Ron said.

Amy nodded, then turned as she felt the phone being pulled from her hand.

"Hey!" she said to Joe. "What the hell are you doing?" She reached out and grabbed at thin air as Joe twisted his torso, held a hand out in front of her face while his other hand held the phone behind his back.

"Sorry, Amy, but I'm under strict orders to check your phone."

"Under strict orders?" she said, then slapped his hand away from her face. "What are you, twelve?"

Joe ignored her and moved into the living room while looking at her screen. Amy watched him accidentally stepping in a pool of brown goo. "Shit," he said, then lifted one foot to inspect the sole.

"Nah," Amy said, then chuckled. "That there is puke."

Both Ron and Maggie giggled as well.

"And Joe?"

Joe looked up.

"How are you going to access my phone when you don't have the code to unlock it?"

Joe's shoulders slumped.

"Hey, we're partners," Amy said. "I'll save you the embarrassment of having to tell Gregory that you missed that minor detail, so why don't I just give you the code? It's four zeros. That is, press the zero button four times. Think you can manage that? Partner?"

Joe's facial expression told her he himself couldn't believe that he'd missed that bit. Amy saw a spoiled brat with a spine like a gummy bear.

"What's that all about?" Maggie asked.

Amy turned to face her, sighed. "Something to do with a certain boys' club and too much testosterone, I think. I'd consider taking out a membership but, given my intellect and sex, I'm afraid I wouldn't qualify."

Maggie laughed a muffled laugh, the mask making her sound like a vintage baby doll on batteries. She cackled and cackled. The absurdity of the situation was complete, yet also understandable. It was an absurd job and everyone coped differently.

Ron shrugged. "Maggie cracks up at the weirdest of times," he said. "It's one of the reasons I enjoy working with her."

Maggie laughed a bit more, took her time to let it die out, then nodded. "And Ron here is one of the most knowledgeable forensic examiners you'll ever come across, which is why I enjoy working with him," she said.

Ron looked at Maggie. "So it's not my hair?" he said, pointing at a few stray tufts of gray sticking up from his otherwise bald head.

This got Maggie going again and Amy couldn't help but smile; they clearly had a wonderful relationship, at least professionally, perhaps even personally.

"On a more serious note," Maggie said, "Ron and I agree that there are some timing issues here. The stomach is distended to the point of what we'd normally see several days after death occurring, yet looking at the body, the guy definitely died within the past couple of hours. He's still warm and Rigor Mortis hasn't set in yet.

"And there's another timing issue. If Ron is right in saying that the projectile vomiting is connected to drugs or an aggressive form of cancer, then how does that tie up with the stabbing? With Ron's theory, the stabbing and the vomiting aren't connected, meaning the victim would have coincidentally vomited at the exact same time he got stabbed and that just doesn't sound plausible, which brings about a third issue.

"Assuming the two *are* connected, what on earth could cause such a powerful reaction in the victim?" Maggie paused, then shook her head. "Anyway, the only fact right here and now is that the victim has been stabbed within the past couple of hours."

Amy nodded. "Do you think the stabbing could have somehow triggered the vomiting?"

Ron shook his head. "No way."

"Any indication of the size of the knife?" Amy asked.

Ron nodded. "About an inch and a half wide. We'll give you an estimate of the length after the autopsy," he said. "At a glance, I'm guessing double-bladed, extremely sharp, probably pointed, making it ideal for stabbing. Something akin to a small dagger."

"Would it take a lot of force to stab someone like that?" Amy said. "I'm trying to find out whether there would have been noise or a struggle."

Maggie shook her head. "Looking at where he was stabbed, just below the ribcage, around the kidney, the tissue there is a lot softer than, say, the tough cartilage surrounding your neck. And not only that, but as soon as the kidney gets stabbed, the body goes into shock, making it even easier for the attacker."

Ron cleared his throat. "Plus, even if the victim tried to scream, the killer would have been in a perfect position to cover the victim's mouth with one hand while stabbing him with the other." Ron frowned, seemingly rethinking what he'd just said. "Although in this case, the killer probably wouldn't have covered the victim's mouth, not with all that spray."

"Sneaking up from behind and sticking a sharp dagger silently into a very effective area," Amy said. "Could this be a professional hit?"

Maggie shrugged. "Depends on what you mean by professional. If it was supposed to be a silent, hit-man type job, then he failed. Whether or not the victim screamed, all that vomiting and spraying would have been noisy enough."

"So, just to confirm, these bodily discharges don't normally take place when someone is stabbed in the kidney?" Amy said.

"No way. Unless it was somehow done deliberately, you know, to send a message. To tell someone to back off," Maggie said. "But if that's the case, I still don't understand how he would have managed to produce such a mess."

Amy nodded, reached inside her pocket and took out a card. "Whenever you find out more about what happened here, please get in touch," she said, and held out the card.

"Absolutely," Maggie said, grabbed the card with two bloodied fingers, then looked down at her white protective suit and seemed to realize that she didn't have any pockets available. Eventually, she turned and put the card on top of her workbag, then turned back to Amy. "We found a shoe print and a few strands of hair. You'll hear from us as soon as we get the results back."

"I see," Amy said, just as Joe appeared next to her.

Without a word, he held out her phone. He looked defeated, then shook his head. "Nothing there."

Amy took her phone, pocketed it and put a hand behind her ear. "I couldn't hear that."

"There's nothing . . . incriminating on your phone."

Amy left her hand where it was. "Still can't quite hear."

"What?" he said.

"That word," she said, then winked at Maggie. "It starts with *s* and ends with *orry*."

Joe bowed his head and mumbled, "Sorry."

Maggie's cackles started up again.

Thirty-Four

It was gray and misty outside the AFP Commissioner's office window on the top floor of the Edmund Barton building in Canberra. He stood behind his desk, back straight, held his manicured hands behind his back. The Molonglo River lay like a wet carpet underneath the King's Avenue Bridge, a single pair of red taillights floated into the distance, another two pairs of yellow headlights were approaching. Behind the flat bridge, the tiny island of Queen Elizabeth II would have been impossible to spot had it not been for a decades-old gift from the British Government in celebration of fifty years of the Australian Capital: a brutalist, concrete tower known as the National Carillon, its gray, vertical surface almost perfectly camouflaged behind the drizzle.

Walter Roscoe was pondering whether the phallic imagery the tower conjured had been intentional when the phone on his desk rang. He turned his head and stared at the creamy plastic communications device as the display lit up and a discreet, electronic ring tone escaped its invisible speaker.

Landlines had been superfluous for years, but, for good reasons, offices and institutions still used them; professionalism, credibility, traditions and expectations among some of those good reasons. But for the AFP, the reasons related to safety protocols: storms could blow out cell towers, faults and usage could drain batteries and calls could easily be tracked. Which meant that when this particular phone rang, it was to report on clandestine developments. And now it was as if the phone itself knew of its importance; the ringtone amplifying and tearing at Roscoe's nerves. He had a hunch what it could be about and, at this moment, he'd rather listen to nails on a chalkboard than to this damn phone.

He tentatively walked over and picked up the handset, watched the curly cord extend as he put it to his ear.

"Yes?"

"We have a problem," Gregory Fordham said.

"You calling from a scrambled line?" Walter Roscoe asked.

"Yes, of course," Gregory said. "You know I always do."

"What's the problem?"

"Frank is closing in."

"I know. I already took care of it and contacted my boss."

"The Attorney-General?"

"Do I have any other boss?" Roscoe said, not bothering to hide his irritation. "He spoke with someone within the Department of Home Affairs. Frank will be leaving this lucky country of ours very soon."

"Perfect. That's great news," Gregory said. "And how soon is very soon?"

Walter looked down at his agenda. Some things he liked to keep old-fashioned. He turned a few pages. "Seven days," he said.

There was silence at the other end.

"Fordham?"

Gregory cleared his throat. "That may be too long," he said. "This guy is wickedly smart. He just left my office—"

"Listen," Walter said. "It's at your end. It's your responsibility. I've done what I could. You pull your finger out and contain that son of a bitch. Keep him guessing. Throw red herrings at him if you have to. For Chrissake, it can't be that hard!"

Another silence.

"Fordham?"

"Eh . . . what do you mean when you say red herrings?"

"I mean, present him with misleading clues, distract him with useless information that'll keep him occupied until we throw his sorry ass out of here."

"I'm doing that already, but I'm telling you, Walter, seven days may be—"

"Then take care of it now! I've done what I could from here. He's in your town, so you better deal with it," Walter said, then added: "For both our sakes."

"You mean—"

"Now!" Walter said, then hung up.

THIRTY-FIVE

T he boom gate automatically rose and Frank floored the pedal, squealing up the concrete ramp and leaping onto Commercial Road. He skidded through a right turn, heading straight for the river. He screamed out loud and punched the already scarred steering wheel, yelling obscenities and cursing the higher powers.

Frank kept going until he hit a cul-de-sac. He bumped up over the curb, leaving two wheels on the sidewalk, the other two resting in the bicycle lane. He pushed himself out with a grunt and walked around the hood, heading for the Teneriffe wharf. Frank kept walking until he reached the floating pontoon deck where a Brisbane City River Cat was berthed. A half dozen passengers were embarking on a small catamaran, ready to take them farther upriver.

Frank sat down on a bench and watched the catamaran glide sideways out, then listened to the diesel engine as it revved up. As the back of the cat got smaller, the stench of the diesel exhaust reduced to a smell, which eventually faded into a whiff before dissipating altogether. Frank leaned forward and put his elbows on his knees. Up close, with the sun poking out from behind a white cloud, the river was blue. The soothing caroling of nearby magpies and the gentle lapping of waves as they reached the pontoon all helped in lowering Frank's pulse. He breathed deeply, peeked around to check that he was alone, then stuck a hand in his right pocket and took out a flattened pack of cigarettes. Frank hoped they'd survived being squashed inside his khaki, elastic-waist Bermuda shorts. Delicately, using both hands, he straightened the pack and tapped out a cigarette that, not surprisingly, had a bend in it. Frank shrugged to himself, stuck it between his lips, then reached for his lighter in the other pocket. He'd decided a while ago that smoking was good for him: it lowered his insatiable appetite for food and brought him closer to his dead wife and the children they never had.

Frank lifted the lighter to the tip of his cigarette, tensed his thumb, then flicked the spark wheel against the flint, igniting the butane gas flowing out through the top. A tall, yellow flame reached the tip of his cigarette and Frank was about to inhale when a gust of wind blew it out.

He twisted and looked toward the city. The blue sky was dominated by a growing cumulonimbus, the cauliflower cloud growing rapidly upward, sucking in hot, humid air and pumping it forcefully ever higher into the atmosphere. With the top of the cloud reaching the troposphere, it had no choice but to grow outward, its anvil already taking shape. The path of least resistance, Frank thought. Adapting to your surroundings. We're all forced to grow, sometimes in areas we choose, sometimes not. But, occasionally, improvisation becomes an integral part of the growth; we adapt, change course, pretend, ignore, cheat and lie. On a hot, humid day, the rising of a thundercloud is inevitable, but not even the smartest meteorologist will know exactly where it'll grow, how tall it'll become, or how much water or hail it'll spit out. That's partially up to the cloud, partially governed by the conditions of that particular day. Something in the case connected in Frank's brain, but it disappeared with the next gust as the cloud blew in front of the sun, darkening the world and once again turning the river into a slithering brown snake.

Frank turned and shielded his cigarette with his body and hand, then flicked the lighter again. The gusts came frequently now and blew his red hair around, making his shorts flap in the wind. But now, at least his cigarette was lit. Frank inhaled the sweet nicotine and felt the familiar itch being scratched inside his chest as a comforting warmth spread through his lungs. He inhaled deeply and frequently, closed his eyes and let the buzz and lightheadedness carry him to happier times.

A cool and clear February day where they'd celebrated their first wedding anniversary by going for an eight-mile run together. Frank saw his sweet Caroline laughing, running through their backyard up to the forest edge, the back of her purple jogging gear disappearing in between the tall spruce and pine trees. He checked the backdoor was locked, then sprinted after her, the cold, bright sun quickly replaced by even colder shade and the smell of childhood; the pungent aroma of sap and prickly needles, mossy wood, earth and recent rain. He easily caught up with her as she ran along the path, then teased her by jumping in and out between trees, showing off his physique by crushing thick pinecones under his powerful legs, jumping over dead branches and bouncing across spongy duff, his pace relentless. They followed their standard round trip for just over an hour and ended up at their backyard again. Caroline leaned up against the fence, bent over and gasped for air, thick puffs of misty clouds forming with every exhale, exhausted and pushed to her limits. Frank simply stopped and began stretching. The weekly run relaxed him and was a welcome break from the rigorous training he endured to prepare for his re-appearance at the Ironman Germany in Frankfurt the following summer.

They showered together, put on thick robes and Caroline made her signature coffee floats. They sat under a pale winter sun in the backyard and talked about their careers, how to fit in family life and raise their future children. Caroline was an esteemed criminal psychologist with the local judicial authority, and Frank's eminent move from detective with the *Kriminalpolizei* to a fully fledged agent with the German Federal Police; the *Bundespolizei*, consumed their days.

Caroline's goal of opening her own business as a psychologist was within reach, and Frank's dream of catching violent criminals was coming true. As always, toward the end of the conversation, they came to the inevitable conclusion that it was difficult to fit in children at the time and that their careers would have to take priority. The conversation had ended with Caroline slurping coffee through her plastic straw and Frank stabbing at a melting ball of vanilla ice cream. The understanding was mutual; they were young, time was on their side, so it made sense to wait. Then the slurping was replaced by an empty sucking noise and Caroline flicked her blonde hair around and sent Frank a teasing smile, grabbed the tie around her robe and undid it, then gently pushed one side down, exposing a shoulder. Frank immediately jumped up and Caroline shrieked and ran as fast as she could into the house, where Frank chased her all the way up the stairs and into the bedroom.

Afterward, lying in bed, both on their backs staring up into the ceiling, Caroline said, "I love you, Frank." Then she turned onto her side and placed a hand on one of his substantial pecs, stroked his chest hair and looked up at him. "And I always will."

Frank smiled, raised his hand and found his cigarette extinguished; it was rain-soaked and disintegrating—just like Frank himself. Water crashed through the surface of the river and drummed loudly as it lashed down onto the deck of the pontoon, the drops bouncing back up to knee height.

Frank stood up, then flicked the rest of his wet cigarette into the river just as his phone chimed. He dug a wet hand into his pocket, which momentarily got stuck in there, but in the end, he managed to pinch the phone with two fingers and slide it out. He attempted to swipe at it, but nothing worked as huge drops covered the screen and Frank's thumb slid around fruitlessly. With all the water running off his brows and into his eyes, he couldn't see what he was doing, anyway.

Eventually, Frank gave up and, with squishing shoes, sauntered through the tropical storm back along the wharf.

It wasn't until he was halfway back that he could barely make out the outline of two vehicles through the dense, gray, torrential curtain of water: yellow halos doubling through the rain, Frank's car stealthily crawling forward and up, pulled by an invisible metal cable screeching from the front of an elevated tray.

Thirty-Six

"So, finally some action, eh, partner?" Joe said.

Amy stopped chewing on a pencil, then turned on her chair. "Get your butt off of my desk, Joe. It's creepy when you sit there. That's what Gregory does."

Joe sighed, stood up. "I'm really sorry about the whole thing. It's just . . ."

"Yes?" Amy prompted.

Joe crossed his arms over his chest. "It's just, I thought I saw you using your phone to record the crime scene, that's all."

"And why would I do that, Joe?"

Joe shrugged. "To show it to Frank?"

Amy threw the pencil on the desk and stood up, looked down at him. "Even if I did, what the hell has that got to do with you, Joe? Why are you so interested in my actions? Have you been offered a job with Internal Affairs? Are you an in-house spy now?"

Joe shook his head. "It's not Internal Affairs," he said. "For your information, within the AFP, it's called the Professional Standards Team. And no, I'm not."

Now Amy crossed her arms, began smiling. "Wait a minute," she said. "Now I get it."

"What do you mean?"

"You've become Gregory's pet, haven't you?" Amy said. "Ever since that little boys' night out, you've been all over me."

"I have not—"

"And what do you know about Professional Standards?"

"That's common knowledge, Amy. It's not my fault if you watch too much television."

Amy's smile didn't falter. "What exactly did Gregory tell you? What did he ask of you?"

Joe put his hands in his pockets and looked down. He stayed silent for a while before speaking. "Nothing."

Amy shook her head. "I don't believe you, Joe. I think you've been recruited for Professional Standards and I think you had a hand in getting rid of Frank as well. You have an agenda and I'm going to find out what it is, so why don't you just tell me yourself?"

Joe sighed and exaggeratedly grunted, pushing air out through his nose. When he looked back up, he appeared defeated. "What do you want me to say, Amy? Obviously, you've been acting weird ever since Frank got sacked and, well, Gregory wanted someone to keep an eye on things to make sure confidential files are not leaked or anyone gets hurt."

"I've been acting weird?"

"Not like that—"

"Anyone gets hurt?"

"Well, yes," Joe said.

"And who the bloody hell would get hurt?"

Joe looked up, his eyes flickering around the ceiling before settling back on Amy. "Well, you know."

Amy's eyes went wide. "I don't," she said. "Kindly fill me in."

"You know, if files are leaked, people could get killed."

"You're just repeating what Gregory told you, aren't you?"

Joe didn't say anything.

"Do you ever question anything he says, or do you happily just swallow his shit?"

"That's not fair, Amy," Joe said. "He had some good points."

"Like?"

"Like . . . saving valuable time."

"Do enlighten me," Amy said.

"Well, for example, I don't remember the exact details, but basically, if Internal . . . if a Professional Standards Team would have to get involved, they would assume some sort of corruption, which would lead to a commissioner having to interfere and perhaps also a regulatory bondsman."

Amy burst out laughing. It was so loud and so sudden that Andrew Koh—who sat down at the other end of the room in a cubicle with two computers—flashed a smile and shook his head. Amy laughed and laughed, then held up an index finger, giving it time to calm down, but then it started all over again. She wheezed and howled anew. When the fit finally subsided, Amy's throat was sore, her eyes felt puffy and her cheeks were lined with dried salt.

"Listen, Joe," she said, then took a break as another fit threatened to return. "It is true that if an investigation somehow leads to evidence of corruption, then the AFP Commissioner will get involved—not interfere, like you said—that's just the procedure. In that case, and only in that case, he'll have to escalate it to the Australian Commission for Law Enforcement Integrity, which is overseen by the Commonwealth *Ombudsman,* Joe, not a regulatory bondsman, which is not even a thing."

"Point is, it's a lengthy process that's simply too slow," Joe said, then seemed to consider his next words: "Which is why Gregory asked me to keep an eye on you, to save time."

"Okay, Joe, how long do these internal investigations take?"

"Gregory said a very long time."

"Addams vs Commonwealth of Australia," Amy said.

"What's that?"

"A case we went through when I became an agent. It's a good example of the swift, efficient procedures put in place by the government to deal with rotten AFP agents."

"It is?"

Amy nodded. "Addams was an agent in Canberra a few years ago who misused his position and was subsequently targeted by Professional Standards. How long do you think it took from when they got involved until they found him guilty?"

"That would take years—"

"Six weeks, Joe," Amy said.

Joe looked perplexed.

"Police cases get automatic priority and case management is accelerated. In addition, queue jumping within the courts is a built-in feature of Professional Standards' legal rights and procedures."

"But Gregory said—"

"I know," Amy said, then leaned in, lowered her voice. "It's time for you to choose sides, Joe. Think about yourself and your future. Don't be so gullible and don't be so eager to impress. Just stick to your job, stick to what you're good at."

Joe took a deep breath. "And what exactly am I good at?"

Amy was pleasantly surprised by his question. There was a refreshing honesty to it. "I was hoping you could show me that. As my partner," she said. "No more bullshit."

Joe looked at Amy. Whether he wanted to say something, Amy wasn't sure.

In the end, he simply nodded, turned and headed back to his desk.

THIRTY-SEVEN

G regory Fordham had parked under a huge fig tree at the back
of the building, directly opposite the entrance to the parking
garage. He checked the dashboard clock. Sighed.

Frank should have been here by now.

His conversation with Walter Roscoe was still echoing through his
head. There was no way he was going to let Frank ruin his plans and
destroy his life. He breathed deeply, then took out his Glock 22 and
checked that it was loaded before replacing it in his shoulder holster.
He closed his eyes and fantasized about shooting Frank through the
head, watching his huge body fall like a felled tree. Then walking over
and repeatedly kicking him in the ribs and the head, stumping on his
groin and knees.

Where was that fat piece of lard, anyway?

From the corner of his eye, he saw a large sedan turn into the street
and head straight to where he was sitting. As it approached and was
nearly beside Gregory's car, its front dipped as the driver hit the brakes
and turned into the underground parking. Red brake lights lit up the
darkened concrete as the car nosed down the ramp. The car was dark

blue and only about ten years old. Wrong color and way too new. Definitely not Frank's.

Gregory slammed both his hands onto the steering wheel. "Fuck!"

THIRTY-EIGHT

The storm had passed and died out somewhere over the Coral Sea as Frank—exactly an hour and four minutes after leaving the Teneriffe wharf—walked the last few yards up his street. Once he reached the entrance to the lobby, he placed his round plastic gizmo in front of the reader and heard a click. He pushed the door open, then walked over to the elevator and pressed the up button. His shirt and shorts were almost dry, his socks slightly damp and his shoes no longer squished. While waiting, Frank pulled out his cigarettes. Holding the crumbled pack with one hand, he used his other to pull away the rest of the foil, then splayed two fingers inside and glared down. All that remained was exposed, wet tobacco scattered among soaked pulp and loose filters. He sighed, turned sideways and attempted a hook shot toward the lobby bin. Missed. The elevator doors opened and Frank left the pack where it had landed and entered the car.

Once inside his hallway, Frank kicked off his dank shoes and peeled off sticky socks. He walked into the living room and sat down on the couch, dug out his phone. He wiped the screen with a nearby pillow and saw that he'd received a text:

Don't lose any of the videos I've emailed you. I've deleted them from my phone already. Amy xxx

Frank's heart began racing, and he found himself trembling as he wrote a reply:

You're a star! F

He opened his inbox, started the video and saw two white-clad figures kneeling next to a body lying in a pool of blood. Frank squinted, but couldn't make out any details. He turned his phone ninety degrees to make the screen larger, but that somehow made it even worse. He sighed, put his phone down and walked into his bedroom where he found his laptop, came back and placed it on the coffee table. He opened it, then rummaged around his small TV furniture until he found a long HDMI cable, which he connected from the laptop to his TV. He sat back down, entered the same email on his laptop, opened the same video clip and grabbed his TV remote. Columbo's smile disappeared as Frank changed the channel and turned up the volume. He was now looking into a kitchen that was exactly seventy-five inches from corner to corner; he could discern the color of the blood, study the pattern of the surrounding splattering of cupboards and view the entire crime scene in ultra high definition.

Frank coughed as a pungent mix of bodily fluids, feces, stomach contents and blood entered his nostrils. He was there, right next to Amy. Logically, he knew that it was the visual sensation combined with years of crime scene experience that made his brain produce these smells, but phantosmia was nothing new to Frank; it was all part of

CONRAD BUX

his past trauma, something he'd come to live with and put to good use rather than shy away from.

Caroline had once told him that we could all learn a lot from nature, simply sway and bend and make room, like the branch of a young tree, or the rocks that yield to persistent water pressure. Rather than fight and put hard-to-hard—a solution which always results in mutual destruction—a relatively healthy life was grounded in flexibility and adaptability. Keyword being relative, but she hadn't put too much emphasis on that word, hadn't known what life would bring.

Or, to be more Frank, what it wouldn't.

The kitchen disappeared in a blur as Amy walked down the end of a small hallway. She stopped in an open doorway where a room appeared with a queen-size bed and two bedside tables. Two brown towels were lying on the floor in a heap next to a rumpled bed, and Frank could see a partial outline of a round, long handle; probably a baseball bat. A half-open bedside table drawer revealed a dark outline of something he couldn't quite make out. Frank jumped as Amy's whispering came through the loudspeakers as though she had stuck her mouth in his ear and blasted as loudly as she could: "This is the bedroom, Frank." His heart galloping, Frank grabbed the remote and turned the volume down, chuckling at her statement.

Thirty-Nine

Gregory Fordham once again checked the dashboard clock.

He swung open his door, exited the car and slammed the door shot, then ran across the street. He jogged around the building, found the security intercom system and was about to dial Frank's apartment number when he decided that surprising him face-to-face would be much more effective in getting the message across.

He'd only waited for a minute when a young man exited the building. Gregory pushed past him and into the lobby.

"Excuse me?" the young guy said.

Gregory turned and stared him down.

The guy hiked up his knapsack and hurried down the street.

Gregory grabbed the banister and stomped up the steps until he reached the sixth floor. He walked down a long hallway, found Frank's apartment and rapped on his door.

He put his ear to the door and listened for a television being turned down, perhaps followed by grunting he imagined would naturally come from the obese bastard trying to get up from the couch, then shuffling of chunky feet on . . . what? Tiles? Carpet? Gregory didn't know—had never had the urge to see this man privately.

In the end, nothing stirred.

Gregory knocked again. Sighed.

He turned and began walking back down the hallway. He'd almost reached the staircase when a faint clicking sound came from far behind him.

FORTY

With no spy hole to rely on, Frank had tiptoed into the hallway and was standing with his ear up against the door, listening for quiet conversations, whispering, shuffling of feet or anything else that could give away who was outside. His belly was rumbling and something told him that whatever was on the other side of that door was bad news. Normally, people would have rung the intercom downstairs first, giving him a chance to see them standing in front of the camera. But since the intercom hadn't been used, logic dictated it had to be a neighbor, the property manager, or perhaps a janitor. And for the almost two years that Frank had been living here, not once had either of those knocked on his door.

Frank waited until he heard the person begin walking back down the hallway, then counted to ten before opening. He stuck his head out and recognized Gregory even before he'd turned around.

"What are you doing here?" Frank said.

Gregory looked angry. "Frank," he said, then walked back, stopped in front of the door again. "I didn't think you were home."

Frank looked him in the eyes.

"Because you didn't open," Gregory said. "Why didn't you open your door?"

"What are you doing here?" Frank repeated.

Gregory seemed to consider. "Can I come in?"

"The odds of that are extremely high."

Gregory gave him a questioning look.

Frank shrugged. "I gave my maid the week off."

Gregory shook his head and huffed.

"You know what?" Frank said. "'Some cause happiness wherever they go; others *whenever* they go.'"

"That's very funny, Frank. Did you come up with that yourself?"

Frank shook his head. "Oscar Wilde did. But you can guess which category you belong to."

Gregory's cheeks bounced in and out as he clenched his jaw muscles. He reached into his pocket and took out an envelope, held it out to Frank. "This is for you."

"What's that?"

"Have a look. I'm pretty sure that you'll be pleasantly surprised."

Frank grabbed the envelope, took out the paper and unfolded it. The top left corner showed a white kangaroo on a red background, then QANTAS next to it. The top right corner had a barcode and a booking reference number. Below that, Frank's full name and an e-ticket number. There were flight numbers and departing and arriving airports. The price was also printed on the paper, as was the travel class.

Frank stuffed the empty envelope in his pocket, held up the paper. "You bought me a business class ticket back to Hamburg for tomorrow afternoon?" he said, a wide smile on his face.

Gregory mirrored the smile and nodded. "It was the first one available. It's the least we could do. It's top-notch service, only the best food and drinks. The ticket even gives you access to their lounge at the airport."

"Hmmm."

"They have a huge buffet there. Eat and drink as much as you can, all included. I've tried it. It's amazing, Frank!"

"But what if I've lost my appetite?"

"What if you've lost . . ." Gregory said. "That's very funny, Frank! It really is."

Frank folded the paper and held it out to Gregory. "I don't want it," he said. "So you should take it back, get a refund."

Gregory shook his head. "But you're due to leave in a few days, anyway! And like this, you can go back home in style. And save a ton of money."

"I have money," Frank said. "And how do you know I only have a few days?"

Gregory held up his hands. "I'm not taking it back. You'll be on that flight, Frank!"

Frank shrugged, then lifted the paper with both hands. He slowly tore it in half, put one piece on top of the other, turned it ninety degrees, then repeated the process until the bundle was tiny and thick and Frank threw the lot into the air and watched as the small white squares drifted down, some into his apartment, some just outside the door. The corner piece with the white kangaroo on a red background landed on the tip of Gregory's polished right shoe.

Frank chuckled. "You've got a 'roo on your shoe," he said, pointing at it. He looked up and saw that Gregory's face had turned red; a big

157

vein on the side of his throat was pulsating and his scar had turned chalk white.

Before Caroline's demise, Frank had been a tactical fight instructor in both the army and the police. He'd trained recruits in the art of aggressive combat and self-defense. Apart from the physical knowledge of joint locks, pressure points, disarming techniques and kill points, the much deeper and more interesting area for Frank was the psychology behind fighting. Hence, Frank's decision to provoke Gregory as much as possible. It was a sure-fire way to figure out if Gregory was really a part of all this; in Frank's experience, genuine anger was a much more powerful truth serum than any drugs or alcohol. Just like people going through difficult divorces; they were living proofs of that theory.

Gregory stuck a finger in Frank's face. "Now you listen to me—"

"Who paid for the ticket?" Frank asked.

Gregory removed his finger, folded his arms across his chest and lifted his face in what came across as pride. "I did," Gregory said. "Personally."

"So, this is personal to you?" Frank said. "So you *are* trying to hide something, after all."

That did it.

Gregory twisted his torso while unfolding his arms and bending his knees, and a split second later, his left fist moved back toward his own hip while his right fist rocketed toward Frank's bulging belly. Remembering lessons from long ago, in his mind, Frank saw the twist of the torso first and turned his hips, his left arm blocking low, his right fist heading straight for a pressure point on the inside of Gregory's right arm, instantly turning it limp. And long ago, that was definitely what would have happened. But now, all these years later and—more importantly—a hundred pounds heavier, what actually happened was that Frank managed to twist barely an inch before his insides imploded. Frank doubled over, cradling his gut with one arm while putting his other hand on the wall.

Frank's stomach muscles cramped and ceased up and he tried desperately to pull in air, but was unable to breathe, despite how hard he tried. It was as if his lungs had collapsed. A huge weight on his chest turned his pain into panic as pressure in his head kept building.

But then, ever so slowly, he managed to gasp in small bursts that grew deeper with each agonizing pull. After what seemed like forever, Frank forced himself to straighten up.

Gregory's finger was back in Frank's face. "This is your last warning, you fat bastard! Unless you're on that plane tomorrow, I'll fucking kill you myself. You got that?"

Frank took a step back, then slammed the door shut.

FORTY-ONE

P ink skies, parrots and palm trees dominated the view from inside
the courtyard garden behind Frank's building.

He readjusted the pillow he'd brought along and shifted his seating
position on the bench. His belly was aching, somewhat from hunger,
mostly from Gregory's fist. Frank tore out a brown ramekin from a
dual-pack, removed the top plastic, looked up and absentmindedly
steered a teaspoon of crème brûlée into his mouth. A small colony of
fruit bats soared across the pink square of sky visible between the four
towers of apartments surrounding him. One of the bats was hanging
upside down in a nearby palm; its large, dark, inquisitive eyes were
staring at Frank while its tiny jaws pistoned swiftly up and down to
crush the small, yellow, jelly palm fruits.

Frank tried to move his mouth as quickly as the bat, resulting in
a blob of the French dessert slipping through the side of his mouth
and dripping onto his shirt. He scooped it up with an index finger
and sucked the tip, then resumed normal chewing. The creamy vanilla
combined with the crunch of caramel sent happy chills down his spine
and his arms prickled with goosebumps. His clothes had stiffened after
drying as he'd been glued to the TV for a couple of hours, rewinding,

pausing, skipping and freezing until he was sure that he'd taken it all in and he could let his mind begin creating connections, forming theories, teasing out details that would later always become important. Vital, even.

Frank emptied the first ramekin, opened the next one and got stuck in.

Upon closer inspection, the dark outline in the drawer had turned out to be a pair of sunglasses and an open pack of condoms. A piece of torn foil was lying under the bed, the used rubber nowhere to be seen. Frank surmised it had probably been flushed down the toilet.

The bathroom had been disgusting but—for some reason—the vomit had communicated something. It felt logical, but Frank was still not quite able to grasp what it was, so he left it to simmer.

The living room was full of leads and evidence, a jungle of clues with a rich story to tell. Obviously, the aftermath of a party. There was always the possibility of performing any number of lab tests, analyzes and high-tech undertakings using nanotechnology to probe at a molecular level, or polynology to trace pollen and grains and seeds that could aid in geographical tracing of matter introduced to the crime scene, and then there was DNA sequencing, fingerprint identification, laser ablation, mass spectrometers and a myriad of other things Frank only really had a vague idea about. And more interesting would be the results of the autopsy and, specifically, what had caused the victim's stomach to balloon. But, by far, the most fascinating part was—and always would be—the human factor. Long before any search for fibers, threads or fingerprints came the hunt for the why. Only when Frank could thoroughly understand the motive, would he be able to tune in on the culprit, and then, at the very end, could he begin looking for evidence. This last part was not to find out who'd done it—because by that point Frank would already know—but was merely an exercise in making sure the guilty party would end up behind bars.

But Frank didn't have the resources. Moreover, he didn't have time. He emptied his last ramekin, put it on the bench next to the other empty one, then stood up and began pacing around the garden.

Normally, gang members liked to cut off tongues or genitals or fingers or gouge out eyes, killing while sending a powerful message to anyone else considering encroaching onto their territory. But where was the psychological warfare? Where was the message? Frank thought of a few examples, one being the well-known Colombian necktie dating all the way back to the fifties. But no, every single victim had been killed swiftly and professionally. No message, not even an indirect attribution of guilt. But if Frank's theory was right, that someone was targeting people in witness protection and gangs had nothing to do with it, then what? Perhaps this particular killer was simply not interested in sending a message, because the killings were not related to organizations, but were done for personal reasons?

Another chill went down Frank's spine as he imagined a serial killer out there, deliberately picking off people previously connected to crime, simply to cover his own tracks. What if this guy was smart and the whole thing was a ruse designed to satisfy his own needs for killing? What if there was no pattern? No, there was always a pattern. The trick was to find it. But to Frank's dismay, two of the victims had backgrounds that seemed genuine enough, and there was no way for him to prove that they'd been in witness protection. That was the whole point of a witness protection program, despite the victims already being dead. Because there would be other considerations, such as protecting involved officers, as well as the victims' families, friends and colleagues, and pretty much any human being the victims had ever been in touch with during their existence. The secret could simply never be revealed, no matter what. The only reason Frank had added the two victims to the pile—making it his final eight—had been their names. Frank had dug and dug and not been able to come up with a single, suspicious thing about their backgrounds. However, they'd both been stabbed in the kidney from behind, and both had had names that, at least according to Frank, had sounded somewhat anachronistic. A fifty-three-year-old man named Jayden Summers. A forty-five-year-old woman named Nevaeh Springs. Jayden and Nevaeh. Someone had made another blunder coming up with those names.

Frank stopped at the end of the pool and leaned up against the glass fence. The underwater spot lights shone through the chlorinated water and lit up the bright blue ceramic mosaic. Eight empty deck chairs lined one side and a paddling of ducks sat on the other. A duckling had evidently fallen into the pool and was now floating on the surface, struggling to get back up. Frank walked around to the side, opened the gate and the paddling waddled away as he kneeled and scooped up the duckling. He carefully positioned it on the edge, then watched as it hurried back over to the flock. Frank's knees clicked and crunched as he struggled to get back up before walking over and lying down on a deck chair.

He interlocked his fingers behind his head and closed his eyes. Loud lorikeets were getting louder and fruit bats shrieked as the parrots were trying to find their nightly resting spots while the bats searched for food. He let silent fragments of movies play on the inside of his eyelids: Gregory spending money he shouldn't have—combined with his anger—was enough proof for Frank to know he was involved; individuals from made-up backgrounds being systematically killed without an obvious motive; a stomach blown up like a watermelon; Rebecca being followed by someone working for Jacaranda Security Group, the same company her dead husband's friend was now the CFO of; Frank's damn letter throwing him out of the country; Frank's newly acquired diabetes; Amy's asshole of a boyfriend; the little, helpless duckling; the sudden and violent appearance of the storm at Teneriffe.

Frank opened his eyes and sat up. Stared at the pool. Something clicked. He couldn't lose it now—not now. He pushed his index fingers against his temples and closed his eyes again, focusing. Felt his panic rise as the image slipped away, then slowly returned. And then it stuck. And it became clear. An article he'd read in a scuba diving magazine in a doctor's waiting room.

Frank opened his eyes again and reached into his pocket, grabbing his phone. He dialed the number he knew from memory.

Or, to be more Frank, by heart.

Amy answered immediately.

"I've got it!" Frank said, his heart racing in his chest.

"Frank?" Amy said. "I'm at my parents' place. We're just about to sit down for dinner. My brother's here and—"

"I think I've figured it out, Amy. How it could all connect."

There was silence for a short while. "Let me just step into the hallway, Frank."

Frank felt his heart drumming up against the inside of his breastbone as he waited for Amy to say something.

When she finally came back, she spoke in a half-whisper. "Are you talking about the murders?"

"Yes, Amy. I have a theory that fits, that makes sense, and I need to discuss it with you."

"Okay, where would you like to meet?" she said.

Frank thought about warm bread and places that stayed open until late. "What about Patrick's Patisserie?"

Amy took a moment. "Ah yes, I know where it is. What time?"

"Now!" Frank thought he heard Amy sigh.

Then he remembered. "Actually," he said, "you'll have to pick me up."

"Why do I have to pick you up?"

"My car was impounded by the council a few hours ago. I'll tell you all about it when you come."

This time, Frank was sure he heard Amy sigh.

Forty-Two

F rank stood under a streetlamp on the sidewalk in front of his apartment block when a small cherry-red convertible—roof folded down—pulled up next to him.

Amy smiled up at him, and Frank looked down in disbelief. Amy had parked all the way up against the high curb, making the access even lower. "How am I going to get into that?"

Amy leaned across and opened the door for him. Because of the high curb, the bottom part of the open door hung two inches over the sidewalk. "Don't be difficult, Frank. Hop in."

Frank turned, pointed his butt toward the car, stretched his arms out in front of him, then lowered himself into a semi-squat position. When his behind was two feet over the passenger seat, his knees gave in and Frank dropped the rest of the way. The car bounced on its shock absorbers and the bottom part of the door slammed into the sidewalk. He twisted his upper body, heaved his legs in and pulled the door shut.

Frank grunted. "I haven't been this low to the ground since driving a go-cart as a kid."

Amy shook her head, looked at Frank's shirt, pointed. "What the hell is that?" she said.

Frank's double-chin was squashed against his chest as he looked down himself. "Crème brûlée."

"Jesus," Amy said, then pushed the lever up into first gear, revved the engine and released the clutch. Frank's skull bounced off the headrest—they were underway.

"Are you upset?" Frank said.

"You're wrecking my car," she said. "You really need to lose some weight, Frank. You know that?"

"Now you sound like Gregory."

Amy sighed, took a few turns in silence, then, eventually, glided onto Coronation Drive.

"Gregory paid me a visit today," Frank said.

"What?" Amy said, raising her eyebrows. "You mean at your home?"

Frank explained how it had unfolded.

"Shit!"

"Don't worry—"

"I *am* worried. This is because of me and my big mouth. That idiot Joe has been feeding Gregory information. He's his little pet and I probably talk too much about you."

Frank shrugged. "Joe's loyalty is misplaced. He's young. He'll grow and learn."

"Says who?"

"I remember meeting Joe on a few occasions. He has no substance. As a matter of fact, he doesn't have much of anything. Don't worry about him. He's a follower, and a weak one at that."

"I hope you're right," Amy said. "So, what's the big revelation?" The Riverside Expressway lights brightened up the interior of the car every few seconds as they glided in and out of beams.

Frank rested an arm on the door, raised his voice to vie with the wind. "I figured two things," he said. "First, we need to find the guy who called in the murder."

Amy shook her head. "Already tried it. He called from the victim's phone, left the phone there, no fingerprints. There are another twenty different prints or so that forensics are currently working through, but we simply don't know who called."

Frank nodded. "Did you check for DNA in the vomit?"

"Yes. It came up positive to a guy already in the system. Brad Jenkins."

"Any other people matched the puke?"

Amy shook her head.

"That's your caller," Frank said.

Amy turned her head, stared at Frank, then returned her attention to the road ahead. "How can you be so sure of that?"

"Just common sense," Frank said. "The murder was called in during the morning, meaning the guy who called was probably still hanging around because he'd slept over. People normally sleep over for three reasons: sex, difficulties finding transport, or being too sick to go anywhere. And I'd say all that gagging makes him the ideal sleepover candidate."

Amy changed lanes, nodded and stared ahead. "And the second thing?"

"I think I figured out the reason for the distended stomach," Frank said.

"Oh?"

"Did you hear back from forensics?"

"Maggie called me earlier. They're still waiting for results to come back."

"From where?"

Amy shrugged. "Databases, I guess."

"Could we go and see Maggie?"

"When?"

"Now."

Amy nodded. "I guess," she said. "Call her, put in on speaker. I'll do the talking."

Frank did as he was told, then held the phone up. After three rings, a positively happy-sounding woman answered, cheerily stating that she was still at work and that Amy was more than welcome to drop by for a chat.

Frank hung up, threw the phone back in the glove compartment, then pointed at a transparent plastic pouch, roughly three-by-three inches, a dark orange paste of sorts inside. "What's that?"

Amy took a peek. "Salad dressing. I think from last week."

"Ugh," Frank said, then shut the compartment and looked up, spun his head around. "*Scheiße!*"

"What?"

"You just passed the turnoff for Patrick's Patisserie. I was looking forward to a cronut."

"I'm sure you were," Amy said. "Think you'll survive until we get to Coopers Plains?"

"Hmmm."

FORTY-THREE

Amy swung her tiny convertible through a roundabout, cruised along the front of the white two-story building, then followed it around the back, where she nosed into a spot right next to a pair of sliding doors. Humidity was on the rise again, and thick clouds slipped in front of the waning moon. Amy pressed a button and closed up the roof before exiting the car. She walked over to the keypad stuck into the large concrete door frame and punched in the combination Maggie had given her over the phone, then waited.

Ron's voice came through the small loudspeaker grille. "That you, Amy?"

"Sure is. And I've brought Frank with me."

There was a moment of silence. Then: "Who's Frank?"

Amy thought for a moment about that question. Who exactly was Frank? Mentor? Funny freak? Ex-colleague? A man possessed?

"A good friend," Amy said.

By the time the doors slid open, Frank had finally made it out of the car and hobbled in behind her. They walked into the bright lights of the elevator together. "I don't suppose we're going up?" Frank said, a hopeful tone to his voice.

170

Amy shook her head. "B3," she said. "Bottom basement."

Frank pressed the button and the elevator dropped in sync with his guts. Despite having studied dead bodies his entire career, Frank had never learned to view it as just another part of the job. Surmising, proving, or instinctively knowing a person's dark sides were bad enough. Seeing, smelling, and feeling were much worse. Frank had always thought that the day these things stopped affecting him would be the day he'd call it quits—for good.

The doors slid open and Amy led the way down a narrow corridor with linoleum floors, yellow walls and rows of exposed neon tubes stretching out endlessly before them. They kept walking until Amy finally stopped in front of a brown door on the left which had a small metal sign below a tiny square of wired security glass: *436*. Amy rapped on the window and a few seconds later the door opened, revealing a plump lady with a smiley face, waxy skin and a bloody apron. The woman smiled broadly, reached out an arm and stepped in for a hug.

Amy stepped back. "Whoa!"

The woman looked confused for a moment, then down at her apron. "So sorry. This damn job is always so messy and I forget," she said, then looked over at Frank, a question mark on her face.

Amy held out an arm and pointed. "Maggie, this is Frank—Frank, Margaret."

Maggie kept smiling and tilted her head. "And you are a . . . friend of Amy's, I understand?"

Frank shrugged. "I suppose," he said. "We used to be colleagues before I got suspended and thrown out of the country. I'll be gone in a few days, but in the meantime," he said, "I'm here to help."

Maggie shifted her gaze to Amy, not moving from the doorway.

Amy sighed. "Frank is a really accomplished agent. He's originally from Germany, has worked for the federal police there, various criminal divisions and basically," Amy said, then stole a glance at Frank before looking back at Maggie, "he's weird yet brilliant. His social manners leave a lot to be desired, I admit, but I brought him along because I think he'll be able to shine a light where we may not be looking."

Maggie didn't say anything, didn't move.

"And he's apparently onto something," Amy said.

"Is he here . . . officially?"

"Is who here?" Amy said, then put on a hysterical laugh that quickly died out and fell flat.

Maggie seemed to think about it for a while, but in the end, she moved aside. "Come on in then."

FORTY-FOUR

Four masked faces surrounded a stainless steel table on braked wheels: Amy and Frank on one side, Ron and Maggie on the other. The table held the naked body of a skinny male lying on his back, arms spread at an acute angle, palms up, legs slightly apart. Two huge spots hung overhead, illuminating every cut, bruise, scar, puncture, texture and blemish. The victim's eyes were closed and long, elegant eyelashes fanned downward onto gaunt cheeks. His hair was sandy brown, longish and brittle, as if he'd spent every day surfing under the sun. A heavy odor of alcohol, preservatives and death hung in the air.

Frank pointed to a small tattoo on the victim's right biceps, then spoke through the blue paper facemask Ron had given him after preliminary, cautious introductions. "Satan's Sharks," he said. "Big scale drug importers and distributors in Australia."

"Exactly," Amy said, nodding excitedly. "Hence the AFP's involvement."

Ron looked at Frank. "You know about them?"

Frank shrugged. "Heard about them," he said, then pointed to badly healed puncture wounds on the inside of the left arm. "Track marks?"

Ron, who stood directly opposite Frank, nodded. "Don was a heroin user, bloods confirm it."

Amy looked across at Maggie. "Anything that stands out?"

"Stands out?" Maggie said.

"You know, compared to other murders."

"Well," Maggie said, "it's not as though we go through a dozen a day here. Murders in Queensland are still somewhat rare."

"How rare?" Frank said.

Ron cleared his throat. "Queensland sees roughly twenty a year that we know of, most of which are straightforward and obvious, investigated with a suspect apprehended and a case filed to the local courts, usually within a week; killers such as scorned women, jealous husbands, robberies gone wrong, that type of thing," he said, then paused. "But a murder like this one with motives we can only guess about, with the assailant in hiding and no apparent leads, well . . ."

Maggie turned her head and looked at Ron. "I think the last one was about a year ago or so, wasn't it?"

Ron nodded. "Also stabbed."

"Charles Grainer?" Frank said.

"I believe so," Ron said, then tilted his head. His bushy eyebrows furrowed. "But as far as I remember, that case was handled by the Queensland Police, not the AFP, so how do you know about it?"

"I studied that case with Amy," Frank said. "We think it's connected."

"Connected?" Maggie said, then looked at Amy. "You think it's connected?"

Amy shook her head. "Not we! Frank . . . I'm not sure if . . . it's a work in progress, let's put it like that."

Frank scratched the back of his head, then stopped as the friction from his rubber gloves pulled at his red hair. "What about the distended stomach?" he said, then pointed. "It looks deflated now."

Maggie's head shot up. "Compared to when—exactly?"

Amy looked in fear at Frank, who spoke immediately. "Amy explained to me that, at the crime scene, the stomach was as big and round as a large watermelon. That there looks more like a flattened cantaloupe."

"Right," Maggie said, then gave Amy a look that Frank interpreted as somewhere between warning and disbelief. She took a deep breath, her exhale clearly audible through the mask, then shook her head, looked at Frank. "I'm sorry, but I really need to know what you can contribute because I'm beginning to not like this one bit, and I actually regret letting a suspended agent in here."

Frank nodded. "Understood. I'll be as quick and precise as I can," he said, then took a moment to find his words. "And please object if I'm completely wrong. This is evidently your area of expertise, not mine, so watch out!"

"Excuse me?" Maggie said in a loud voice.

Amy quickly raised a hand. "It's a German translation issue. What Frank means to say is 'please pay attention'".

Ron shook his head. "Why doesn't he just say that, then?"

"Apologies," Frank said. "It's a direct translation of *pass mal auf.* Anyway, from what I know, when putrefaction occurs, a process involving microorganisms creates bacteria that release a mix of gases, right?"

Maggie shook her head. "Yes and no. I already explained this to Amy's partner. The victim's death was far too recent for the putrefaction process to have even begun, which it doesn't until earliest after three to four days, *then* the decay of organic matter commences, and we sat next to this body maximum three hours after he was killed."

"Maximum three hours?" Frank said.

Ron nodded. "The body was still warm, and Rigor Mortis hadn't set in yet—that puts it at maximum three hours."

Frank nodded too. "And putrefaction—"

"I just told you—" Maggie began.

"—because of the organic process, would produce a mix of gases, is that right?"

"Yes," Maggie said, then lowered her gaze onto the partially deflated belly as she spoke. "Among the gases often found are hydrogen, methane, carbon dioxide and hydrogen sulfide."

Frank nodded. "Did you analyze the makeup of the gases in this guy's stomach?"

Maggie turned and walked over to a table, removed one rubber glove, then rummaged through the printouts. She found one, then lifted it up, read it with her back to the rest of them. "Ron?"

Ron turned to her. "Yeah."

"These results show ninety-nine percent carbon dioxide."

"What?" Ron said.

Maggie nodded. "Yeah. Even if the murderer was extremely clever and somehow managed to camouflage the time of death, wouldn't putrefaction show a high content of *both* carbon dioxide *and* hydrogen?"

"Absolutely," Ron said.

Maggie put the paper back on the table, put her rubber glove on again and walked over to Ron. "What's going on here?"

Ron shrugged. Shook his head.

Maggie waited a beat, looked him in the eyes. When Ron stayed silent, both of them turned and looked at Frank.

Frank cleared his throat. "I think the victim's stomach was blown up using compressed carbon dioxide released into the stab wound under high pressure. It would account for the concentration of carbon dioxide, as well as the projectile spraying through his mouth and anus."

Now all three of them stared at Frank. The silence was thicker than the stench of death.

In the end, it was Ron who spoke. "What are you talking about?"

Frank looked at all three of them in turn. "I'm talking about the murder weapon."

FORTY-FIVE

"It's called an injection knife," Frank said. "I read about it in a diver's magazine. Originally designed as a weapon of defense for divers. Most of the companies I've found offer models with blades that are six inches long, two inches wide, double-edged, with a standard sharp edge on one side and a serrated edge on the other. Where the serration ends, just short of the tip of the blade, there's a small hole. The handle is hollow and holds a carbon dioxide cartridge that is activated by the press of a button on the handle, instantly pushing eight hundred psi of carbon dioxide through the hollow blade, through the outlet, injecting the high-pressure gas into the animal, which then expands, all while its wound freezes."

"Why would divers want something like that?" Maggie asked.

"The idea is that a diver who's attacked by, say, a shark, will stab the shark and then press the button. Injection of high pressure gas will inflate the part of the animal around the stabbing site, making the animal ascend quickly, just like an inflated ball underwater, thus removing the threat physically. And not only does the injected gas pull the shark up to the surface rapidly, but, theoretically, because of the immediate freezing of the wound, there should also be little to no blood spill into the water. According to the article, that's a fortunate byproduct as it'll keep the diver relatively safe against other nearby predators smelling blood."

Ron whistled. "That sounds effective."

"But this guy exploded from the inside," Maggie said.

Frank shrugged. "He's not a shark. Smaller body, shorter distance between the stab site and his orifices. Basically different biology, different physics."

"Guess you have a point," Maggie said.

"Plus," he added, "a nice little bonus, as you can imagine, is that the rapidly expanding carbon dioxide freezes tissue as well as any organs in the vicinity of the wound, making even a poorly placed stab much more effective."

"And these things really exist?" Amy said.

"Not in Australia, at least not officially, because they're illegal to possess," Frank said. "But if you're willing to part with roughly six hundred US dollars and you manage to smuggle one in, you'll get a top model with a blade of hardened steel, a slip-resistant neoprene handle and a dozen cartridges."

Ron looked at Maggie, then pointed to the wound. "This guy's wound is about two inches wide, could very well match."

Maggie nodded. "And the freezing from the carbon dioxide could account for the ruptures we found in some of the fibers from his right kidney."

Everybody looked back at Frank. It was Amy who spoke. "But, if you believe that this is connected to other stabbings, I'm pretty sure that none of them were injected with carbon dioxide, and we know with an absolute certainty that Charles Grainer wasn't, so why would you think they're connected?"

Frank shrugs. "Patterns. He's getting bored. Maybe he's evolving."

"Jesus," Amy said. "What now?"

Frank turned his head to face her. "Now we have to find the owner of the injection knife."

FORTY-SIX

T wenty minutes after leaving Forensic Services, heading southeast, Amy zigzagged her way through Slacks Creek until finally entering a dead-end street sparsely lit by a single streetlamp down the end. She slowed down.

The headlights illuminated cracked asphalt and Frank watched bulgy, black tar snakes slither underneath the hood. The low suspension obediently fed back every imperfection in the road, making Frank grunt and moan as tiny bolts of lightning shot up his lower back and into his sore belly. Their recent visit to Forensic Services had left him nauseated, and the driving had made him dizzy.

Halfway down the street, spotlights suddenly powered up on their left and shone an exaggeratedly bright light on a neglected front yard. The edge of the beams spilled over the front of a dilapidated red-brick house. Amy kept going, rolled farther down the street, pulled over and parked behind a battered utility truck that had passed its use-by-date about two decades earlier. She switched off the headlights and killed the engine, leaving both of them enveloped in silent darkness.

Amy jumped out of the car. Frank opened his door, turned and grabbed the frame with one hand and the hardtop with his other, then pushed up. He lost his balance, almost fell back into the car, but kept pushing and eventually managed to get himself out. Now that the transition to Homo erectus was complete, Frank closed the door, reached into his pocket and took out a brand new pack of cigarettes he'd purchased earlier from his local corner shop while waiting for Amy to pick him up. He removed the tiny plastic ribbon, tore off a corner of the foil and held the pack sideways, tapped it and watched three filters appear. He closed his lips around the one sticking out the most, pulled it out and lit it up.

"What are you doing?" Amy whispered.

"I need a cigarette," Frank said. "I haven't had anything to eat in ages. No cronut, remember?"

Amy pointed three houses back in the direction they'd come from, at the red-brick house. "They'll see you a mile away with that fire stick."

Frank shook his head, inhaled again, blew smoke out through his nostrils. "Not with those spots," he said. "The place looks brighter than the Suncorp Stadium on game night."

They walked back slowly until they arrived at the corner of the front yard belonging to the red-brick house, then positioned themselves halfway behind a white van that had its back wheels lifted onto wooden blocks, both license plates missing.

From the cracked curb, roughly five feet back, chain links stretched out between rusted steel tubes from Frank's left, all the way across, stopping at a wide double gate on the right that was hanging on its hinges, forever stuck in the open position. The small house was set back about fifteen feet from the fence, and from just inside the open gate, Frank's eyes followed dusty wheel ruts running through a sunburnt lawn, all the way up along the right side of the house. Where the ruts stopped, toward the back of the property, Frank recognized the shadowy outline of a shaker scoop poking through the hood of a muscle car.

The house was elevated, with two square windows set on either side of a front door accessible by three concrete steps. Underneath the right window stood three rubbish bins, all with different colored lids, none of which worried Frank. To the right of the bins, a tap protruded between the bricks, and a wide hook—with a garden hose repeatedly looped around it—hung just next to the tap. Not a concern either.

What troubled Frank was on the left side. An item set beneath the window. Probably bought as a self-assembly kit, it was the only thing that looked fresh and well maintained on the property: tinted, treated timber; a large, arched doorway; a tall A-frame roof. In other words, high-quality, spacious living quarters. For a distinguished member of the family. What disturbed Frank even more was the size of the partially empty water bowl and the condition of the chew toys: thick ropes shredded to pieces; rubber bones with deep teeth imprints that were visible even from where Frank stood. And then there were the shattered remains of a small, brown teddy: no head, right arm and left leg missing.

"So this is Brad Jenkins's house?" Frank said, then took another drag of his cigarette.

Amy shook her head. "He's registered as living here, but officially the house belongs to a woman named Stephanie Taylor."

"His girlfriend?"

"We can only assume."

"Have you seen the dog anywhere?"

"Probably inside."

Frank shook his head, then took a last drag of his cigarette and threw the butt under the van. Suddenly, and with an explosion of energy, Frank pushed off the van and ran up to the fence.

In the same instant, a slim yet muscular, black dog with erect ears and rust spots on its muzzle and chest sprinted out of the kennel, then stopped just as fast, sat down and looked at Frank; a Doberman.

"Let's go," he said, then quickly turned and headed for the car.

Frank made it back first and was already inside when Amy opened the driver's door.

She'd never seen Frank walk that fast.

Forty-Seven

A my was about to turn the key in the ignition when the *Mission: Impossible* theme song filled the car. She retrieved her phone from a jacket pocket. "Hey, Maggie," she said, then listened as Maggie conveyed the latest findings. While listening, Amy saw Frank sway gently in his seat, his skin seemingly damp.

Frank leaned back and closed his eyes.

"Thank you," Amy said, then hung up. "You're shaking! Did the dog scare you, or was the run too much?"

Frank shook his head. "What did Maggie say?"

"They ran a boot print they lifted from the scene. They're not sure about the brand yet, but it's a size fourteen."

"So?" Frank said.

"They also got the results back from the hairs they found next to the boot prints."

"Someone in the database?" Frank said, opening his eyes.

Amy nodded. "You won't believe it."

"What?"

"It's someone you already know."

"What?"

Amy nodded again. "William Forrester."

"William Forrester?" Frank repeated. Then: "William Forrester from JSG? The CFO from the company who's having Rebecca followed?"

"The one and only," Amy said.

"How is that possible?"

Amy shrugged.

Frank looked out the front windscreen, not saying anything for a while. When he finally did speak, his voice was low and measured. "Rebecca told me that William Forrester was involved in some bar brawl years back."

"Really?"

Frank nodded. "Apparently he must have been found guilty, hence his DNA already in the database."

"Makes sense," Amy said.

Frank looked out into the darkness for a while, then slapped himself on the forehead, keeping his hand there.

"What?"

"And since he now works for JSG, the same company that's currently following Rebecca, what does that tell you about the company?"

Amy turned to Frank, shrugged. "Not sure where you're going with this. Are you okay? Why are you sweating? Do you need the AC on?"

Frank didn't reply. He ran a hand over his face, removed it, then wiped it on his shorts.

Amy thought he looked pale, and she was beginning to worry when Frank finally spoke again.

"Rebecca told me that William was involved in some bar brawl years back," he repeated.

"Okay," Amy said. "But if you're referring to an assault and battery conviction, that's still a far cry from committing murder."

Frank shook his head. "I'm thinking about JSG," he said. "When did William start working for them?"

Amy looked out her window, mentally accessing the files she'd printed for him. She looked back at Frank. "Sometime after Carl's death, so maximum five years ago?"

"Exactly," Frank said. "Meaning that William Forrester would have already had a criminal record when they hired him."

"So?"

"You think a person with a criminal record would be able to get a job in a security firm?"

Amy's eyes grew large. "Of course not."

"Exactly," Frank said. "JSG must be a front, which means they're all crooks, hiding illegal activities behind the legal facade of a security firm."

"Not a bad idea, driving around selling drugs and then deducting the company miles from their annual tax bill," Amy said. "Wouldn't surprise me if they have asset depreciation schedules on everything they own."

Frank ran a hand over his face again. "Plus, no one would ever question why they drive around at all hours of the night," he said. "That's what security companies do. They patrol. Survey. Go on the occasional stakeout. It's the perfect cover."

"Bloody brilliant," Amy said.

Frank nodded, swayed slightly and put a hand on the dashboard. "Which means that Brian Hearst, the CEO, is the leader of a criminal organization."

"Yeah."

"And we know that William Forrester is the CFO, his right hand. Meaning he's no ordinary accountant. He's their wizard, tweaking numbers and laundering the dirty dollars as they come in."

"Probably. I still don't understand why they're following Rebecca, though. What could she have that's so important to them?"

Frank shrugged.

"Maybe all of this connects to her dead husband?" Amy said.

"Okay," Frank said. "But how? He's gone. If they wanted to blackmail her, they would have done so already. If they wanted to kill her, she'd already be dead. Why follow her now?"

"From what you've told me, they've only been following her for a short while, so that could simply be them wanting to work out her whereabouts, cataloguing her movements to plan the perfect strike."

Frank shrugged. "But Carl died five years ago. If this all connects to him, then why wait five years?"

"Bide your time and all that?"

"Maybe," he said, then opened the glove compartment again, looked inside.

"What are you looking for?" Amy asked.

"A cheeseburger, spareribs, maybe a couple of hotdogs?"

Amy chuckled. "Let's go get you some food. I know just the place. They're open late and you're going to absolutely love it!" Amy said, then started the car and put it in first. "Put on your seatbelt."

"*Jawohl!*" Frank said, giving her a mock salute.

Amy pulled a U-turn, then sped off down the street.

Frank tugged at his seatbelt. "I could use . . ." he began, then his head lulled forward, his chin landing on his chest before his upper body slumped.

Amy hit the brakes, causing Frank to smash his forehead onto the dashboard, his arms still hanging slack, the back of his hands resting on the floor of the convertible.

"Frank?" Amy said, then put the gear selector back in neutral and pulled the handbrake. She shook his shoulder. "Frank?"

Frank's head rolled off the dashboard and disappeared between his legs.

"FRANK!"

FORTY-EIGHT

Darkness enveloped the hilly expanse as Rebecca walked between a seemingly endless row of erect rocks in various shapes and sizes. Chiseled, edged and carved by skillful hands decades—even centuries—earlier, Rebecca saw each and every one of them as a story; lives ranging from short stories to full-length novels, as well as a few rare, epic sagas. And although people's life stories varied greatly in both form and length, in Rebecca's mind, there was one thing that they all had in common: the lack of a happy ending. Only fairytales had happy endings and no life was ever just a fairytale. And it was for that reason that she always visited after nightfall; Rebecca wanted the unfairness, the inhumane and the brutal to be kept in perpetual darkness so that she could enjoy sunny days with no associations to death, destruction or despair.

She stopped at a spot she'd visited regularly over the past five years, kneeled down, then felt her knees get wet as her tracksuit pants soaked up dew from the pristine lawn. She pulled back her hood and placed the bouquet of white lilies in front of the headstone. A small, single lamppost positioned on a dimly lit gravel track that ran four rows farther back from where Rebecca was sitting, spilled its orange light over the headstone, just enough to cast a weak shadow across the engraved epitaph: Carl Benjamin Wright – beloved husband and cherished friend. Taken too soon.

Rebecca folded her hands in her lap and closed her eyes. She apologized to Carl for not being a better wife, for lying to him, for keeping things from him. But she thanked him for a sweet, albeit short, time together. She thanked him for looking after her, for making sure that she, at least, didn't have to worry about money, and for always being so gentle, loving and caring throughout their relationship. She told him she missed him and that she knew he was in a better place now, that God would look after him.

Rebecca opened her eyes. "What do you think about Frank?" she asked out loud, then put a hand to her mouth. If Carl wouldn't have been able to answer a question like that when he was alive, what did she expect him to say now that he was dead? She almost felt ashamed to have asked, shook her head, and removed her hand. "I'll see you again soon, my love," she said, kissed her index and middle fingers and placed them on his name, then stood up and headed for the gravel path. Rebecca took a few deep breaths, set the counter on her smart watch for an hour and headed off.

The familiar, rhythmic crunch under her sneakers reassured Rebecca as she jogged alongside thousands of dead people. She steadily sped up, took random turns at forks and junctions while her muscles warmed up, crisscrossed the vast cemetery while her breathing deepened, and sweat coated her skin.

And one thought kept pushing through to the front of her mind: What would Carl have thought about Frank?

Forty-Nine

F rank ran his tongue around his mouth for the umpteenth time. "What is that taste?"

"That there is the luscious flavor of a thousand islands, thankfully factory-made with way too much sugar."

Frank didn't say anything.

"You know, Frank. You could have at least told me."

Frank scratched his red goatee. He wasn't sure what to say. He could feel her looking at him.

"I . . . eh . . ."

"Yes, Frank?" she prompted.

Frank didn't speak.

"Is this how you see a partnership? A friendship? You feed me random bits of incomprehensible, work-related bullshit while keeping all the juicy stuff for yourself?"

Frank turned his head and looked at her. "Juicy stuff?"

"Personal stuff, Frank! I thought we were friends!"

"Of course—"

"Then why treat me as if I'm stupid?"

"I would never—"

"But you *are*, Frank! You are! By keeping your private life from me, and not letting me in," Amy said, shaking her head. "You surround yourself with an invisible wall. And I just don't get it. I thought . . ." Amy began.

"You thought what?" Frank said.

Amy took a deep breath. "I thought I meant more to you."

"I . . . eh . . ." Frank said, then looked down. Sighed. "How did you know, anyway?"

Amy turned back and looked out the front windscreen. "My brother has been a diabetic his whole life," she said. "God knows how many times I had to save his ass when we were younger."

Frank shrugged. "The doctor said that I have type 2, but maybe I'm only borderline. Maybe I still have time to turn the boat around."

Amy began blinking rapidly. "Frank, you can't play with this. You can't hide from it. And you definitely can't ignore it." She put an index finger to the corner of one eye. She turned back to face him. "Do you realize you could have died?"

Frank looked her in the eyes and watched as her lower lids filled with water. Any moment now and they would overflow and drops would run down her cheeks. He wanted to say that the doctor had probably been mistaken, and that he could seek a second opinion. He also wanted to tell her he was dieting and had begun exercising. But most of all, he didn't want to lie to her.

"Say something, Frank."

Frank sighed. "I'm sorry, Amy," he said. "I really am."

Amy nodded, then wiped her left cheek. "Come on, put on that seatbelt and let's get you some dinner."

FIFTY

A my pulled up at the curb.

Frank took off his seatbelt. "You're picking up William Forrester first thing tomorrow?" he said, then put two fingers inside the doorhandle, ready to exit.

Amy nodded, let the engine idle and put it in first. "I'll head back to HQ now to brief the team. We'll come up with a plan."

"Good luck," Frank said, then opened the door, twisted and swung his legs out.

"I'll keep you informed," Amy said, while Frank pushed himself out and up.

Frank nodded in appreciation and turned and put one hand on the door, the other on the roof, then bent and stuck his head in. "Be careful," he said. "Follow procedures. Don't be brave, be professional. There's something wrong with Gregory."

Amy nodded. "Don't worry, Frank, I'm sure he's just pissed at you for not respecting your suspension."

Frank shook his head. "It's more than that," he said, then moved to swing the door shut when Amy spoke again.

"Also, Frank?"

Frank stuck his head back in the car. "Yeah?"

"Thanks for punching Jason in the nose," Amy said. "He's history now. Gone. Moved out."

"Thanks for saving my life, albeit with disgusting salad dressing."

"I'm sure you'll find something to cleanse your palate with in there. Just keep it healthy, will you?"

Frank nodded, then shut the door and watched the red taillights speed into the night.

He turned back and found himself in a large parking lot in an abandoned area of the old Brisbane River Docks. Frank walked slowly toward the murky river. The old docks were littered with boarded up warehouses, rusted loading cranes and cracked storage silos. Straight ahead, in the direction Frank was walking, sat a colorful array of renovated containers: blue, green and yellow. Double stacked, brightly lit, with neon tubes bent into WELCOME, HELLO and EAT STREET.

Frank walked inside, and immediately his nostrils were attacked by culinary aromas from around the world. A sea of people strolled along brightly lit stands offering Japanese sushi, Greek gyros, American burgers, Thai beef salads, Chinese pork dumplings, British fish and chips and Italian pizza. Some were drinking beer, others colorful cocktails prepared in pimped-up pineapples. His ears filled with something that sounded like eighties pop music performed by a band on a small stage farther up, and Frank tried to discern what song they were playing, but the thumping bass from a nearby DJ distorted everything into a frantic noise. His belly roared.

He found a stand with Mexican street food and ordered himself a share platter with gorditas, nachos, tacos, tamales and quesadillas. While waiting for his order, he got a large beer and sat down at a small, round table. The glow from bare bulbs slung between poles reflected off the surface of the white metal table. Bright green, artificial lawn stretched around the whole area, and the tops of metal rubbish bins glinted under thousands of fairy lights. He emptied the beer, felt it line the sides of what was a bottomless crater in his guts. He got up and ordered two more.

He sat back down and was halfway through the second beer when the round fast-food pager began vibrating violently across the table; it emitted a high-pitch beep and a red light flashed. Frank grabbed it and walked over to where a smiling woman in a colorful dress was finishing up his order. He handed her the pager. "Would you like to wait with your churros and café de olla?" she said, all while piling up his tray.

"I'll have them now, please," Frank said. As soon as she turned, Frank grabbed a gordita and stuffed it in his mouth—the whole thing. Felt the meat and cheese push up against the back of his gums and slide down his throat. A small tear escaped the corner of his left eye, and Frank left it there, stuffed the next gordita down.

His head was spinning, and Frank swatted tiny black flies hovering in his periphery. Then he remembered they didn't actually exist. His optometrist had explained that they were age-related eye floaters; something about a jelly-like substance inside the eye getting old, causing scattered lumps of collagen fibers that would sometimes cast tiny shadows on his retina. Sometimes annoying, sometimes not. It was only disturbing when Frank thought about it, like now, for example. Like criminals and connections. He could try to think about other things so that—at least for a while—the world was a beautiful place, and his wife had never been killed, and there were no criminals, no misfiring of his synapses, no scents to pick up or leads to follow, no gut instincts to listen to, no intrusive thoughts in his already busy brain. He could pretend the colorful flowers weren't made of plastic, that he actually was in Mexico right now, that he didn't know, didn't feel, and then life would have meaning and make sense, and he could come up with valid reasons for waking up again tomorrow morning.

But, deep down, he did know, didn't he? And Frank couldn't look the other way. It was simply not in him. He had to feel, despite the pain. Heck, no. *Because* of the pain. It was a shitty excuse for an existence—no doubt about that—but it was also equally valid. Perhaps even more so than the happy alternative of not caring. Someone had to be Frank.

The woman brought his dessert and coffee, and Frank walked back and sat down. He put his elbows on the table, his face in his hands and closed his eyes. It was at times like these he thought he was going to lose his mind.

Someone was out there killing people in witness protection. Now, earlier today, another one. Same MO; stabbed and killed, swiftly and efficiently. Bar the distended stomach. Maybe the victim had known the day would come. That the program would eventually fail him. Maybe that was why he had done drugs, as an escape. Then William Forrester from Jacaranda Security Group had been there, taking him out. The victim had never seen it coming, which could mean he knew Bill personally.

And now Rebecca was being followed by the same people. Now Rebecca was a target. The Rebecca, who looked so much like Frank's dead wife that he hurt every time he saw her. Felt a need to get close to her like nothing he'd ever felt before. This was his second chance. Yet now he only had a few days left. He could choose between abandoning it all, voluntarily boarding a plane heading for Germany, or hide in some godforsaken town in the Queensland hinterland or outback New South Wales, pretending to be someone he wasn't. But the result would be the same; people would continue to die, and, slowly but surely, so would Frank.

He lifted his face and dug in. He threw food in his mouth and chewed and swallowed aggressively until the platter was empty and the beer gone. After that, he made quick work of the churros and then downed his cinnamon-spiced coffee.

His belly rumbled and groaned louder than ever before. Something didn't sit right.

Or, to be more Frank, something did.

Frank dug out his phone and found the number he'd saved, pressed call, put the phone to his ear.

"Frank?" Rebecca said.

"I need to see you!" Frank hadn't meant to say it like that; it had simply flown out of his mouth, and now he'd ruined the only chance he'd ever had.

"Why don't you come over tomorrow morning?" Rebecca said. "Let's say nine am. I'll make breakfast for us."

Frank was still staring at his phone long after she'd hung up.

FIFTY-ONE

A my had donned a helmet and a bulletproof vest and held her
Glock 22 down in front of her, arms straight, both hands
clutching the Austrian semi-automatic pistol.

Dawn was still twenty minutes away, and the pink light that
would normally be visible at this time of day was hiding behind
the surrounding steep hills of The Gap. The crowns of gum trees
stood silhouetted against a clear, dark blue sky. Wildlife sounds were
scattered. Somewhere deeper into the dense growth, farther up a hill,
a single kookaburra began laughing.

Amy walked sideways, her back tight up against lush landscaping.
Broad, waxy, dark green leaves stroked her back as she continued
up along the side of the steep driveway, Joe right behind her. The
large Queenslander was still shrouded in darkness, two vehicles parked
below the front of the house, between fat timber poles. Tactical
response team members in full combat gear, carrying assault rifles, had
surrounded the stilted house, waiting for Amy's command.

"Ready?" Amy said.

The leader of the tactical response team whispered into Amy's
earpiece. "Affirm."

Amy took one last look around, then took a deep breath. "Go! Go! Go!"

Two team members sprinted up the stairs and breached the front door at the same time as two others mounted the back patio and burst through the double doors. Another four—two on either side of the house—came out of hiding, their rifles raised, aiming them at the windows. A bright flash and a loud boom preceded screams coming from inside the house. A huge flock of cockatoos awoken by the commotion joined in; the screeching and wailing was deafening.

"Clear," the team leader said in Amy's earpiece. "We're in the master bedroom."

Amy and Joe ran up the stairs and entered the house.

"In here," a voice said.

Amy heard a woman scream and followed the sound up the end of the hallway, where she turned into a large, high-ceilinged room dominated by a king-size bed.

Four tactical team members were aiming their weapons at a man sitting up against the headboard, his upper body bare, his arms above his head. His mouth was open, and he blinked repeatedly into the brightness of the flashlights attached to the tactical rifles. The woman sitting next to him—Amy presumed it was the man's wife—was screaming and holding her hands over her ears. She was shaking so much that the lace on her pink teddy vibrated.

Amy found the light switch and flicked it. "Australian Federal Police!"

The woman stopped screaming.

Amy looked at the man. "Mr. William Forrester?"

The man nodded.

"Yes or no," Amy said. "Are you Mr. William Forrester?"

"Y-yes," he said.

Amy holstered her Glock, walked over to his side of the bed and produced a set of handcuffs. "Mr. Forrester, I'm now placing you under arrest for the murder of Donald Robinson. Hands behind your back."

"Who?" Bill said.

Amy clicked the cuffs in place and helped him out of bed. She was grateful to notice he was wearing boxer shorts.

"What's this all about?" he said.

"You really need to keep up," Amy said, then began leading him to the doorway.

"You didn't read me my rights!" he said.

"Mr. Forrester, this is Queensland. We'll get to all that when we question you at the station."

"Question me?"

The woman on the other side of the bed leaned over and reached down, and four rifles instantly covered her, followed by loud warning shouts. She screamed again and began crying. "I just want to give Bill his robe," she said. "Can he at least have that?"

Amy nodded to Joe, who walked over and grabbed the robe off of the floor, then came back and draped it around Bill's shoulders.

"Let's go," Amy said.

"Where are you taking him?" the woman asked.

"AFP in Newstead," Amy said, then pushed Bill in front of her into the hallway.

"Can I put on my boots?" he said, then nodded to a pair of brown, leather slip-on boots just inside the front door.

"No," Amy said, then nodded to Joe. "Pick them up, bring them back as evidence."

"It's okay, Paula," Bill yelled over his shoulder. "We'll sort it out. Call Brian. This is clearly a misunderstanding."

Fifty-Two

F rank was back on his balcony.

The sun had just come up, and the rainbow lorikeets were restless and loud, jumping between branches and talking to one another. Frank supposed they were making plans for the day ahead.

To celebrate their wedding anniversary, he'd bought a bouquet of red roses and placed them in a vase. Then he'd made himself a coffee float, following Caroline's recipe: a tall glass of cold, percolated, black coffee, no sugar; two scoops of vanilla ice cream; a generous dollop of whipped cream on top. Exactly five years ago, they'd gotten married in front of their friends and family at the Glücksburg Castle with its white plastered walls, red roofs and octagonal corner towers. Caroline's white dress and red roses had contrasted the dark blue castle pond, which had been flat and still, mirroring the cold winter sky of a clear February day. Exactly four years ago, they'd been sitting in their backyard after their run through the adjoining forest, drinking coffee floats, celebrating their first anniversary, talking about a future that would never be.

Frank thought about Caroline's parents, who'd probably suffered even more than Frank himself, or at least in a different way. Perhaps they were still devastated; perhaps they'd moved on. Who knew? Sometimes, like now, he would have liked to ask them, but he couldn't, and probably never would be able to. They'd blamed him for her death and cut him off. His own mother had suggested that it shouldn't be a big deal; after all, as she'd said, Frank and Caroline hadn't even had children yet. The last time Frank had spoken with her was a month before he'd come to Australia. And he had no siblings to think about, and only one friend: Hans Richter, his former boss from the German Federal Police.

A thick, uninterrupted layer of gray clouds hovered high above Brisbane, the underside murky and undefined and heavy. Frank grabbed his glass, thought about something to do with family and friends at a wedding, all while stabbing at a melting ball of vanilla ice cream with his teaspoon. It was something recent, too. Family and friends at a wedding. Then Frank remembered: the only person he'd spoken to about that was Rebecca, about her wedding, the first time he'd visited her. Something had snagged at his mind when she'd talked about it, and now Frank realized what it was. It was the way she'd said it. And that now sparked another idea.

Frank put the coffee float on the table, then walked into the living room and retrieved his laptop and his file on Rebecca. Once back on the balcony, Frank booted up the computer, then accessed the AFP database and used the login credentials Amy had given him. He thought he was going through a VPN, but—if Frank had to be completely honest—he simply couldn't be sure. His IT skills were close to non-existent, and his knowledge of all things digital severely limited. While waiting for the computer to complete the login, Frank knew that Andrew Koh could have helped with both access as well as a clandestine, untraceable setup. But, although Andrew had been a good colleague and at times seemed like a friend—he was a wizard with computers, hence his little joke putting *The Love Boat* theme song onto Frank's phone as a ringtone—Frank didn't feel he knew him well enough, hence his decision to reach out to Amy.

While the computer whirred and hummed and files loaded, Frank closed his eyes and sent his dead wife love and happy thoughts, as well as an apology for having to work on their anniversary. Instead, he promised that he'd visit her grave the following week, when he'd be back in Hamburg. He imagined she smiled and told him it was okay to move on, that enough time had passed and that he should start his life anew. And soon. But not with *her*. Then he opened his eyes and thought that maybe he hadn't imagined it after all.

Frank typed using solely his rude fingers, and he slowly but surely progressed in his searches, eventually finding a Queensland marriage certificate showing that Rebecca Wilson had indeed married a Carl Benjamin Wright six years ago, meaning that they'd only been married for around a year when Carl died. She'd taken his name and had since been known as Rebecca Wright. He dug back further and found a single tax return showing that she'd been employed for a few months at a high-end designer boutique in the city center. He deduced from the timeline that she'd probably met Carl while working at the fancy retail store, and a few weeks before the wedding, she'd stopped working altogether.

Going back further, Frank located a high school certificate issued to Rebecca when she was eighteen, by a public school less than a mile from her last foster home: her results had been mediocre, her absence high and her suspensions many, but she'd at least gotten the certificate.

She'd enrolled at fifteen, transferring from another school eight miles away where she'd been living with another foster family for a couple of years.

Before that, she ceased to exist. No other schools. No other foster homes. Frank delved deeper and struggled to find where—at thirteen—she'd moved from.

He did, however, find a birth certificate. It said Rebecca was born in Scotland to parents Fergus and Bonnie Wilson. Frank couldn't find anything wrong with the birth certificate, but he'd met Rebecca twice, and she was a tall, beautiful woman; her naturally blonde hair and blue eyes were features more reminiscent of someone from Scandinavia, perhaps even Germany or Holland, but he couldn't see any hint of Scottish.

Frank sighed, grabbed his glass; the brown sludge of sun-heated coffee and melted ice cream looked unappealing, so he put it back down.

He decided to gamble. If this was what he suspected it could be, then Rebecca would have been moved as far away as possible. He opened a map of Australia, then located a city far away from Brisbane. As big cities went, this one was as far away as it got. Frank nodded to himself. It could very well fit. He'd have to do a bit more research, but his rumbling gut told him he was on the right track.

And it could also explain William Forrester's involvement. He'd have to tell her, but, at the same time, Frank couldn't rush it. Scaring her off could easily do more damage than good. Reality was, there was only so much Frank could do, and if she panicked and made a silly move, the results would be disastrous.

Frank decided then and there that he would breach the subject delicately.

In a couple of hours. At breakfast.

Fifty-Three

Frank stepped out of the SUV, thanked the driver and shut the door. He crossed the sidewalk and found the gate already open. He stepped inside the front courtyard and closed the gate just as the car sped away. The hum of the engine faded into the distance, and then Rebecca appeared at her front door. She'd put up her hair in a complicated bun, with blonde strands hanging down in all the right places. She was wearing a fluffy, pink hoody, matching track pants and oversized bunnies as slippers. Floppy ears, long plastic whiskers arching above permanent, sewn-in smiles.

Frank's heart ached. He pulled at the front of his red checkered shirt, damned himself for not taking the time to iron it.

"Good morning," he said.

"Good morning, Frank," Rebecca said, gesturing for him to come inside.

Frank climbed the steps and stuck out his hand, but Rebecca shook her head.

"Don't be silly, Frank," she said, then leaned in and gave him a hug and a kiss on the cheek. Frank had a second to put a hand on her back and realized to his astonishment that she felt even softer and warmer than he'd imagined.

He followed her out onto the porch and sat down in the same seat he'd sat in when he'd showed her the video. Frank leaned up against the baby-blue cushion. The clouds were growing, their bases compacting, and a breeze made Rebecca's colorful flowers sway. The river remained still and brown.

She sat down across from him and pointed and informed. The table was full of plates, bowls and trays. There were fresh strawberries. Oranges peeled and sliced. A tray of toothpicks with honeydew melon cubes and serrano ham. Organic granola. Whole-grain quinoa crackers. Low-fat Greek yogurt. Smashed avocado. Poached eggs. She'd even served smoothies with several types of fruits, nuts and seeds—most of which Frank had never heard of.

He smiled and took a sip of the smoothie. "Hmmm."

"Do you like it?"

"Delicious," Frank lied, then put it back on the table.

"Help yourself," Rebecca said. "Would you like anything else?"

Frank thought about her question, wondered if it would be rude, but, in the end, decided to ask anyway: "Could I please have a cappuccino?"

Rebecca laughed. "Of course. I should have remembered," she said, then stood up. "Three sugars, right?"

"Yes, please."

Frank leaned back in his chair again. A Jet Ski zoomed past, heading upriver. Frank's gaze followed the wake as it spread across the river, eventually forming a giant, inverted V. Humidity was building up rapidly, and Frank grabbed his napkin and wiped his brows and forehead. He enjoyed the heat but disliked the sweating. He grabbed a strawberry and popped it into his mouth. His cheek muscles contracted, and his left eyelid began twitching; despite its fullness and deep red color, the strawberry was extremely sour.

Frank smiled as Rebecca returned with a mug of cappuccino. "Thank you," he said, then took a large gulp and let the sweet hit of full-cream caffeine coat his insides. In contrast to the strawberry, the cappuccino was pure bliss. Frank took another mouthful, then set the mug down.

"This is incredible, Rebecca," he said. "Thank you."

Rebecca waved a hand to show that Frank's gratefulness was completely unnecessary and sat down across from him.

"So, it sounded sort of urgent, this breakfast meeting. Have you had a breakthrough?" she said, then reached for a jug and began pouring herself a glass of orange juice.

Frank nodded. "You could say that. William Forrester has been arrested."

Rebecca put the jug down, looked at Frank, her mouth slightly open. After a moment, she seemed to realize that she was still holding onto it. She let go and put both hands in her lap. "What for?"

Frank looked Rebecca in the eyes. "Murder."

Rebecca's eyes began darting around the table before they settled back on Frank. "Murder?"

Frank nodded, then explained in detail how Bill had become a suspect, the evidence found, and that he was now in custody.

"I just can't believe it. Bill?" she said, then shook her head, shrugged. "I suppose he always did come across as aggressive. Maybe even sociopathic. But murder?"

Frank nodded again, turned his head toward the backyard. The flowers were swaying even more now. "You've been very lucky."

Rebecca leaned forward. "What do you mean?"

Frank turned his head and faced her. "You remember the first time I came here?"

Rebecca put her elbows close together on the table, interlocked her fingers, raised her hands and nested her chin on top. "Of course," she said. Her pink lipstick glistened.

"You said something that sort of stuck with me, and I hope you don't mind my asking about it," Frank said.

"Whatever it is, it can't be that bad."

Frank shrugged. "When you described your wedding, you said that—and I believe these were your exact words—'we got married in front of a hundred of Carl's friends and family.'"

Rebecca grabbed her orange juice, leaned back in her chair and crossed her legs. "Yes, that's right."

"Okay," Frank said. "And once again, I'm really sorry. I don't want to come across as being rude."

"Please," Rebecca said, "don't worry about it."

Frank took a sip of his cappuccino, shifted his seating position to alleviate the pressure on his lower back. "Where were *your* friends and family?"

Rebecca sighed, took a sip of her juice and fiddled with her glass. "I don't know," she said.

"Because?"

"I can't tell you," she said. "I'm sorry, Frank."

Frank nodded, sipped his coffee. "That's okay, Hannah."

211

Rebecca smiled, then lifted her glass to her mouth where it stayed hovering for a few seconds. "Wait," she said, then put her glass back on the table, stared at Frank. "What did you say?"

"I think you know."

Rebecca kept staring at Frank. Her mouth had fallen open.

"I studied a fourteen-year-old cold case of a family gunned down execution-style, in Perth," Frank said, looking at Rebecca for a reaction. "The mother and father, as well as a little boy. The teenage girl was nowhere to be found until, two days after the murders, a distraught thirteen-year-old girl walked into a police station.

"You've been in hiding your whole life, haven't you?" Frank said. "Your parents were Jeremy and Eileen Collins, your little brother Sebastian. A happy, typical Perth family until the day they were murdered and that all changed."

Rebecca closed her mouth.

"And now this. Another murder. And you being followed. William Forrester in custody."

Rebecca's eyes turned watery. "You think I was next on the list?"

Frank ignored the question. "Why were your parents and brother murdered?"

Frank thought she was about to speak when a violent sob escaped her throat, and her hand flew up to her mouth. Tears began streaming down her cheeks. She stood up, turned, and faced the river as guttural, primal, ancient sounds wailed from her throat. Her lips moved and her moaning gave way to wailing, and soon after, she screamed from the tops of her lungs. She spread out her arms, leaned forward and screamed and screamed and screamed.

For a moment, Frank considered walking over to comfort her, but in the end, he let her stand there and scream, get it all out.

FIFTY-FOUR

Amy sat next to Joe. Behind them, Gregory Fordham leaned up against the wall.

Across the table sat William Forrester, his hands in his lap. They'd removed his handcuffs, and William had stuck his arms through the sleeves of his robe and done it up. William was now wearing a pair of slightly small flip-flops that someone at the station had found lying around from a previous arrest. The AC was cranked up. Amy felt like she was sitting inside a fridge, yet William's chest was glistening with sweat. A drop ran down one temple, which he caught with a flannel sleeve.

Amy leaned forward, looked him in the eyes.

"Questioning Mr. William Forrester," she began, then introduced the parties present and stated the obligatory items necessary to begin the process.

"Mr. Forrester," Amy said, pointing around the room, "we are obliged to inform you that this interview is recorded using video and audio, and with that, let's begin. Where were you the night between the sixth and the seventh of February?"

William Forrester smiled. "I have nothing to say."

Amy nodded. "I understand you would like to exercise your right to remain silent?"

William Forrester kept smiling.

Joe cleared his throat. "How well did you know the victim, Donald Robinson?"

"I have nothing to say."

Amy thought about her conversation with Frank; that Jacaranda was a front, although she hadn't shared that with Joe or Gregory. She had, however, done some more research on both William and JSG.

"Mr. Forrester, tell us about your employment with Jacaranda Security Group."

Amy thought she caught a glimpse of malice behind William's brown eyes. His facial muscles tightened, and his brows dipped ever so slightly. "I would like to wait for my lawyer to arrive before I answer any questions."

"And, this lawyer, is he also employed by JSG?"

William Forrester stayed silent for a while, but Amy had a feeling that he'd eventually want to flex his muscles, show his power.

"Sure," he said. "It's a big company. We have people for everything."

"We?" Amy said. "As in, you're part owner of the company?"

"We, as in, us employees hired by the company."

"Who hired you?"

"The company," William said.

"Come on, Mr. Forrester," Amy said. "Who in particular? Tell us about the application process, who you did the interview with, how you got the job."

William shrugged. "I responded to an online ad, sent off my CV, got called in for an interview with the CEO."

Amy nodded. "So, not Human Resources? Not a regular staff member? Not an employee from the accounting department?"

William chuckled. "I was hired as their Chief Financial Officer. The CEO is the only person above me, hence he had to hire me."

"And that CEO is Brian Hearst?"

"Hey," William said, "look at you. Congratulations, at least you got one thing right today."

"Is that a yes, Mr. Forrester?"

William rolled his eyes. "Yes, ma'am."

"The same Brian Hearst that's suspected of being involved in organized crime, corruption, drug dealing, blackmail, extortion, bribery, intimidation, weapons trading and human trafficking?"

"I don't know anything about that."

"Would it surprise you to know that you're looking at guaranteed jail time, unless, of course, you become a bit more cooperative?"

William laughed. "You can't prove anything. I've never met . . . what did you call him? Donald Robinson? Plus, doesn't this thing need to go to trial first? You know, innocent until proven guilty?"

Amy looked surprised. "Oh, I'm not talking about jail time because of murder. No, I'm talking about giving false statement during questioning."

"What?"

"Lying to the police, Mr. Forrester."

"I haven't said one lie here today."

"Funny," Amy said. "Before this interview, I asked our IT experts to scour the net for job ads placed by JSG in the past ten years, and they didn't find one. Not one!"

"So?"

Amy pointed at a camera mounted above them. "You said, and I quote, 'I responded to an online ad', end quote."

William Forrester's jaw muscles bulged in and out.

"That's three years behind bars, Mr. Forrester."

William looked Amy in the eyes. "That's bullshit! You can't jail me for something as minor as that."

"On its own, you'd probably be right; that would be quite a weak case. But," Amy continued, "catching you red-handed? Lying to us while questioning you during an active murder investigation? That's a different ballgame. Add to that the fact that you're our prime suspect as we found your DNA at the murder scene? Well, that gives you a powerful motive to lie, and that, Mr. Forrester, gives us one hell of a strong case. We could keep you locked up during the entire trial on those grounds."

Amy let the ensuing silence work for her, hoping that William was imagining his near future behind bars, praying that he wouldn't call her bluff.

Almost a minute had passed when William cleared his throat, leaned forward, and opened his mouth.

FIFTY-FIVE

Rebecca was back in her chair. Faint black lines ran down her cheeks as tears diluted carefully applied mascara.

"You were all in witness protection, weren't you?" Frank said.

Rebecca nodded.

"What happened?"

Rebecca shook her head. "My father saw something he shouldn't have."

"Right."

"My dad, who never took a wrong step in his life, headed out one night to get a jar of pickles." Rebecca laughed. "My mum was pregnant and craved them. Pickles. Can you imagine anything more innocent than that?"

"Hmmm."

"As he strolled up the street, heading for the local convenience store, he noticed two people walking up ahead. Didn't think anything of it. Then a car sped past him, pulled up alongside the two guys, guns came out the windows and cracked through the still night. A moment later, the car was gone."

"What did your father do?" Frank asked.

"My father was very attentive in everything he did. He was mentally always present. He remembered the license place and gave it to the police," she said. "And with that information, the killers were apprehended, prosecuted, and eventually jailed."

Frank nodded.

"But that was only the beginning. Then the threats began, and as they escalated, my parents got really scared."

"So you were all offered a spot in the National Witness Protection Program?"

"Yes," Rebecca said. "From what I remember, my father sat us down one day, told us what had happened, and that the right thing to do would be to help as much as he could," she said. "He tried to explain what was about to unfold. See, we were living in Nightcliff, a suburb of Darwin. My brother had only just been born, and that added to the stress and panic we felt as a family back then."

Frank scratched his red goatee. "I've recently studied the history and structure of the National Witness Protection Program, and, back when you were in Darwin, there were a few localized witness protection programs, but they were specific to individual states and territories. There was no central coordination, and people were simply moved to another town, often within the same state. On top of that, sensitive information was scattered everywhere for criminals to pick up because of local amateurs who cared more about jurisdiction and dick measuring than witness protection.

"And so, because Darwin is a small place, and because the National Witness Protection Program had been formed by then, you would have been the ideal candidates."

"Right," Rebecca said. "Well, we all got new identities."

Frank nodded. "I haven't been able to find any information, so I'd like to ask you. Ever since coming to Brisbane, you were Rebecca. In Perth you were Hannah. What was your real name before the incident in Darwin? What I mean is, what were you born as?"

Rebecca sighed. "I grew up as Astrid Svensson. It sounds so strange when I say it now. My parents migrated to Australia from Sweden just after they got married. Olof and Johanna Svensson. Both my brother Ulf and I were born in Darwin."

"It must have been incredibly hard."

Rebecca nodded. "After we'd been accepted into the program and got new identities, they put us on a plane. We didn't know where we were going until it landed and we could read the airport signs." Rebecca laughed.

Frank chuckled along. "What?"

"Funny," she said. "I was ten at the time, and I haven't thought about it since, but I just remembered now. I was hoping that we were going to Hawaii." Rebecca's laugh contrasted her wet cheeks and red eyes.

Frank laughed as well, felt ill at ease. He looked at his watch.

"Are you in a hurry?" Rebecca asked.

Frank nodded. "Now that I know with an absolute certainty you're in witness protection, things are making more sense."

Rebecca nodded. "You won't tell anyone, will you, Frank?"

"Of course not," Frank said. "Besides, that would mean breaking several laws. Your secret is safe with me."

"Thank you."

Frank sighed, took a moment. Wondered how to move things along. Eventually, he said. "I'm going back to Germany."

"What?"

Frank nodded. "In a few days, and I have so many things to settle first that . . ."

"That what?"

"Could we meet again tonight? For dinner? I'll take you out wherever you want to go."

A huge smile lit up Rebecca's face. "Nonsense. You come back here, I'll make the most amazing dinner you've ever had, and you can go home with a beautiful memory."

Frank felt his cheeks get hot. His heart hammered in his chest. His belly growled.

"Six-thirty?" Rebecca said, then stood up.

Frank stood up as well. "Six-thirty," he said, then leaned in and kissed her on the cheek, tasted salt.

As he walked up her street, whistling louder than the magpies, Frank hoped he hadn't lingered too long, and wondered what she thought about him.

Frank took out his phone and began fiddling with the rideshare app while questions began forming. He thought about their conversation and wondered what had interested her.

Or, to be more Frank, what hadn't.

FIFTY-SIX

F rank thanked the driver and pulled himself up and out of the small hatchback. He crossed the street and pushed open the door to his local kebab shop. A small man with a big smile, freshly shaven with black sideburns was lighting up vertical gyro grills and arranging the salad bar.

"Hi Velat," Frank said.

"Good morning, Frank. How are you?"

"Just came back from a breakfast date," he said, then began reading the menu board above Velat's head.

"Date, hah?" Velat said, then continued talking about things closer to his own heart; the humid weather, his disappointment in the quality of his latest batch of cucumbers, and his unhappiness with soaring prices in general.

When Frank felt there was a natural break in Velat's monologue, he ordered two kebabs: one chicken; one lamb.

Velat turned and pointed behind him. "I haven't loaded the spits, Frank. You're a bit early. I'm not even open yet, officially."

"Hmmm," Frank said, then turned and walked over to the glass door fridge, grabbed himself a bottle of iced coffee and a large ginger beer, then put the bottles on the counter.

"I can heat you up a lahmacun if you want?" Velat said.

Frank nodded, held up his index and middle finger. "Two, please."

"What would you like in them?"

"Everything," Frank said. "And have you got any of those sweet, succulent, square things that melt in your mouth?"

Velat laughed. "You mean baklava?"

Frank snapped his fingers. "That's the one."

Velat nodded.

"A large tray of those, please," Frank said.

"Coming right up," he said, then turned and grabbed a flat, round piece of bread with mince, stuck it in a small oven to heat. Velat then walked out the back and came back a moment later with a small cup of black, sweet coffee. "Here Frank," he said. "On the house. Have a seat."

"Thank you," Frank said, then went to a small table and sat down, watching Velat work. "What about that powdery, fluffy cake, tastes wonderfully nutty, and has a texture that's almost like compressed cotton candy?"

"Now you're pushing it," Velat said, shook his head. Then: "Oh! You mean halva?"

Frank nodded. "I'll have some of that, too," he said, then sipped the sweet coffee.

Velat rummaged around in small fridge drawers and slid items into paper bags. Then he took Frank's lahmacuns out of the oven, loaded them up and wrapped them. He gathered all the food items, grabbed the bottles and put everything in a large bag, then placed it on the counter and began pounding on his small cash register. Frank saw green digits on a black background come and go, interrupted only by intermittent beeping and clacking of buttons.

Frank emptied his cup, then stood up and walked over to the counter, dug into his pocket and retrieved a yellow fifty-dollar bill.

"So, all done, that'll be seventy-eight dollars."

Frank blew raspberries and studied the menu again, to see whether Velat had upped his prices, then replaced the bill in his pocket and dug into another one where he'd stashed two green one-hundred-dollar bills. He handed one over.

"I'm so sorry, Frank," Velat said, then pressed a button to open the till and began counting the change. "Prices have gone nuts. Believe me. I pull hair out of my head every time I get a bill from one of my suppliers."

Frank looked Velat straight in the eyes.

"And the quality is going down. How do you explain that, huh? Rotten tomatoes at double the price, bruised onions that are tasteless, mince that is so full of water that half of it evaporates during cooking."

"Say that again," Frank said.

"Right?"

"No," Frank said. "I mean, could you say that again?"

Velat gave him a questioning look. "Mince that—"

"The hair," Frank said.

"The hair?" Velat asked.

Frank grabbed the bag and turned, walked toward the door, spoke over his shoulder as he exited. "Keep the change my friend."

Fifty-Seven

Gregory Fordham was back in his office.

He stared at the phone on his desk, wondering if he should make the call. He tensed his jaw, made a fist and closed his eyes, willing this whole mess to go away. Then he took three deep breaths, opened his eyes and picked up the handset, pressed speed dial one.

While it rang, Gregory imagined an identical-looking phone on a similar yet larger desk which was probably made of some rare dark wood, placed in an office that was much larger than the one he was presently sitting in. He imagined it being a corner office, perhaps overlooking a park with some stately monument no one but people living in Canberra had ever heard of. After the fifth ring, he was about to hang up.

"Yes."

"Frank didn't take the bait."

"And?"

"Well . . ."

"Why haven't you dealt with it yet?"

Gregory sighed. "I bought him a business-class ticket, with lounge access, buffet, the works, all paid for. The man loves food and comfort, and you know what he did? He tore the ticket up right in front of me!"

"A fucking business-class ticket?"

"Well—"

"Just how stupid are you?"

"But Walter—"

"This man is driven! Focused! He has more investigative experience than you and I combined. Do I really need to spell it out for you?"

Gregory didn't say anything.

"He's playing you, you idiot!"

"With all due respect, I don't think—"

"I don't give a rat's ass about what you think, so I'm going to issue an order now. Think you can follow orders?"

Gregory swallowed. "Yes, sir."

"Kill him tonight, then wrap his fat body in tarp and fill it with lots of rocks and dump him out in the fucking Coral Sea! You hear me?"

"I—"

"Is that understood?"

"Yes, sir!"

Gregory's hand was shaking so badly that the handset rattled as he carefully placed it back on the cradle.

Fifty-Eight

"Say no more, Bill!"

The man who entered the room was stocky. The edges of his mouth turned down naturally, pulling deep grooves up to his nose. He had slicked-back, gray hair and sunspots scattered all over his face, as well as on his large ears. He looked to Amy to be at least sixty-five, but his physique seemed more like that of a fit man in his forties. His trimmed, gray mustache matched his gravelly voice.

"My name is Brian Hearst, and I'm William Forrester's lawyer. Unless you have something—"

"*The* Brian Hearst?" Amy said. "The one who's also the CEO of Jacaranda Security Group?"

Brian's cool, blue eyes bore through Amy. She doubted his face had any other settings than angry.

"JSG has got nothing to do with this. Right now, I'm here as Mr. Forrester's lawyer, that's all."

"JSG has nothing to do with what?" Amy said.

Gregory shifted his position behind Amy, then cleared his throat. Whether he'd decided to speak and then changed his mind, Amy didn't know, but for the time being, he kept quiet.

Brian looked from Amy to Gregory to Joe, then back to his client. "Mr. Forrester, we're leaving now," he said, then turned to open the door.

Joe put up a hand. "Mr. Forrester is not going anywhere," he said.

"That's right," Amy said. "We found his DNA at a murder scene, as well as a print which, as it looks now, will come up a match with a pair of boots located at his home."

Brian Hearst walked over, leaned forward and put both hands on the table; his fingers looked thick and stiff, the nails polished and hard, the backs of the hands scattered with an unhealthy dose of age spots and scars. A gold watch was squashed between a white shirt cuff and the wrinkles formed by the angle of the left hand. "What's Mr. Forrester's motive for this . . . alleged murder?"

Amy shrugged. "We haven't figured that out yet, Mr. Hearst, but what we can say for sure is that Mr. Forrester doesn't have an alibi for the night in question."

"Meaning?" Brian said.

"Meaning the night Donald Robinson was killed, according to Mr. Forrester here, he was at home sleeping."

"Mr. Forrester is married. I'm sure his wife could corroborate that story."

Amy shook her head. "She was at work."

Brian gave William a look; he clearly wasn't happy. He stood back up, put his left hand in his pocket, walked over and stood behind William. "What is this DNA that you claim to have?"

Joe cleared his throat. "We found three strands of Mr. Forrester's hair on the floor, in a pool of blood, right next to the victim."

"What type of hair?" Brian asked.

Joe looked at Amy, who took over again. "Hair from Mr. Forrester's head," she said.

Brian nodded. "Could have rubbed off on an earlier occasion, or transferred between several people before ending up at the scene."

"Of course," Amy said. "The only problem is, Mr. Forrester claims to not know the victim at all. Has never even heard of him."

Brian walked back to the end of the table, looked at William. "Anything else you told them here today?" he said. "Before I arrived?"

William shook his head, and Amy thought she saw his cheeks flush.

There was a knock on the door. Brian turned as it opened.

A stout woman in her fifties with brown curls walked over, whispered something in Amy's ear, then left again, closed the door.

Brian's eyes followed her from the moment she entered and until she left. "What's going on?"

All eyes were on Amy.

"Well, well, well," she said. "As we suspected, the boot prints have come back a match."

Brian Hearst sighed. "Can we bring an extra chair in here?" he said. "And before we continue with these charades, I'll need a moment alone with my client first."

Fifty-Nine

F rank took a bite of his lahmacun while waiting for Amy to pick up. He was back on his favorite bench in his landscaped courtyard, which was unusually quiet. Birds of all sorts were out and about doing whatever birds do, and the nocturnal fruit bats were probably sleeping in caves and trees elsewhere. He took another bite just as she answered her phone.

"Hey, Frank," Amy said.

"Hey," he said. "How did the arrest go?"

"Are you eating again?" she asked.

"Lahmacun," Frank answered. "Velat said it was too early for kebab."

"What?"

"Never mind," Frank said.

"Listen, Frank, we're in the middle of the questioning now, but let me give you the highlights," Amy said, then quickly filled Frank in on the DNA, boot prints and Brian Hearst also being William's lawyer. "I really have to go now. I just ducked out to find a chair for Mr. Hearst."

"Hmmm," Frank said, then stuffed his mouth again, thought about what Velat had said.

"Okay, Frank," Amy said, "I'll call you later."

"Actually, I was going to ask you a question," Frank said, hoping she hadn't hung up yet. "But I just realized that Maggie would be better equipped to answer it. Could I have her number?"

Amy gave Frank the number and had to repeat it three times as Frank saved it on his phone.

"I have to go, Frank."

"Before you go, could you tell me about the boots?"

Silence filled Frank's little phone, not even static entered his ear.

"What do you mean?" she said.

"Just tell me about the boots, anything you remember."

Amy sighed. "They're a type of farmer's boots, size fourteen, from an Australian company called Nanango. They're brown, ankle-high, slip on boots, made of leather, sort of half cowboy, half dress boots with a raised heel, meaning the print shows a gap between the heel and the front part of the sole, just as you would expect from a boot like that."

Frank nodded. "And how old are they?"

"I don't know, Frank. My guess is at least a year, maybe more. Depends on how often he's used them. The upper part has that look of leather that's been polished frequently, but all of that doesn't matter, because we're in luck."

"Yeah?"

"Yeah. This brand is rare, the model even rarer. Nanango is a company that sells high-end footwear at an extortionate price. They're apparently great quality, but it's also a designer label, and William Forrester is just the man who'd be able to afford a pair of boots like that. He's a man who would enjoy showing off in a pair of boots like that, and, guess what? William Forrester *has* a pair of boots like that. They were sitting in the hallway when we arrested him, and he asked if he could put them on before we left, and those same boots were used at the murder scene."

"Hmmm," Frank said, then swallowed the last bit of his first lahmacun, wiped his mouth with a napkin. "Seems convenient."

"Convenient?"

"Could be a setup."

"I really have to go, Frank."

"Thanks," Frank said, and hung up.

He took a sip of his iced coffee, unwrapped his second lahmacun, took a bite, then looked up Nanango, found the number.

The phone rang.

SIXTY

"This guy, William Forrester," Maggie said to Ron, then took a sip of her breakfast tea. "He must be wired in a different way."

Ron sipped his black coffee, nodded from across the expanse of two large desks. "You'd have to be one cold-blooded creep to kill someone like that."

The room they were sitting in had originally been designed for six science technicians. However, the combination of generous government funding, heavily subsidized medical programs, attractive incentives as well as a lower than predicted crime rate meant that Maggie and Ron had the large office space to themselves.

Behind them, unused PCs with dark monitors and silent printers were sitting on top of another pair of unused double desks boasting ergonomically correct office chairs that had never supported a single backside. The same setup followed down the back of the large space.

Seeing as it was just the two of them, Ron had taken the water dispenser from the middle of the room and pushed it up to the end of their desks, upon which they'd placed photos of their daughter in various stages of her life from birth up to and including the latest:

her wedding photo. The rest of the desk space was filled with potted succulents Maggie had brought in, as well as some of Ron's model airplanes. Occasionally, during quieter times, he would sit there and cut and file and glue and paint, spending weeks on perfecting the little plastic planes—perks of working as a forensic scientist in an incredibly rich, and relatively safe, country.

"Amy says he's part of some big criminal organization," Maggie said.

"Not surprised to hear that," Ron said. "Probably related to drug dealing. Maybe he's against Satan's Sharks."

Maggie took another sip of her tea, looked out one of the large windows, then back at Ron. "What do you think about that Frank fellow?"

"I'll tell you what," Ron said, turning a Jetstar Airbus 320 in his hands before looking up at Maggie. "He's either stupid and lucky, or incredibly intelligent and strategic. That's my feeling."

Maggie nodded. "He made some very valid points regarding the murder weapon and the bloating of the victim."

Ron nodded, put the plane down and sipped his coffee.

Electronic music filled the bright space, and both of them looked at Maggie's phone vibrating its way across the desk.

Maggie picked it up. "Blocked number."

"Put it on speaker," Ron said.

Maggie answered the phone and put it on speaker. "Hello?"

"Margaret? Sorry to bother you, it's Frank here, we met—"

"Frank? Ron and I were just talking about you."

Ron leaned forward and whispered. "Is he eating?"

Maggie shrugged. "How can we help?"

"I've been thinking about the hair that you found at the murder scene, the hair belonging to William Forrester?"

"Right."

"What type of hair was it?"

"Hair from his head," Maggie said.

"Did it have roots attached?"

"Yes," Maggie said. "And, although we can extract DNA from the hair alone, when available, we also extract it from the root and both match Mr. Forrester's DNA, if that's what you were thinking."

"Hmmm," Frank said. "I was thinking more along the lines of the shape of the root."

"The shape?" Maggie said, then gestured for Ron to get the file. Ron got up and walked over to a file cabinet and began rummaging.

"Yes," Frank said. "Was it club-shaped? Or was it stretched? Perhaps even partially broken? Was there tissue attached to it?"

"Hang on, just give me a minute," she said, just as Ron came over and placed a file in front of her. She found what she was looking for, took a few seconds to study it yet again, but she already knew the details of this case inside out.

"We found three strands of hair from his head. All three had been cut at one end, and the roots at the other end were slightly elongated. One had a few fibers attached, probably from a follicle."

"The hairs had been cut at one end?" Frank said.

Ron rolled his eyes. Maggie spoke: "You know, probably from the last time he went to the hairdresser?"

"Oh," Frank said. "I see. What does it mean when the roots are elongated?"

"That the hairs were pulled out."

"That's what I thought," Frank said.

"Your point?"

"Someone else could have planted them to frame William."

Now Maggie rolled her eyes. "Not likely. I mean, who'd be able to pull hairs from Mr. Forrester's head to plant at the scene without him knowing?" she said, then shook her head. "Anyway, a much more likely scenario is that the victim managed to pull a few hairs out of the assailant's head during the attack. As a matter of fact, that's something that happens quite often."

"But, didn't you tell Amy that when someone gets stabbed in the kidney, the body goes into shock?"

Maggie thought about what to say. Ron scratched his head, looked at another one of his airliners.

"Yes, but . . ." Maggie said. "Look, in some ways, forensics is an exact science, but in other ways, not so much. What I mean is, we do occasionally have to make presumptions based on known facts, and my educated guess in this case is that the victim reacted quickly and managed to pull Mr. Forrester's hair during the attack."

"Hmmm," Frank said. "There's something else."

Sixty-One

"What the hell is happening here?" Brian said, walked over and sat down across from William.

"I don't understand any of this," William said.

Brian lowered his gaze and looked at his thick, newly polished nails. "You better not lie to me, Bill."

"I swear," William said. "I have no idea what the hell is going on!"

"And why was Paula out the very night you get accused of murder?"

William shrugged. "She works in home care. She manages the night shifts on the weekends."

"How convenient!" Brian said. "You think I'm fucking stupid, Bill?"

"Of course not."

"You think you can speak to me like you speak to everyone else?"

"No, Brian—"

"Don't insult my intelligence," Brian said. "Tell me what's going on. Now!"

"What do you want me to say?"

"I want you to tell me what you were doing the night in question."

"What makes you think—"

"Last chance, Bill! If I have to repeat myself one more time, I'll fucking jump across this table and beat it out of you."

William recoiled in his chair. "I can't tell the police that I wasn't home on the night in question because Paula will find out."

"Find out what?"

William sighed. "That I was with a hooker. Okay?"

Brian guffawed. "You think your marriage has any weight compared to the success of my business?"

"Well—"

Brian leaned forward. "Let me tell you something," he said. "I've spent years building up JSG to what it is today."

"I know—"

"Don't interrupt me! You dilettante!"

William bowed his head. "Sorry."

"Do you realize how it's going to look if the police start investigating my CFO of murder? We'll have every law enforcement agency breathing down our necks for months, maybe even years. The whole of JSG will get tangled up in endless enquiries. The cops will scrutinize every single member of my staff and use the case as an excuse to harass us every fucking day of the week, unraveling this corporation that has taken me a decade to set up."

"What do you want me to do, Brian?"

Brian leaned back, smiled. "I want you to make sure the investigation stops right here!"

"And how am I supposed to do that?"

"I need you to confess to the murder."

William's eyes widened. "But I didn't do it, Brian. I swear! I had nothing to do with it."

Brian laughed again. "They all say that, but your ugly hair and even uglier boots say otherwise, don't they? What an amateur you are!"

William shook his head. "I'm being set up, don't you see? I would never murder anyone. I'm not a killer. I'm the numbers guy. And this Donald whatever-his-name-is, I don't even know him!"

Brian nodded. "If you say so, but it doesn't make a difference. I can't have any unnecessary heat on JSG."

William's breathing quickened as his eyes darted around the room before settling back on Brian. "What about the hooker?"

"What about her?"

"She's my alibi. I can contact the escort company. It'll be on file that the girl was with me," he said, then shrugged. "Paula will find out, and it won't be pretty, but at least the hooker will be able to vouch for me. And the alibi will clear my name and take the heat off JSG."

Brian nodded. "Okay," he said. "You have a point. What escort company did you use?"

William turned his head to look at a window that wasn't there. "Dinner and More," he said. "They're in Chermside."

Brian nodded. "Name of girl?"

"I don't know her real name," Bill said. "But she works under the name Alison."

"Very well," Brian said, then stood up. "I'll take care of her; you just make sure to confess."

"Thanks . . . what? What do you mean, 'you'll take care of her'?"

Brian smiled, walked to the door.

William began breathing in short, shallow bursts. "You're going to remove my only alibi, you son of a bitch! You are, aren't you? I'm looking at life behind bars if you do that. Brian, please."

Brian shrugged. "Still better than the death penalty, which is what you'll get if you walk free. I'll make sure of that—personally," he said, then opened the door and left.

SIXTY-TWO

"What is it?" Maggie said.

"I'm thinking about the boot prints. Are you sure about them?" Frank asked.

"A one hundred percent match," Maggie said. "No doubt. It was a visible, bloody print lifted from the tile floor in the kitchen. The outsole has a unique tread that only this particular company produces," she said, then turned a page, scanned it. "Nanango Farmer boots size fourteen."

"A perfect print, you say?"

"Every square inch of that outsole was imprinted in the blood, the tread complete in all its detail."

"What do you compare with?"

"We have an extensive digital database that has all known prints from brands around the world."

"Hmmm."

There was silence for a moment. Eventually, Ron lifted his hands, palms up, a question mark on his face.

"Anything else?" Maggie said.

"When you find shoe prints at a crime scene, are they often as perfect and complete as this one?"

Maggie sighed. "No, and that's the amazing thing about it. We rarely get this lucky."

Frank was silent again. Only chewing sounds came through the phone.

"Frank—"

"Are you telling me you've had a perfect print like this before? As in, ever?"

Ron picked up a Virgin Australia Boeing 737, leaned back, blew air into the left engine. When he looked back up at Maggie, he shook his head.

"No," she said. "We can't say that we have. But, theoretically, it can happen."

"But more often it would be a partial shoe print which could come from a perfect set of boots. You know, boots with a whole, complete outsole with ruts and ridges and a tread, but only part of that tread gets transferred as a print, because of the way the person steps or because only part of the sole gets covered in blood or whatever else the person steps in, right?"

"Yes."

"But what I'm talking about here is the other way around."

"What do you mean 'other way around'?"

"I'm talking about a situation where you have a complete print of the whole outsole of the boot, with the entire area of the tread shown, but where the outsole of the actual boot in question isn't complete," Frank said. "In other words, a perfect print, made by an imperfect boot."

"An imperfect boot?" Maggie said.

"Yes, due to wear. Say, for example, the tread on the outside of the sole is worn down, because of the particular gait of the owner of said boots. That wear would show in the print, but you're saying it's not: The print was perfect, as if the boots were brand new and have never been used."

"That's right."

"And since you compare the print to a digital database of all known prints, perhaps you neglected to study the boots themselves?"

There was silence for a moment. "What are you saying?"

"Amy told me over the phone that, in her opinion, the boots are at least a year old, maybe more," Frank said.

Maggie shrugged. "If they're good quality and haven't been used that much, the sole could still be perfect."

"I agree," Frank said. "Which is why I called Nanango."

Maggie and Ron looked at each other. Ron put the Boeing back on his desk.

"Only two pairs of this model of boot in size fourteen were sold last year."

"Well, that's not unusual," Maggie said. "From what I could gather from our initial research, the footwear from this company is generally custom-fitted, very expensive and somewhat of a luxury."

"You're right, that's not unusual at all," Frank said. "What's unusual is that both pairs were ordered on the same day. By the same person."

Ron's mouth fell open. Maggie stared at him with big eyes.

Maggie was about to speak when Frank beat her to it. "And before you ask, they were purchased by a male, paid for in cash, picked up at their production facility in Redcliffe."

Maggie took a moment to gather her thoughts. "So, Mr. Forrester bought two pairs?"

"Mr. Forrester only has one pair," Frank said, then hung up.

Maggie looked at the phone incredulously, then up at Ron. "Quite a character," she said.

Ron nodded.

Sixty-Three

A my entered the canteen and spotted Joe over by the coffee machine. She walked over.

"Where have you been?" Joe asked, pouring coffee into a couple of mugs. "You practically ran out of that interview room."

"William Forrester confessed thirty seconds after we returned with a chair for Brian Hearst?"

"So?"

"What do you mean, 'so?' You were there. Didn't that confession seem weird and awkward?"

Joe shrugged.

"I've been surfing the net and making a million phone calls," Amy said, then sat down at a nearby table.

"Look," Joe said, came over and put the mugs on the table, sat down. "It's not only the confession," he said. "We also have an abundance of evidence. What more do you want?"

"I want the truth," Amy said. On one hand, she didn't hope she was beginning to sound too much like Frank. On the other hand, what he'd dug up couldn't just be ignored.

Joe shrugged. "I think a confession is as true as it gets. Even his lawyer was there, and when your own bloody lawyer recommends you confess, that sort of says a lot, don't you think?"

Amy looked at her own mug, smiled, took a sip. "But that's just it," she said. "He wasn't."

Joe looked confused. "Who wasn't what?"

Amy looked Joe in the eyes. "His lawyer wasn't there."

"Have you been smoking—"

"Brian Hearst is not his lawyer," Amy said.

"And how would you know that?"

"Because Brian Hearst is *nobody's* lawyer."

Joe's brows furrowed.

"I called the Australian Legal Profession Register and the Queensland Law Society," Amy said. "No one has ever heard of a Brian Hearst, so I expanded my search. I called the Legal Practice Board in Western Australia, searched the Register of Solicitors in New South Wales, contacted the Victorian Legal Services Board, the ACT Bar Association, the Register of Practising Certificates in South Australia. No one has ever issued a legal certificate to a Brian Hearst. Not one single organization has any record of a Brian Hearst registering as a solicitor. So, I thought, maybe he just never sat the bar exam."

"Right."

"So then," Amy said, "I contacted every single university on Australian soil that currently has, or has ever offered, a Bachelor of Law, a Master's of Law, a Juris Doctor or any other course even remotely connected to anything law related, and I think you can guess what I found."

"He's never studied law in this country?"

"That's exactly right," Amy said.

"But, even if he's just pretending to be a lawyer, what has that got to do with William Forrester, the evidence and his confession?"

"Don't you see?" Amy said. "Brian Hearst is the head of a mob. For whatever reason, he obviously came here to threaten Forrester into a confession, and that's evident because Forrester's story changed dramatically after their talk. So we need to find out why Brian Hearst so desperately wants William Forrester to take the fall for this killing, and we need to find out why Forrester simply agreed to confess, although that's probably fairly straightforward."

"Brian would have threatened to kill him if he didn't?"

Amy nodded. "Talk about a coerced confession."

"Well," Joe said. "If what you're saying about Brian Hearst being the gaffer of a criminal organization is true, then I suppose it would explain it to some degree."

"Gaffer?" Amy said. "Is that Scottish?"

"You know, head honcho," Joe said. "Boss."

Amy took another sip of her coffee. "Frank suggested the whole thing could be a setup."

"You think JSG set William up under the leadership of the great Brian Hearst?" Joe said.

Amy shrugged. "Why else would Brian show up here to make sure William confessed?" she said.

"So JSG wanted to get rid of Donald Robinson, and they needed a scapegoat, so they chose William?"

Amy nodded. "But why choose their own CFO?"

Joe shrugged. "Maybe they're not happy with his services anymore, and that's a great way to kill two birds with one stone."

"That could be it," Amy said. "We'll need to contact forensics, ask them to look through all the trace evidence again, particularly at anything that could place Brian Hearst at the crime scene. I have a feeling he's a do-it-yourself kind of guy."

"You think he likes to get his hands dirty?" Joe said.

"For sure," Amy said. "Old mobsters often do. It's a macho thing."

"So Brian himself killed Donald, then planted the hair?"

"Could be," Amy said, then took out her phone.

"Who are you calling?" Joe asked.

Amy gave Joe a look. "We need to look for mistakes, and we need help."

"Mistakes?" Joe said.

Amy nodded, punched in a number. "People make ten thousand mistakes when planning a crime," she said. "And we only have to find one."

"That's a nice way to look at it," Joe said.

Amy nodded, pressed the green call button. "Frank said that."

Sixty-Four

F rank took the coffee cup from the so-called-barista, thanked her and put a two-dollar coin on the desk. His local supermarket had been doing cheap coffee for a while, and since he didn't yet have his car back and didn't want to spend any more money on rideshare trips to go to Mugs & Marmalade, semi-lousy coffee would have to do. He exited the shop, walked in a large half-circle to avoid a pit bull tied to the shopfront, and was about to wrap his lips around the hole in the plastic lid when *The Love Boat* theme song began.

Frank lifted his phone out of his shirt pocket. "Yeah," he said.

"What have you got?"

"Amy? There's something fishy going on."

"Convince me," Amy said.

"William Forrester's hair was found at the scene, but there's evidence to suggest that it was planted."

"Aha," Amy said.

"Margaret found the roots were damaged, meaning the hair was pulled out rather than fell out naturally."

"Right."

"And theoretically, if someone placed the hair there on purpose, that same someone may own a pair of boots identical to Forrester's and could have simply worn them while committing the crime."

"I see," Amy said.

"And the prints are too perfect. Did you check the soles of the boots?"

There was silence for a moment. "That's Maggie's job."

"Okay, but she's cross-referenced a database of prints, not the actual boots."

"Well," Amy said. "She should receive the boots soon, so she can have a look at them then, I guess."

"I called Nanango," Frank said. "Turns out they sold two identical pairs on the same day to a guy who paid in cash. I spoke to a woman earlier today who works there."

"Really?"

"Did you go through the house where Brad Jenkins lives? Did you get a warrant? Or are you going to? He may very well be the one setting up Mr. Forrester."

"No, no, and no."

Frank paused. "You don't seem very excited about my discoveries," Frank said.

"I'm sorry, Frank," Amy said. "If I don't, it's only because William Forrester has confessed."

Frank was silent for a while. "And what do you think?" he said. "You. Not the AFP."

"I think you make valid points, Frank. Brian Hearst showed up here, barged in and presented himself as some hotshot lawyer, but I found out that he's never studied law in his life."

"So that would go hand in hand with our theory about JSG being a front?"

"Yes. And I'm pretty sure William confessed because Brian threatened him. He seemed terrified. Panicked, even."

Frank nodded.

"I just don't know what to do with all this information. I don't get what Brian's motive is, and for the time being, we have no way of proving that he's involved, so I think Gregory will lean toward letting Mr. Forrester take the fall, if for no other reason than to put more pressure on him, to somehow try and get to the truth that way. Play it out until the very end, you know what I mean?"

"Do me a favor," Frank said. "Go to Nanango. Use your flashy credentials to dig some more."

"Will do," Amy said, then hung up.

SIXTY-FIVE

Forty-five minutes after leaving AFP in Newstead, Amy swung the unmarked sedan left onto Marine Parade and cruised due north. On their right, Moreton Bay lay deep and blue, partly visible through scattered cottonwood trees hiding access stairs to stony beaches down below. On their left, run-down hotels and overpriced restaurants were dotted in among bottle shops, drugstores and real estate agencies.

"Did you know that Barry, Maurice and Robin Gibb lived around here when they first came to Australia?" Amy said.

"Who?" Joe said.

"The Bee Gees," Amy said. "They came to Redcliffe in 1958 as young boys and were pretty much discovered here."

"Oh," Joe said.

"As young teenagers, they would sometimes play at the Redcliffe Speedway, during intervals, on the back of a truck. While doing their rounds and playing their hearts out, the crowd would throw money onto the speedway track in support."

"I did not know that," Joe said.

Marine Parade became Redcliffe Parade and Amy found a spot just across from the jetty. She parallel parked the shiny sedan right outside a souvenir shop.

Joe jumped out of the car, pointed farther up the street. "Should be four or five shops up," he said, then began his brisk walking. Amy circumnavigated metal baskets stuffed to the brim with koalas, hand-painted boomerangs and tea towels with kookaburras. She stopped for a moment as she noticed a display unit with kangaroo-scrotum bottle openers. She shook her head, then continued walking.

Joe was waiting as Amy reached the entrance to Nanango. Above the entrance door, a rusty metal bar protruded from the brick wall, suspending a three-foot-high outback boot made of plastic. It gently swayed in the breeze.

Joe pushed open the door and an electronic chime announced their arrival. Tasteful, dark wooden shelves held all the latest models and designs, and Amy savored the smell of leather and polish as she approached the counter.

"How can I help you?" a man said. He was wearing a brown tartan suit, his hair was more salt than pepper, and he wore blue-rimmed glasses.

"Are you the owner?" Amy said.

The man smiled, nodded. "I am. Carlton Jones is my name."

Amy took out her credentials and put them on the countertop. Joe followed suit. Carlton glanced at the IDs, furrowed his brows and then looked back up at Amy.

"How far back do your sales records go?" Amy asked.

Carlton's silk jacket whispered against his white shirt as he shrugged. "I normally keep the details for at least three years," he said. "Sometimes longer, if it's a special, high-end customer."

Amy nodded. "We're particularly interested in the sale of two pairs of Nanango Farmer boots, size fourteen, in brown, purchased sometime last year."

Carlton's eyes moved up and left, and his focus seemed to blur as he accessed a memory. A moment later, he looked at Joe, then back at Amy. "A gentleman called about those boots. Another one of your colleagues from the police?"

"Aha," Amy said.

"But he spoke to one of my assistants because I wasn't here when he called, and she told him what she could see in our system."

"That's right," Amy said.

"I wanted to speak to your colleague, but he didn't leave a number with my employee," Carlton said.

Joe looked at Amy.

"One moment, please," Carlton said, then turned and disappeared out the back.

Joe looked at the ceiling, nodded at a corner high up behind the counter. "Look at that."

Amy followed his gaze and spotted the camera. "Could work."

Carlton came back and put a piece of paper on the counter, turned it and pointed. "This is a copy of the receipt," he said. "I personally sold them just before Christmas a year ago. A man picked them up here in person, paid cash."

"So I guess he didn't leave any details," Amy said. "Otherwise your assistant would have passed them on to my . . . colleague?"

"That's right. But I remember he made a big deal out of it, refusing to give me any contact details whatsoever."

"So," Amy began, scanning the receipt on the counter. "Looking at this date, he was here fourteen months ago?"

"Yes," Carlton said.

Joe pointed at the camera behind Carlton. "We're going to have to request a copy of the recording from that day," he said.

Carlton smiled. "I'm so sorry, but that will not be possible—"

"We'll come back with a warrant, if necessary, Mr. Jones," Joe said.

Carlton kept smiling. "I'm sure you would, and I'd love to help—"

"Then help," Joe said. "Or would you rather talk to us at the station?"

Amy gave Joe a look.

"What?"

"Maybe let Mr. Jones finish what he was about to say?"

Carlton smiled at Amy. "Thank you," he said, then looked at Joe. "As I was saying, it will not be possible to give you a recording from fourteen months ago, for the simple reason that I had the cameras installed just last month."

Amy sighed. "Do you remember what he looked like?"

Carlton's carefully plucked brows shot up. "Of course I know what he looks like," he said.

"That's impressive," Amy said.

Carlton's suit jacket once again whispered against his shirt. "Not particularly," he said. "In this case, I know exactly who he is because I recognized him."

Joe cleared his throat. "You recognized him? From where?"

"The Aspley Hotel," Carlton said. "Many moons ago, I worked there as a bartender, and I remember Doug because he was a kitchen hand there for a few months."

"And didn't he recognize *you*, then?" Amy said.

Carlton shook his head. "Unrequited love. Plus, I looked very different back then, had a full beard and always wore jeans and a T-shirt. Besides, it's almost twenty years ago now."

"Unrequited love?" Amy said.

Carlton looked down at the counter, stroked it with a finger. When he lifted his face, his cheeks were flushed. "I had a huge crush on him," he said. "But Douglas Glenmore had a fling with one of the female cooks, which is probably why he didn't remember me when he came into my shop last year," he said, then smiled and let go of what sounded like a slightly sad chuckle.

Sixty-Six

The mirror reflected a Hispanic man standing right behind Frank. His gray stubble suggested that his black hair was colored, the layers somewhat complicated and the style intricate. He looked like a man who put on a brave face, but his facial creams and stiffly starched collar still weren't enough to conceal that he was tired and run down. And Frank knew he wasn't suffering from a type of exhaustion obtained by a single late night; this was bone-dense, repetition-related, long-term fatigue. A clown's makeup wouldn't have been enough to hide the bags under his eyes.

The man rotated a pair of large scissors in one hand and twirled a comb in his other; he was as smooth and deft as an old Hollywood gunslinger. He stepped forward and looked Frank in the eyes through the mirror.

"So, what would you like?" His Spanish accent was thick.

Frank shuffled under his black cape and looked at his own red hair as if for the first time. "Sides and neck shortish, top a bit longer?" Frank said.

"What number?" the skinny hairdresser said. He sounded as though he'd had after-work drinks every day for the past thirty years.

Frank shrugged. "Whatever you think," he said. "You're the professional."

The man smiled, revealing teeth that looked fake and way too white. "And how long on top?"

"I sometimes like to style it with gel, so, whatever length that is."

The man nodded, stuck out a leg, hooked his foot under the metal frame of a stool and pulled it over. He sat down and bounced a few times to get comfortable. "You have a nice hair," he said. "I think I'll do scissors for volume."

"Hmmm."

"I'm Hector, by the way."

"Frank, nice to meet you. This your shop?"

"Yes, been here one year now."

Frank enjoyed the sensation as Hector sprayed his hair with water before combing and cutting. "So, you like gel?" Hector said.

"Hmmm."

"Powder is much better. I've got some here; it's *increíble*. It lifts and thickens and gives your hair a beautiful, matte finish."

"Powder?" Frank said.

"That's right," Hector said. "Gel can look a bit . . . young, for men our age, if you know what I mean."

Men our age. The tank of life working its way toward empty, time sinking away as quick as the needle of his car's fuel tank, the halfway mark passed some time ago. Only, with the tank of life, refilling wasn't an option. It was one fill, one ride, then pull over. For good. It was a depressing, terrifying thought. At other times, it could be strangely comforting. But, if for nothing else, at least it provided perspective. Frank's belly rumbled.

"Are you Australian, Hector?"

The man smiled. "Arrived from Spain with my wife two years ago, but I've been a citizen ever since I was a kid. Came here with my parents, became a citizen in six months, then my *papá* wanted to go back to Spain, so we did. But, you know, back then the Australian government handed out visas and citizenships like candy, not like now."

Frank nodded, accidentally pulling at the comb and making Hector lift the scissors away from his head. "Sorry," Frank said. "But, yeah, tell me about it. I'm going back to Germany. Return to sender."

"When are you going back?"

"A few days."

"And how long have you been here, Frank?"

"Almost two years."

"Do you not like it here?"

"No choice. I lost my job, meaning my work visa was canceled."

"Oh," Hector said. "May I ask what you do for a living?"

"Sure," Frank said. "I worked as an agent for the Australian Federal Police."

Frank caught Hector's eyes in the mirror, sizing up his considerable bulk under the cape. Back when he'd been in the shape of his life, training with professional assault teams and competing in various triathlons, he'd eaten schnitzels with French fries and chocolate and ice cream, yet still had a six-pack and effortlessly done twenty chin-ups. Frank wondered if he'd ever get his old physique back. If he'd ever feel in control again. Heck, just getting out of bed in the morning without grunting in pain would be an improvement.

"I know," Frank said. "My obesity is, at least officially, the reason why I lost my job."

"And . . . not officially?" Hector said, his left eyebrow arching.

"I have a sense of what could be the reason, but it may be too little, too late. Story of my life, really."

Hector smiled his bright smile again. "Well, at least you can go home looking great," he said. "Not to, how do you say, honk my own horn, but I do a good job. I had my own salon in Madrid as well, which is where I met my wife."

Frank looked at Hector. "I have one shot left at extending my stay here."

"One shot?"

"The reason for my haircut. I don't really care how I look when I go back to Germany," Frank said, then smiled, swung an arm out from under the cape and pointed at his hair: "This is for a date."

"A date?" Hector said, then lifted his arms above his head and did a little dance on his stool.

"That's right. Tonight."

"I see," Hector said. "So you need this . . . girl?"

"Aha."

"You need this girl in order to stay in the country?"

"You're spot on," Frank said.

"So, she is an Australian citizen?"

"And beautiful as a summer's day."

Hector laughed.

Under the black cape, Frank's belly rumbled again.

Sixty-Seven

A s was the case with most people, Douglas Glenmore hadn't moved far from where he'd grown up, gone to high school, gotten his first job and later met his wife.

Amy drove while Joe got in touch with HQ, who sent all the basic details they had on Douglas; his birthdate, home address, school papers, workplace, marital status, current financial situation, as well as another few bits and pieces they had on file. Then Joe had called Doug's workplace just to discover that he'd taken a day off.

A half hour after leaving Redcliffe, the AFP sedan hummed up a hill in Aspley, its tires sticking on the hot blacktop. Almost at the top, Amy reversed into a driveway and stopped just short of an older-style roller door that was halfway open. Even through the rearview mirror, the amount of clutter in the single garage told Amy that a car probably hadn't been parked in there in years. She stepped out and watched Joe bounce up the stairs to the front door.

The front yard was a mess of lackluster lawn, wild weeds and busted bins. Cracks in the concrete driveway and footpath looked beyond repair, and Amy guessed the house to be about forty years old. It was set on top of the garage, the yellow bricks faded and dusty with age, the mortar stained and brittle and crumbling. Amy made her way up the stairs while scanning the street; the houses were an eclectic mix of newly built and rendered, old Queenslanders and Californian bungalows.

Joe knocked on the door. When there was no answer, Amy pressed the doorbell, and chimes reminiscent of the Brisbane Clock Tower came from inside the house. Amy was considering leaving when the door finally opened. A woman, wearing a tight sports outfit that revealed a bit too much cleavage, smiled at them.

"Yes," she said.

Amy and Joe both showed their IDs. "I'm agent Lamborne," Amy said, then nodded to Joe. "This is my partner, agent McAvoy. We're here to talk to Mr. Douglas Glenmore?"

The woman's smile disappeared. "My husband is out bicycling," she said. "What's this about?"

"Where did he go?" Amy asked.

The woman crossed her arms, revealing even more cleavage. "I'm not sure that's any of your business."

"Mrs. Glenmore," Joe said, "this is an ongoing investigation, which is why we can't share any details, but what we can say is that we need your cooperation."

The woman looked perplexed. "An ongoing investigation of what?"

"Let me just be frank here," Amy said, then silently kicked herself for using *that* word. "We know a lot already. For example, we know what gym Douglas frequents, that he works as an accountant with Cradley and Bronson in Chermside, how many sick days he had last year and when his holiday is due, plus a bunch of other things. We just need to fill in a few blanks, and if you refuse to help, and we find out that you're withholding information vital for this case, then you'll be charged with hindering an investigation, which is a criminal offence. And the truth is, we'll get the information one way or another, so why don't you make your life easy and cooperate with us on this one?"

"Well," Barbara said. "If you know all that, I can't see what you need from me?"

Joe put his hands in his pockets. "Could we come in and talk for a second?"

Barbara Glenmore stayed where she was, looked at the both of them in turn. After a few more moments, she uncrossed her arms and stood aside, then gestured for them to enter.

Sixty-Eight

A respectful knock on a reinforced, bulletproof door made Brian Hearst look up from his desk.

"Come in."

Hank Bussey, second in command of JSG, even stockier than Brian but ten years younger, with a gray buzz cut, gym muscles and a shirt that was at least two sizes too small, came in and sat down.

"What happened at the station?" Hank said.

"I convinced him to confess," Brian said.

Hank nodded, his wide neck muscles flexing, his disproportionately small head bopping back and forth. "What do you want to do now?" he asked.

Brian ran a hand over his gray top. He removed his hand and slammed it onto his desk. "God dammit!" he said. "Bill was an amazing accountant."

Hank nodded again.

"How the hell could this happen?"

"I've looked into Donald Robinson," Hank said. "He was a regular member of Satan's Sharks, and I simply can't see what he's got to do with anything. We've never had anything to do with them."

"Keep looking," Brian said. "There must be a connection somewhere."

Hank thought for a moment. "How much do you trust Bill?"

"I trust him," Brian said. "Period."

Hank didn't say anything.

Brian continued: "He's the best accountant we've ever had. He's a talented money launderer, and he's a goddam wizard when it comes to tax evasion. What's not to trust?"

"He hasn't been with us that long, Brian."

Brian put up a hand. "I know, I know, but, far as I can tell, our numbers look fine, and we're making more money than ever. But . . ."

"But what?" Hank said.

"Why did he kill someone without involving us?"

"But he said he didn't do it, right?"

"Well, if Bill didn't do it, that means someone is trying to set him up."

"Perhaps," Hank said, shrugging. "But who would want to do that?"

"Maybe someone trying to get to us," Brian said. "Someone who wants a piece of our turf. A competitor who knows how much money we're making, and how we're making it. Maybe someone hoping that Satan's Sharks will start a war with us."

Hank nodded. "As far as I've figured out, this guy, Donald, was stabbed in his own home after a party with his mates."

"And?" Brian said.

"You really think someone from the inside would off one of their own just to set up Bill, to ruin us?"

"Ever heard of pyromaniacal firefighters?"

"Huh?"

"You know," Brian said. "An arsonist who also works as a fireman. Could be something like that. A power hungry beast, someone who has something to prove."

"But wouldn't we have to protect Bill, then?"

"No way," Brian said, then pinched his chin between thumb and forefinger. "Bill is going to go down for this murder. JSG can't be associated with him anymore."

"Why?" Hank said.

"What? Are you stupid? Because the police would be all over us. We can't afford that kind of attention. It would ruin us."

Hank's mouth fell open.

"We'll find another accountant. An even better one."

"But if Bill was set up, don't you think the police will find out and release him?" Hank said.

Brian put his hands on the table, leaned forward. "If they do, you better make sure you're there to pick him up and . . . take care of it."

Hank nodded. "Even if he's innocent?"

"Who knows? He could just look innocent because he cut a deal with the police, his freedom in return for feeding them information about us."

"Right . . . I see."

Brian opened a drawer, leaned over and retrieved an envelope, put it on the desk and closed the drawer again.

"What's that?" Hank said, nodding to the envelope.

"The reason I called you in here," Brian said. "She's an escort with Dinner and More, a small independent outfit up in Chermside. Her working name is Alison. You need to take care of it."

"Why?"

"She's William's alibi. His only chance to prove his innocence."

Hank stared at Brian for a while, then nodded again, grabbed the envelope and left the office.

SIXTY-NINE

They were sitting in the shade of a large lemon tree, around a small table on folding camping chairs that creaked every time someone crossed a leg or in any way moved. They were in a small backyard surrounded by semi-ramshackle borders; an overgrown hedge facing one neighbor, a wooden fence facing the other, and a chain-link fence running across the back of the property.

"Sorry if I seemed hostile. You showing up here is a bit of a shock," Barbara said. "Consider this my official apology, made with fruits from this very tree," she said, pointing at it before pouring lemonade from a pitcher.

Behind the chain-link, dense vegetation hid the source of a familiar burbling sound.

"You have a creek running through here?" Amy asked.

Barbara nodded while pouring. "Little Cabbage Tree Creek."

"And I thought we had weird names for things in Scotland," Joe said.

Barbara filled the last glass, then put the pitcher back on the table. "I believe it was named after the slender cabbage fan palms that grow along its course."

"Ah," Joe said, then took a glass. "Thank you. Have you lived here long?"

"We bought this house the year after we got married," Barbara said. "Which must make it twenty-one . . . no, twenty-two years ago now."

Amy took a sip of lemonade. "Mrs. Glenmore—"

"Call me Barbara."

Amy nodded. "Barbara, we're here because we're investigating a crime, and through our investigations, we came across a print left by a boot that we believe your husband purchased just before Christmas the year before last."

Barbara downed half of her lemonade, then put the glass down. Whatever training she'd been doing, it had clearly made her thirsty. "What?" she said. "What crime?"

"As mentioned, unfortunately, we can't discuss the details," Joe said. "But we'd appreciate your cooperation."

Barbara crossed her arms. "Surely you can't be serious. How would you know a thing like that? Kmart and Target and Big W, they sell thousands and thousands of pairs of shoes each year."

"Not this particular boot," Amy said. "It's a high-end, classy, unique type of boot only produced by one manufacturer. And as it stands, only two pairs of this model have ever been sold. They are super expensive."

Barbara's brows furrowed. "And how much are these boots?"

"This model is just over three thousand dollars," Joe said, turning the lemonade glass in his hand. "A pair."

"Three thou . . . ?" Barbara shook her head, then laughed. "Doug would never spend that amount of money on a pair of boots. Our car doesn't even cost that much!"

Amy cleared her throat. "And what about two pairs?"

Barbara looked at Amy incredulously. "Are you trying to tell me my husband is supposed to have spent over six thousand dollars on footwear?"

Amy nodded.

"Then I ask, where's your proof? Doug and I always talk about all things money. We know what we have, we know what we spend, and we know what we spend it on. And I can tell you, as an example, the other day when we were in Kmart, Douglas tried on a new pair of pants and put them back because he refused to pay forty dollars for work trousers," Barbara said, then shook her head. "No. I'm afraid you're not making any sense."

"They were paid for in cash," Amy said. "So the transaction wouldn't have showed up on, say, a credit card statement."

"I'm sorry," Barbara said, then smiled. "You've messed up. You clearly got some details wrong."

"The owner of the boot shop recognized him," Amy said. "Apparently, your husband and the shop owner used to work together at the Aspley hotel."

"The Aspley Hotel?" Barbara said. "My God. That must be twenty years ago! Douglas worked a short stint there just after we got married." Barbara shook her head. "That shop owner must be mistaken. Besides, there's no way Douglas would be able to take out that much money without me seeing it. And why would he hide something like this from me in the first place?" she said, the last few words diminishing in volume. Barbara took another swig of her lemonade, put the glass back down. "When exactly is this supposed to have taken place?"

"Fourteen months ago," Amy said.

Barbara seemed to consider. "So, as you said, just before Christmas the year before last?"

Amy nodded. When she looked at Barbara, she recognized the mix of doubt and fear she'd seen in so many eyes of spouses who knew more than they would admit. Some people needed time, others prodding. Amy kept quiet.

After a while, Barbara nodded, looked at Amy, then back at her lemonade. She opened her mouth, then closed it again. Amy watched her eyes go from doubtful to wondering to determined. As soon as Barbara sat up straighter in her chair, Amy knew their visit had come to an end.

"You must be mistaken," Barbara said, then stood up. "I'm sorry, but I can't help you any further."

Amy had an idea. It should have been the obvious first question, but, for some reason, it simply hadn't occurred to her until now. "May I kindly ask you, Barbara, what size shoe is Douglas?"

Barbara seemed to consider for a while. "Doug is a size ten."

Amy and Joe looked at each other, then back at Barbara.

"Thank you for your time," Amy said, then stood up. "You've been very helpful."

"So am I right? This is all just a big misunderstanding?"

"We'll be in touch if we need anything else," Joe said. "Thank you for the lemonade."

Barbara's eyes locked on Amy's. "Tell me what's going on here!"

"I'm so sorry, Barbara, but I can't tell you anything more," she said. "At least not yet. And if I'm right, I think you and I both have things we'd like to keep to ourselves, at least for the time being."

Barbara bowed her head, and all three remained silent as she showed them through the house.

She was still standing in the open doorway when Amy checked the rearview mirror before turning back down the street.

Seventy

Outside the AFP Commissioner's office window on the top floor of the Edmund Barton building in Canberra, the sun struggled to penetrate the drizzle. Limited visibility obscured the river and the bridge while mist camouflaged the gray concrete of the National Carillon.

Walter Roscoe lifted a piece of paper he'd just taken from his printer. He once again studied the name and address and made a mental note just in case anything should come and bite him in the ass one day. He contemplated possible outcomes—both good and bad—until he shrugged to himself and grabbed the handset off of his secure landline and dialed a number he'd memorized long ago. Seven hundred and fifty miles farther up the coast, a similar handset was picked up on the first ring.

"Yes?" Gregory Fordham said.

"I've got another one," Walter said.

"Go ahead."

"Listen very carefully and don't write this down."

"I never do."

Walter read out a name and an address in Byron Bay.

"Byron Bay, huh? Lucky chap. Not bad for a fresh start."

"How soon can you pass it on?"

"As it turns out, I'll hand the information over personally. Tonight."

"When do I get my share?"

"My client always pays cash, and I'll send you your share via the usual channels. You'll receive it tomorrow."

Walter nodded. "Okay, let me know when it's done."

"Sure thing."

"And what about our chunky friend?"

"It'll all be over by tomorrow."

Walter hung up. He took his black Zippo from his pocket and flicked it. Studied the laser-engraved Ace of Spades hovering over a pair of dice, struck the wheel, and held the flame to a bottom corner of the page, watching it flare up. Then he dropped the paper into his metal basket next to the desk. He flipped his Zippo closed as the flame in the basket momentarily grew before dying down. The glowing edges worked their way toward the middle of the paper until it all ended in a final puff of smoke. When there were only black ashes left, Walter closed his eyes and thought about a break at his usual spot, a well-deserved holiday.

His destination was both wild and exotic, but it could also be tranquil. It was a place where he could let his inner demons loose, the demons that had gathered in his soul over decades of working in law enforcement. He always went somewhere beautiful yet civilized, somewhere relaxing yet entertaining, somewhere far away from this dull town of police and politicians. Walter Roscoe always went to the mecca of entertainment, a gambler's paradise, the ultimate playground for people with money. He enjoyed the nightclubs and the adult entertainment, but, above all else, he loved the casinos. And now, with another payday looming, he couldn't wait to go again.

To Las Vegas, Nevada. In God's own country—The United States of America.

SEVENTY-ONE

"How does this make sense?" Joe said.

His face lit up orange every time they passed under the lights within the tunnel of the Airport Link freeway system. A four-by-four with oversized tires and a loud exhaust passed on their left, its engine roar bouncing between smooth concrete walls. There was plenty of room ahead in its lane, but then the driver cut in front of Amy, who had to step on the brakes.

"Jesus," she said. "And no lights either. Look at that!"

Joe shook his head.

"Anyway," Amy said. "First of all, and that really should have been our first question, the boots are the wrong size. Douglas Glenmore is a size ten. The boots he ordered and paid for in cash were size fourteen. What does that tell you?"

"That they would be too big for him?"

Amy chuckled. "Good one. What else?"

"What if the shop owner . . . what was his name?"

"Carlton Jones," Amy said.

Joe nodded. "What if Barbara is right? What if Carlton Jones remembers incorrectly or thinks he recognized Douglas Glenmore, but, in reality, it wasn't him at all? I mean, he himself said it's been many years since he last saw him."

"Nah," Amy said. "If you met a woman you'd had a huge crush on twenty years ago, don't you think you'd recognize her today?"

"Maybe," Joe said. "Yeah, probably."

The orange glow in the interior of the car was replaced with bright sunshine, and the noise died down to a gentle hum of rolling tires as they exited the tunnel. A suspenseful theme song filled the cabin.

Joe chuckled. "*Mission: Impossible,*" he said. "I don't think I've heard that since I watched the TV series as a wee boy in Scotland. You know the one, with Steven Hill and Barbara Bain—"

"Let me just get this," Amy said, reaching for the phone sitting in its holder. She tapped the answer button and put it on speaker. "Maggie? What's happening?"

"Frank called us about the boot prints."

"Yes, I know. He asked me for your number. Hope that's alright."

"Well," Maggie said. "He's right, Amy. It's not a one hundred percent match. We've got the actual boots here that you took from the home of William Forrester, and although the model and size are a match, the outsoles of the actual boots are somewhat incomplete. That is to say, Mr. Forrester has a gait that results in the outer part of the soles wearing out quicker than the inner part, and there's a quarter inch of tread missing from that area, as its been worn off with use. However, the prints from the crime scene are complete, you see? Frank called it a complete print made by an incomplete boot."

"Okay," Amy said.

"Anyway, the point is, those prints couldn't have been made by William Forrester's boots."

"And what about the hair?" Amy said.

"Frank suggested it was pulled out, and we knew that already, but we assumed it had been pulled out by the victim as he was attacked, but now . . ."

"Yes?"

"Well, seen in light of the fact that we can conclude with an absolute certainty that the boots weren't on scene, I'm leaning toward also changing my explanation about the hair."

"Why?"

"Do you remember we told you that a person who gets stabbed in the kidney will go into shock immediately and won't have the capacity to react?"

"Yes."

"Frank brought my attention to that issue as well, so I suppose there's a good chance that he's right. That the hair was planted later."

"Let me know if I've got this right," Amy said. "Initially, back when you were convinced that the boot print belonged to William Forrester, you chose to also assume that the victim had managed to pull out one of William's hairs. But now that you know the boot print was planted, you choose to reaffirm your knowledge that someone who's stabbed in the kidney goes into shock, and thereby wouldn't have been able to pull at William's hair, thereby making it logical to assume that the hair was planted as well?"

"You make it sound complicated," Maggie said. "But that's the gist of it. Also, Frank said that the boot company sold two pairs of the same model and size to one individual?"

"Yes," Amy said. "We're just coming from there now. We know who purchased them."

"Shouldn't that person be your prime suspect, then?" Maggie asked.

"Joe and I were just talking about that. His name is Douglas Glenmore, and we're fairly certain that's he's the one who bought them. But you see, the problem is, he's a size ten himself."

"Oh," Maggie said, "that's an old trick. He could simply have worn boots that were too big and stuffed a bit of newspaper in there while wearing them to remove suspicion from himself."

"We visited his wife in their home," Amy said. "He simply doesn't seem like the man who has that kind of money."

Amy could hear mumbling in the background. "What's that?"

"Ron is saying that he could have been saving up without his wife knowing. Or borrowed the money from someone. He says that if a guy wants to kill someone, saving up to buy two pairs of boots shouldn't be that big of a hurdle."

"I see what you mean, but his wife said that their car cost less than these boots," Amy said.

"Are you serious?"

"Absolutely. The boots cost just over three thousand dollars a pair," Amy said.

Silence filled the cabin for a moment. "What the hell do they drive?" Maggie said.

Amy and Joe both laughed. "Please go through all the prints and DNA again," Amy said. "Whoever did this must have messed up somewhere; they always do. And double-check a man named Brian Hearst, because I'm sure he's on the register. Have another look. And see if you find anything matching Douglas Glenmore, as well as a Brad Jenkins."

"Will do," Maggie said and hung up.

"Someone has been planning this for a very long time," Amy said.

"You think?" Joe said.

"You know what could make sense?"

"What?"

"That Douglas Glenmore purchased those boots," Amy said. "But as a middleman."

"A middleman?"

"I'm almost certain," Amy said, then nodded to herself. "He did buy those boots, but he bought them for someone else, paid with someone else's money, too."

SEVENTY-TWO

F rank held onto the metal handle on the inside of the back doors as he exited the bus, then sauntered across the sidewalk and entered the Brisbane Department Store. He walked over to a large screen placed at a forty-five degree angle on a stand, just inside the entrance doors. He pressed the looking glass symbol and a six-inch curser began blinking. Frank wrote FASHION, then chose the shop at the top of the list, tapped it and studied the digital map.

He walked over to the nearest elevator, pressed the up arrow and waited. Frank couldn't stand department stores or shopping malls of any sort; he absolutely hated the hustle and bustle and stress of people running around like headless chickens, looking for the latest of something they probably already had five of.

Frank found the shop, walked inside and began looking around. After several fruitless minutes, he found himself surrounded by bras and panties. His blood pressure was rising and, despite the cool AC, the agitation was making him sweat. He scanned the large space, desperately hoping to at least spot the men's department, when a friendly-looking shop assistant came over. She looked to be Frank's age and her smile seemed genuine.

"May I help you, sir?" she asked.

Frank took a deep breath and explained he was looking for a suit for himself, for a date. But not just any date. Frank was going on the most important date he'd ever been on.

"Follow me, please," the lady said, then walked ahead past hoodies and tracksuits and sportswear. A minute later, he was finally standing next to shelves and racks of shirts and pants and jackets.

Frank spotted several nice-looking items, but the lady kept walking. "I like that one," Frank said, pointing at a suit.

The lady shook her head and smiled. Kept walking. "This is regular stuff," she said. "I'm taking you to our 'Big Guys' section."

"Hmmm."

Toward the far corner, she stopped and began pulling out a tasteful selection.

Frank entered a small dressing room and squeezed into a dozen different shirts, swearing and fumbling with buttons, every change increasingly difficult as he began sweating profusely. Just as he was reaching the end of his wits—and on the verge of giving up—he tried on a blue suit with a lighter blue shirt. The pants fit. The shirt conformed to his shape, yet didn't stick. The jacket was cut as though tailor-made. Frank thought it was perfect.

Frank changed back into his Bermuda shorts and short-sleeved shirt, exited and thanked the lady. She smiled and pointed him in the direction of brown dress shoes, which he managed to find in his size without too much hassle. Then he scoured yet another area and was lucky to find a matching brown leather belt fit for his girth.

With his arms full, Frank proceeded over to the nearest cash register where a young man rang it all up, then packed it into large plastic bags. Frank dug into his pocket and counted out eight of his green one-hundred-dollar bills. The man smiled as he gave him twenty dollars change. Frank thought the prices were way over the top, but he needed to give himself the best chance possible.

Exhausted, sweaty and hungry, Frank went to the perfume department and—one at a time—sprayed the air with a dozen fragrances until light, pleasant whiffs turned into nauseating, heavy smells. In the end, when he could no longer distinguish one from the other, he decided to stick to what he knew. The cologne Caroline had loved. He scanned the shelves and found the familiar, round, chubby bottle covered in a turquoise label, an ornamental print in black and gold showing a number given to a house in Glockengasse in Köln centuries earlier: *4711—Original Eau de Cologne.*

Satisfied with his haul, he sighed in relief that he was done. As he exited the department store, he began scanning his surrounds for somewhere to take a break. Frank eyed a burger place diagonally across the street, with tables and chairs in the shade of a tall building, a perfect place to sit down and rest his legs and enjoy a large ginger beer. And eat.

And come up with a plan of attack.

SEVENTY-THREE

Amy parked behind the same beat-up utility truck that she'd parked behind the night she'd been there with Frank. Joe hopped out of the car, and Amy caught up with him just as they reached the white van with its back wheels lifted onto wooden blocks.

"Does he live in there?" Joe said, nodding in the direction of the red brick house.

"He does," Amy said, then took out her phone and called the number she had for Brad Jenkins.

"Who is this?" a male voice said.

"Mr. Jenkins, this is the Australian Federal Police. We're outside your house. We need you to contain your Dobermann and then we'd like a word with you," Amy said.

"I'm . . ." Brad began, then Amy noticed two slats on the righthand window being split apart. A second later, the slats were back in place. "I'm not home right now," he said.

"Mr. Jenkins, I just saw you peeking out from behind your blinds. I know you're in there."

There was silence for a while. "Give me a moment," Brad said.

Amy put her phone away. They watched Brad exit the front door, walk down the cracked concrete steps and then chain his dog. He walked over to the permanently open gates on the right and nodded. He was wearing what looked like green swim trunks and a black T-shirt bearing the name of a heavy metal band. "Sorry about the not being home bit," he said.

Joe introduced himself and Amy, then said: "Is anyone else in the house?"

Brad nodded. "My girl."

"Anyone else?" Amy asked.

"No."

Amy gestured for Brad to lead the way. "After you."

Brad walked ahead, and as they walked into the small hallway, a sharp and pungent smell went up Amy's nostrils; it made her think of stale urine mixed with window cleaner.

They proceeded into the front living room, where Brad pointed to a wrinkled, two-seater fabric sofa covered in stained blankets.

"Have a seat," he said, then walked over to the windows and pulled up the blinds.

The dust in the air whirled around in the sun rays, and Amy sat down, feeling part of a metal spring poke one of her ass cheeks. Joe sat down next to her. Brad sat across from them in a matching chair with both armrests all scratched up, suggesting to Amy where the smell could be coming from.

"Where is your girlfriend?" Amy asked.

"She's out the back," Brad said, then looked around the room. "She's sleeping."

Joe looked at his clock.

Brad smiled. "We had a late night yesterday, you know."

Amy nodded. "Mr. Jenkins, we need to ask you a few questions."

"Sure thing."

"Where were you on the night between the sixth and seventh of February?" Amy asked.

Brad scratched his stubble, and Amy saw dandruff float and fall onto his black T-shirt.

"I was at a party at one of my mates'," he said. "I had a little too much to drink, so I ended up crashing on his sofa."

"Donald Robinson?" Amy said.

"That's right."

"And do you know what has happened to Mr. Robinson?"

Brad leaned forward, folded his hands, put his elbows on his knees and looked down. "Yeah," he said. "I heard he was killed."

"What time did you leave Mr. Robinson's place?" Joe asked.

Brad kept looking at the floor, then back up at Joe. "I'm not sure."

"How many guests were there when you left?" Joe said.

"Just me."

"Was he alive when you left the place?" Amy asked.

"What?" Brad said. "What are you . . . of course, he was alive."

"Anything you would like to add?" Amy said.

Brad leaned back, shrugged. "What should I add? What more could I possibly add?"

"Well," Amy said. "You can see how this looks. You've just admitted to us you were there, and now you're saying you were the last one to leave."

"But, no, no, hang on, just hang on," Brad said.

"We'll hang on," Amy said.

"I have absolutely no reason to kill Don. He was my friend."

"Well, Mr. Jenkins, if you were the last one to leave, who called the police?"

Brad shrugged, scanned the living room as if he'd never seen it before. He grabbed a glass from the table and downed the rest of something that looked like cat urine, but which Amy hoped was stale beer.

"Mr. Jenkins?" Amy said.

The smell was stronger here than in the hallway. Cat piss and window cleaner. No, something else, but similar. What was it? Ether? No. Ammonia, that was it.

"Mr. Jenkins," Amy said. "Best case, this odor I'm picking up is your meth use. Worst case, I'm smelling something bigger. Like a lab? Are you a bit of an entrepreneur? Perhaps you have a production out the back?"

Brad wiped his palms on his trunks, his eyes darting around.

"I'll give you one last chance to come clean," Amy said. "If you don't, I'll have the drug squad here in five minutes. Your choice."

A glow around Brad's neck told Amy she'd hit a sweet spot.

"Someone killed Donald while I was in the flat," he said. "Somehow . . . I don't know . . . I was sick, you see? I'd had too much to drink, and I was in the bathroom throwing my guts up when Don yelled at me to clean up after myself. Then it sounded as though he fell, but I couldn't move to go check on him, not in that state. Eventually, all that came up was bile, so I wiped my mouth on a towel and decided to go see if there was any beer left in the fridge. You know, a little hair off the dog? Anyway, I walked into the kitchen, and that's when I saw him."

Amy leaned forward. "Tell me exactly what you saw."

"I saw Don lying on the floor and there was blood everywhere," Brad said. "And the stink was horrendous."

"Tell me about his stomach," Amy said.

"His stomach?" Brad said, looking at the table. "Oh yeah, it was kind of big, like round, like . . . like bloated?"

Amy nodded. "And then you called the police and left?"

Brad sighed. "Yes."

Joe took out a notepad. "In your opinion, Mr. Jenkins, who could have done this?"

Brad shrugged. "I have no clue," he said. "Don was a great guy. Never set a foot wrong, not as far as I'm aware."

"Did Donald fight with anyone during the party?" Amy said. "Any weird phone calls? Texts? Hints of any kind?"

"No," Brad said.

"Was there anyone at that party that Don did not know personally?" Amy asked. "Someone who didn't belong?"

Brad reached for the beer glass, realized it was empty and put it back, rubbed his thighs again.

"Mr. Jenkins?"

Brad Jenkins took a deep breath, then opened his mouth to speak.

SEVENTY-FOUR

B rad took another breath, looked past Amy toward the back of the house and lowered his voice. "Just a few . . . shall we call them ladies of the night?"

"Are you talking about prostitutes?" Amy said.

"No, not . . . well, I suppose, but these were like high-end ladies. Escorts, you know?"

"Did Donald rough up a hooker, give anyone a reason to get back at him?"

Brad shook his head. More dandruff went flying. "No way, but I'm pretty sure Don did one of them at the party."

"How many were there?" Amy said.

Brad counted on his fingers. "Seven."

"You sound sure of that number," Amy said.

"I am," Brad said. "There were three Asians, three blondes and one brunette."

"I don't understand," Amy said. "Why would you remember a thing like that?"

Brad lowered his voice even more. "Because we had a lineup. I really wanted to do the brunette, so I figured I'd have to be quick to be first in line."

Amy tilted her head. "And did you make it?"

Brad smiled. "Yep."

Amy returned a fake smile. "So happy for you."

Joe leaned forward. "Did any of them sleep over?"

"No."

"Which one did Donald Robinson have sex with?" Amy said.

"No idea."

"Did you get any of their names?" Joe said.

"No."

"Do you know what company they were from?" Amy said.

"I asked the brunette," Brad said. "Dinner and More."

Amy nodded. "One last thing, Mr. Jenkins."

"Sure."

"Who paid for the hookers?"

Brad smiled, shrugged.

"Mr. Jenkins—"

"Honestly. We were all drunk, but I remember we spent a lot of the night laughing and guessing which one of us would have done something like that, but in the end, no one took credit for it."

"Are you telling me that you have absolutely no idea who arranged for the hookers?" Amy said.

Brad shrugged again. "Donald was really the only one that we suspected. He has . . . had a bit more money than the rest of us, and seeing as it was his party, we thought he was the one behind the surprise." Brad glanced at his feet before looking back up. "So I asked him, and he looked like he honestly had no idea."

"No idea?" Amy said.

Brad shook his head. "None."

Seventy-Five

A lthough Dinner and More was a high-class establishment, the entry door to the brothel was black and nondescript, and only accessible by descending a set of stairs leading down to a basement at an address in Chermside that wasn't advertised anywhere but online. Joe walked down and rapped on the door, which was opened by a bulky man in a black suit with a shiny bald head. He looked angrily at Joe, then at Amy, but his frown turned into a smile when Joe showed him his ID. The man stood aside and waved them both in.

The reception area was tiny, with a low ceiling. One corner was dominated by a black wooden countertop with red lace of all sorts plastered on the front. A tanned woman was standing behind the desk. She looked to be in her forties, her black hair flowing over a red satin negligee. Amy didn't know where to look, didn't feel comfortable. She looked at Joe, whose eyes were darting around the room, looking everywhere but at the lady behind the desk.

Amy sighed, took out her ID and held it up. "I'm agent Lamborne, this is my partner, agent McAvoy. Could we speak with the owner or manager?"

The lady smiled. "Me or me," she said. "I'm Julia Ambrose."

"Mrs. Ambrose," Amy said, putting her ID back inside her pocket, "is there somewhere private we could talk?"

"Miss Ambrose," the woman said, spreading her arms. "And honey, this is a brothel; it doesn't get any more private than this."

Amy smiled, put her elbows on the counter and leaned in. "We need to speak to you about a booking you would have received for the evening of the sixth of February. A whole harem of women, all sent to the same address."

"Of course," Julia said, clasping her hands. "And do we have a warrant?"

Amy arched an eyebrow. "Seriously? You wanna go down that route?"

Julia smiled. "I'm afraid I have to. You know, client confidentiality and all that."

"What are you? A lawyer?" Amy said.

Joe chuckled. "My colleague has a point."

"Point or not, I'm not giving out any information without seeing a warrant first."

"Miss Ambrose, we could easily come back with a warrant. But if we do, we'll also make sure to bring a copy of the Prostitution Regulation together with a government authority representative to perform a much-needed audit of this place. And I doubt your missing posters, incorrect wording on signs and outdated safety certificates will impress."

"So what?" Julia said.

"Dodgy alarm systems, incorrect lighting, lack of proof or irregularity regarding medical examinations of your employees."

"I have—"

"Current advertisement requirements, legal image usage, records, documents and licenses you're required to keep on the premises, as well as smoke alarms and fire extinguishers and emergency exits. The list is long and the penalties hefty. Would you like me to continue?"

"Alright, fine," Julia said, then began clicking her long, artificial nails on the keyboard in front of her. "Sixth of February, you said?"

"I did, and I need a list of all the women you sent out to an address in Beenleigh on that night."

A moment later, a printer began humming and spat out a piece of paper that Julia picked up and began highlighting. Once done, she put the paper on the counter and turned it so that Amy could read it. "This is a list of all of our girls. I've highlighted the ones who went to Beenleigh that night," she said, a long red nail hovering over the names. "The first column shows each girl's legal name, the next one shows the name they work under."

Amy studied the list. Read it from top to bottom. Then again. She didn't recognize any of the names, highlighted or not, real or aliases.

Joe glanced across at the list.

Amy looked back down the list one more time. "You sure this is all of them?"

"Absolutely."

"And you've highlighted all the women sent out to Beenleigh on the sixth of February?"

"Yes, honey, I have."

Amy nodded. "I'll also need to know who paid for their services."

"No clue," Julia said.

"Again," Joe said, "we could easily get a warrant and come back."

"No, no," Julia said. "All I mean is, had it been an online booking, I would have been able to give you the name and credit card details. But it wasn't, so I don't have any details. It was booked over the phone and the whole job paid for in cash at the address."

"And the person who called, was that a man or a woman?" Amy asked.

Julia looked around the small reception area. "I honestly don't remember. We are a very busy establishment. In between all the running around, I get hundreds of calls a day."

"When was the booking made?"

Julia had another look at the computer screen. "Same day."

"Who handed over the cash?"

Julia shrugged. "I don't know, and I don't really care, either."

Amy ran her finger across every highlighted name.

"What is it?" Joe said.

Amy looked at Julia. "Mind if I keep the list?"

"As if I have a choice—"

"Thank you," Amy said, then nodded to Joe. It was time to leave.

Joe didn't speak until they were back in the car. "Why the rush?"

Amy shook her head. "Didn't Brad say he was certain there were seven women at that party?"

Joe took out his notebook, flipped a page. "Yes. Why?"

"Look at this list," Amy said, then handed it over.

Joe's head moved slightly as he scanned it. "It looks like Julia only highlighted six names."

Amy nodded. "That's exactly right," she said. "Which makes me wonder: Who's the seventh woman?"

SEVENTY-SIX

A my and Joe were cruising south, heading down Gympie Road. They'd reached a point where car dealerships gave way to gas stations that eventually became shops and supermarkets until the cityscape changed again and Amy stopped at a red light.

They were surrounded by fast-food outlets of all sorts. Amy chuckled.

"What?" Joe said.

Amy was smiling and biting her lower lip. "I don't think I would have made it through this area with Frank," she said. "He would have insisted I stop in somewhere."

Joe nodded. "Lucky you're with me then."

Amy didn't comment.

Up ahead was a place that made foot-long sandwiches. Frank had taken her there once and had a steak sandwich with "the lot", as well as a half dozen chocolate chip cookies. Amy had a small ham and cheese and had skipped the cookies. Across from there, a burger joint with flame-grilled burgers where Frank had downed a tower with layers of meat and cheese and bacon, as well as swallowed a bucket of fries and slurped what looked like a gallon of ginger beer. And she never had to wait for him; he had an ability to demolish his monster meals in record time. Frank had a raging hunger for food that spilled into an appetite for life which drove him to—sometimes literally—get to the bottom of whatever he was working on; a burger or a murder case. Hidden behind the burger joint was a place that sold crisp chicken, coleslaw and corn on the cob, a place where Frank had—

"Amy?"

"What?"

Joe pointed at the lights. "It's green."

Amy hit the pedal and the sedan shot forward.

"Whoa," Joe said.

Amy blew air through her lips. "I just don't get it."

"Get what?" Joe said.

"Any of it. Who do you think is lying? Julia Ambrose or Brad Jenkins?"

Joe raised his eyebrows, pushed out his lower lip. "How are we supposed to know that?"

"By understanding the implications of the lie."

"How do you mean?"

"Well, if Brad is telling the truth and Julia is lying, that she in fact did send out seven women, that could imply that Julia is protecting the seventh woman, but why? If Brad is lying and Julia is telling the truth, that she really only sent out six women, what motive would Brad have for saying that? Why make up an extra woman that wasn't there? How does that make sense?"

"Right."

"The answer to that is, it doesn't. Which makes me think Julia must be the one lying. She *did* send out seven women, which ties in with my earlier question. Who's the seventh woman?"

"Indeed."

"And then we have William Forrester's confession."

Joe nodded. "Signed and dated."

"He confessed just after having a conversation with his lawyer. A man who—as it turns out—isn't a lawyer at all. And that makes me think JSG could be involved with Dinner and More. It could be their company, or perhaps they have stakes in it. Either way."

"Right."

"It could confirm my . . . well, Frank's suspicion that JSG is simply a front for some sort of mob. Is Brian framing William? Is this a company-ordered hit? Did Brian really do it, and if so, why do they want William Forrester to take the fall for it?"

"Could very well be something like that."

Amy found a gap in the outer lane and filled it, then sped up slightly. "You know," she said. "When Brian Hearst came charging through that door, pretending to be William's lawyer, I had a sense that William was about to open up."

"You think he was ready to spill the beans?"

Amy nodded. "What Frank seems to be onto makes more and more sense. I don't know yet how it all fits, but there are too many inconsistencies in this case for us to simply accept William's confession, don't you think?"

"I hear you."

Amy nodded. "I'm heading back to the station. I need to have a chat with William again," she said. "And this time without Brian."

Joe nodded. "Aye."

SEVENTY-SEVEN

F rank ran a hand through his freshly cut hair, hiked up his trousers one last time, readjusted his shirt that he'd stuffed into his new pants, buttoned his suit jacket, then pressed the brass bell and smiled up at the camera.

The gate clicked open, and Frank strolled up to the front door, one hand in his pocket, the other holding a bouquet of white roses.

When the door opened, Frank gulped. Rebecca's auburn hair was styled in layers of soft curls caressing her bare shoulders; her silky, short, black cocktail dress stopped teasingly high up her thighs, and the V neckline told Frank that he'd have to concentrate hard on not staring. Which—he now realized—was exactly what he was doing.

Rebecca giggled, walked close to Frank, then pushed up on her stilettos and put her arms around his neck, kissed him on the side of the mouth. Frank's nostrils were filled with a pleasant mix of citrus, soap and lavender.

"Thank you so much for the flowers," she said, taking the bouquet. There was a seductive huskiness to her voice that Frank enjoyed immensely.

"You colored your hair," Frank said. "It looks nice."

Rebecca took Frank's hand and led him through the house and onto the back porch. The light from a low-setting sun couldn't compete with the contrasting glare of flickering candles in silver candlesticks. The table was set with a white linen tablecloth and matching napkins that were draped over large porcelain plates with hand-painted blue patterns. Glistening silverware. A silver dome. Beside the table, on a separate drinks trolley, a champagne bottle was sticking out of a silver bucket.

"Waw," Frank said.

Rebecca laughed. "You say that every time you come here."

"I mean that every time I come here."

Rebecca looked at the roses. "Give me a moment; I'll just go and find a vase."

Frank nodded, stayed where he was.

When Rebecca returned, he walked over and pulled out a chair. When she turned in front of him, Frank had to use all his willpower to not touch her bare back as he pushed her chair in. Her skin looked orange in the fading light. Frank walked over to the opposite side and sat down.

"Will you open the champagne for us?" Rebecca said, then reached past the salad bowl and lifted the large dome. Steam escaped from a tray with pan-fried salmon fillets, blanched asparagus and spinach. It smelled of garlic, parsley and lemon.

Frank leaned over and lifted the bottle out of the melting ice, then used his napkin to dry it off. He removed the foil, then began wrestling with the wire cage. After he gently slid it over the top, he held it out, pointed to it: "You know what this is called?" he said.

Rebecca smiled and frowned at the same time. "No."

"It's called a *muselet*," Frank said, then spelled it for her. "It's French, pronounced moose-ee-lay."

"I never knew," Rebecca said.

Frank wanted to kick himself. His trivia always slipped out at the most awkward of times. He knew he could say the most stupid things when he was nervous, and nervous he was. Scared, even.

No, that didn't cover it. Frank was petrified.

"How do you know something like that?" Rebecca said.

Frank shrugged. "I guess I'm naturally curious," he said, then grabbed the bottle with one hand and began pulling at the cork with the other. "I've always been interested in learning about the things I don't know, rather than what most people do, which is simply repeating what they already know, over and over again." Frank shook his head. "That would drive me nuts."

"So you constantly try to broaden your horizons?" Rebecca asked.

Frank had wriggled the cork halfway out. "I suppose," he said. "And the opposite of that makes most people good at what they do. Driving, for instance. People who revel in repetition can keep fine-tuning and perfecting."

"Does that make you a bad driver?"

Frank smiled, caught the tease in her voice. "Well, there are plenty of drivers out there that are much, much better than I am, that's for sure."

Rebecca nodded. "Well, then, that leaves the most important question of all."

The cork had reached a point where Frank could stop pulling; the internal pressure would be enough to push it the rest of the way, so

Frank let go of the cork and angled the bottle toward the river. "What's that?" he said.

Rebecca lifted her empty champagne glass, leaned in. "Does it make you a good investigator?"

"No," Frank said, then looked Rebecca in the eyes. "It makes me the *best* investigator."

The cork popped, white foam gushed out and Frank filled their glasses.

Seventy-Eight

G regory Fordham looked up from his desk. "You want to interview William Forrester again? But he's already confessed."

Amy remained standing just inside the open door, nodded. "I realize that, sir, but I don't believe that he's telling the truth."

"And why on earth not? He confessed on the advice of his lawyer."

"That's another thing I've found, sir. Brian Hearst isn't a lawyer at all."

"What?"

Amy explained in detail what she'd found.

Fordham scratched his scar with one finger, his eyes moving around all corners of his desk. "And . . . what do you expect to get out of another interview? You think he's just going to withdraw his confession?"

Amy shrugged. "I don't know. I'd just like to try and get to the bottom of all this."

Fordham sighed. "Close the door and have a seat."

Amy followed orders.

Fordham put his elbows on the desk and leaned forward. "And what exactly is 'all this'?"

"Just some minor . . . inconsistencies, you know?"

Fordham shook his head. "I don't."

"Well," Amy began, "the boot print for one. It's almost too perfect, and it comes from one of two pairs, both of which were purchased by a man who has much smaller feet, and who—according to his own wife—wouldn't be able to afford such boots."

Fordham leaned back in his chair, crossed his arms. "And?"

Amy shrugged. "And just the fact that Brian Hearst isn't a lawyer, don't you find that extremely suspicious?"

"You think JSG is behind it?" Fordham said.

Amy was about to object when she remembered what Frank had said the night she'd dropped him off at Eat Street. About Gregory. About there being something wrong with him. "I really have no idea," she said. "But I need to speak to William Forrester again."

Fordham nodded. "Okay," he said. "But don't record it. Let it be an unofficial chat."

"What? Why?"

Fordham spread his arms and put his hands flat on his desk. "Interrogating a suspect *after* he's already confessed could be considered police harassment, and we don't want that on our books here. Also, William could potentially use it against us later, which, combined with him actually withdrawing his confession, would help him get an acquittal. It's a mess we don't need."

"But, surely—"

"Remember our chat the night I caught you working outside of hours?"

Amy's eyes widened.

"That you owe me one?" Gregory said.

Amy nodded.

"You keep this little chat between you and William confidential, then we'll call it quits."

"I see," Amy said, then stood, walked over and opened the door.

"But," Fordham said. "You take notes of what he says, and then you come and hand me those notes, and fill me in. I want to know exactly what you find out. And make sure Joe sits in on it. Got it?"

Amy nodded again. "Yes, sir," she said, closing the door behind her.

SEVENTY-NINE

"I hope you like it black," Amy said, placing a full mug of coffee in front of William Forrester.

"Thank you," he said. "It's nice to get out of the holding cell."

"I bet," Amy said, then placed her own mug on the table and sat down across from him.

Joe closed the door to the interview room and sat down next to Amy, who took a small, personal recorder out of her jacket pocket, pressed RECORD and placed it on the metal table between them.

"Mr. William Forrester, where were you on the night between the sixth and seventh of February?"

"I've already answered all these questions."

"Yes, but your story seems to have changed since you last spoke to us."

William shrugged. "As advised by my lawyer, I've decided to confess to the murder."

Amy nodded. "And who is your lawyer?"

"What sort of game is this?" William said. "You know that very well. Why would you even ask such a question?"

"Humor me."

307

William took a sip of his coffee, then put the mug back down. "Whatever. My lawyer's name is Brian Hearst."

"The Brian Hearst who came into this very room during your initial interview?"

"Yes, that Brian Hearst."

Amy shook her head. "Would it surprise you to learn that Brian Hearst isn't a lawyer at all?"

"What do you mean?"

"He's never studied the law, has no diploma, no certificate, no membership with any legal organization, no registration with any legal body associated with the law. At all."

William shrugged, took another sip of his coffee.

"In other words, he's an imposter. A fraud."

William put his mug down. "And . . . what are you saying?"

Amy shrugged. "I think it's your turn to talk."

William looked at the small recorder on the table.

"Mr. Forrester, would you like to continue off the record?"

William nodded.

Amy turned off the recorder, put it back in her pocket. "Talk to me."

William's shoulders slumped. "Brian threatened to kill me unless I confessed."

"So you did not kill Donald Robinson?"

"No."

"And, despite us having found both a boot print and strands of your hair at the scene, I'm supposed to simply take your word for it?"

William's eyes sought his coffee mug. "No, you don't have to take my word for it," he said, then took a deep breath before looking back up at Amy. "I have an alibi."

Amy sipped her own coffee, then nodded at William to continue as she put the mug back down.

"I'm obviously not proud of this, but I called a hooker that night."

"To your house in The Gap?"

William shook his head. "I have a . . . I guess you could call it a little bachelor's pad in the city that I use."

"A pad?"

William nodded. "I bought it a long time ago, together with my best friend."

"So it belongs to the both of you?"

William shook his head. "Used to, but he died a few years ago."

"What was his name?"

"Carl Wright."

"Always nice with a good friend," Amy said, then something connected in her brain. Amy took a moment, considering how to proceed. "Did you meet up with women at the pad a lot?"

William shrugged. "Define a lot."

"I'm not in the mood," Amy said.

"I guess I meet up with girls there once a month, maybe even twice. I don't know."

"Okay," Amy said. "Tell me about the night in question."

"Well, Paula—my wife—always leaves for work around eight in the evening. On that night, I told her I was going to watch a movie and go to bed early, but I left the house around nine, put the key in the door of the pad just before nine-thirty."

Amy nodded. "Then what?"

"Then I called the . . . company, ordered a girl and hit the shower."

"What company was that?"

309

William sighed, leaned forward and put his face in his hands, mumbled something.

"What was that?"

William removed his hands and sat back up. "I said my marriage is so going to be in the shits. Paula is going to leave me, I just know it."

Amy tilted her head. "Oh, poor William."

"This may come as a surprise to you, but I love my wife."

"Sure," Amy said, nodding. "When did the prostitute arrive?"

William shrugged. "Probably just after ten."

"And how long did she spend with you?"

"About an hour."

"Then what did you do?"

"Had a couple of beers, watched a movie."

"And you paid her for that time as well?"

William's brows furrowed. "How do you mean?"

"Well, I couldn't imagine that she would sit there and watch television with you for free all night."

"No. I mean, that's right, she wouldn't, and she didn't."

"So, how long did she stay?"

"She stayed until . . . after, you know."

Amy shook her head.

"She left around eleven-thirty."

"So, she only stayed for about an hour?" Amy said.

"Yes."

"And you spent the rest of the night in the pad on your own?"

William shook his head. "As I was saying, I had a beer, watched a movie, but then I drove home again."

"What time did you drive home?"

"Probably around two."

"You drove home at two am?" Amy said.

"Yes, arrived home around two-thirty."

"Waw, Mr. Forrester, that's bad."

"I know, and I'm not exactly proud of—"

"No, what I mean is, you have no alibi."

"How can you say something like that? She was there!"

"Yes, but you see, the victim was killed sometime between two and four am that night."

"What?"

"Meaning long after your prostitute left."

"That's crazy! That just can't be."

Amy shook her head. "The timeline says you were alone for at least three hours before the murder, you were alone during the murder, as well as a good few hours after, meaning the prostitute visiting you doesn't qualify as an alibi."

William began shaking. Drops of sweat appeared on his forehead. "Well, Brian certainly doesn't seem to think so."

"Brian doesn't seem to think what?"

"That it doesn't qualify as an alibi."

"How so?"

William took another deep breath. "He wants my alibi...removed."

"Brian is going to kill the prostitute?"

William nodded.

"When?"

William shrugged.

"I need some names, now William. Now!"

William sat up straight. "Okay, okay! Look, all I know is that the girl works under the name Alison, but I obviously don't know her real name."

"Where does she work?"

"A place up in Chermside. It's called Dinner and More."

"What?"

"Dinner—"

Amy shot up and knocked her chair over. "Joe, take that asshole back to his holding cell," she said, then ran for the door. "I'll bring the car out front. Go!"

EIGHTY

J oe jumped into the car and Amy thrust the list they'd been given from Julia Ambrose into his lap, then lurched into traffic.

Joe held onto the handle above the door as Amy screeched left into Ann Street. "Where are we going?"

Amy focused on her driving. "Look at the list, and you'll see a woman whose working name is Alison—real name Lin Bei."

Joe looked. "I see it."

Amy found a lane on the far right and skidded right into Brookes Street. "And you'll notice that her name isn't highlighted, meaning that she could be the one Julia is trying to protect."

"How?"

"Seven of Dinner and More's women attend a party where Donald Robinson was killed. And now William Forrester looks like he's the guy who did it, yet his shaky alibi is that he supposedly spent a night with a woman from the same company, an alibi which doesn't hold up because of the timing issues, the very timing issues that make it possible for Alison AKA Lin Bei to leave William's pad and drive down to Donald's party and murder him. Don't you see? Either she's the seventh woman, which means she could be the killer, or she's not, which means Brian is going to have her killed. Either way, we need to get to her fast."

Joe nodded. "Let's give Dinner and More a call," he said, then took out his phone, dialed a number and held it out for both of them to hear. The phone didn't get through the first ring before it was picked up.

"Good evening, Dinner and—"

"Julia Ambrose? This is AFP Agent Joe McAvoy, we've just—"

"Yes, honey, I remember you."

"We need to get a hold of Lin Bei. She works under the name Alison."

"Lin? Just give me a moment."

Amy couldn't hear any background noise over the engine roar of their sedan, but she supposed Julia was standing behind her counter, typing away on her keyboard.

"Right," Julia said. "Come up tomorrow. She'll be available then."

"I'll need her home address if she's off tonight," Joe said.

"She's at work," Julia said. "She just got called out, that's all, but she should be back—"

"I need the address where she was sent," Joe said. "Right now!"

"Brisbane Tower Hotel."

Amy checked her mirrors, turned her head and did a quick U-turn across all four lanes of Brookes Street and headed back toward the city.

Joe held onto the handle but was still pushed up against his door. "When was she sent there?"

"I guess about an hour ago."

"Name of caller?" he said.

"He didn't say, just gave me a credit card number, paid up front for the entire night," Julia said. "Is Lin in danger?"

"Listen, Julia," Joe said, then, holding the phone in one hand, took out his notepad and pen with the other and placed it on his knee. "I need you to give me all the credit card details, everything you have."

"Okay," Julia said, then went through the numbers while Joe jotted them all down. "What's going on?"

Joe hung up and patched the details through the radio to HQ, who informed they'd get back to him with a name as soon as they could.

Amy joined the Inner City Bypass and overtook a large semitrailer. Despite the descending darkness, the driver had yet to switch on his lights.

"I don't get it," Joe said. "This feels more and more like a scramble, rather than a carefully laid out plan. It's so messy."

Amy shrugged. "Maybe it's just messy to us because we can't see it yet."

"I think William Forrester is double-bluffing us. I think that maybe he himself has set himself up to make it look as though JSG set him up. Maybe JSG did something to William Forrester that he can't forgive."

Amy honked the horn and flashed her headlights at a red hatch that was hogging the outer lane despite going below the speed limit. When the car finally pulled over, Amy squeezed the pedal and accelerated as fast as traffic would permit. She had to weave in and out of lanes to keep moving. "Well, theoretically, I guess anything's possible, but I think that particular theory is a bit far-fetched."

"I guess," he said. "And since Dinner and More keeps popping up, maybe we should focus on them."

"I couldn't agree more," Amy said, just as the radio crackled.

"Unit five?"

Joe lifted the transmitter off the hook. "This is unit five. Go ahead."

"Credit card belongs to Jacaranda Security Group. It's a company card."

"Jesus!" Amy said, then nodded for Joe to hit the buttons.

In the setting sun, the red and blue strobes bounced off a van in front of them. The vehicle moved over and Amy floored the pedal. The engine roared even louder, and for a moment the deafening sirens drowned her deepening fears.

EIGHTY-ONE

F rank heard the distant rumble of thunder. Clouds were thickening and towering and the humidity ever rising. With a thunderstorm approaching and the sun just below the horizon, Frank realized just how much he missed the wonderful brightness of Brisbane daylight already.

"This morning, you said you'd hoped that you were going to Hawaii," Frank said.

Rebecca smiled. "That's right."

"But you landed in Perth."

Rebecca nodded. "I remember the first year as being tense and unhappy. My father was constantly looking over his shoulder. I wasn't allowed to engage too much with my surroundings, just go to school, then straight back home, lock the doors."

"Sounds horrible," Frank said.

Rebecca nodded. "Then, over time, my parents began loosening up a bit, and we all happily agreed that the program actually worked, which I suppose it may have up until the point a man showed up and gunned down my family."

"Where were you when it happened?"

"As you now know, I was thirteen at the time, and just like my dad, I was crazy about the outdoors. It was the first time I'd ever been given permission to camp in our backyard, and I was even allowed to use my dad's tent. I remember how proud I felt. I brought my teddy, my Harry Potter book and a flashlight. I was reading when I heard a loud bang."

"The first shot?" Frank said, then grabbed his mug of cappuccino, put it back as he realized it was empty.

Rebecca nodded again. "I switched off my flashlight, pushed my sleeping bag off, and ran up to the backyard door and looked through the glass. I saw ..." Rebecca began, then pinched the bridge of her nose with two fingers.

"Take your time," Frank said, the growling in his guts intensifying.

Rebecca sighed. "It still hurts so bloody much," she said, then looked up at Frank. "I saw my father on his back near the front door, and my little brother lying on top of him in a bloody mess. Then I heard my mother scream and run straight toward me, and I could see her eyes, and they told me to get the hell out of there. I turned, ran out the back gate and sprinted as fast as I could. I'd just made it past our neighbor's house when I heard another bang, and at that moment I knew my mom was gone as well, and that made me speed up even more. I ran and ran and ran until my lungs were on fire and my stomach cramps were so bad that my legs simply gave way, and I remember crashing through a bush and scraping my face to bits."

"I'm so sorry," Frank said.

Rebecca shrugged. "My world changed in a second. I was frozen with fear, so I just sat there in complete darkness, not sure for how long. After a while, the blackness of the bush turned into a silhouette," she said. "I remember clearly that the sun still hadn't reached the horizon, but there was a faint glow which outlined trees and bushes. Then the sky turned pink, and the light brightened, and I realized I was sitting on the edge of a huge building site. It was a Sunday, so it was dead. I looked around, then chose a nearby house where only the brick walls had been erected, and I ran in there, sat in a corner on the concrete foundation, looked up at the wooden timber frame of the roof, not knowing what to do.

"After what felt like a lifetime, a guy in work boots and a hardhat appeared. I clearly remember looking at his huge, scuffed boots full of caked dirt and gray cement bits. What happened after that, I don't remember exactly, but I remember he spoke gently to me, then drove me to the nearest police station." Sobs escaped Rebecca's throat. "Oh God, Frank. I have never spoken about this to anyone. It's strange, scary, and wonderfully freeing, all at the same time."

Frank smiled. "What did the police do?"

"Once they realized who I was, they took me into protective custody, and the next few months were a blur of officials, overnights in weird institutions, talks, interviews and assessments and then, for the second time in my life, I was entered into the National Witness Protection Program."

Frank nodded. "You're the only one I've ever heard of who's had to go through that twice."

"Apparently, I'm the only one in the history of the NWPP," she said. "At least that's what they told me back then. About two months later, I was put on another plane, this time heading for Brisbane."

Frank's belly roared. "But you were thirteen at the time, so where did they take you?"

Rebecca sighed. "A foster home."

"And is that where you spent the rest of your childhood?" Frank said, already knowing some of the answers.

Rebecca shook her head. "I bounced from home to home for four and a half years until I turned eighteen," she said. "I was a troubled kid, but I was saved. Do you believe in the power of the written word, Frank?"

"I do," Frank said, nodding. "Authors such as Michael Ende, Patricia Highsmith, Jeffery Deaver, Jo Nesbø, Stephen King, Lee Child—"

"No, Frank," she said, furrowing her perfect eyebrows. "I mean the Bible."

"Oh."

"My foster parents, when I was sixteen, they were very religious, and they taught me about the power of the written word. They showed me how to find strength through God, and I did. I really did."

"Hmmm."

"I moved out the day I turned eighteen, bunked with a friend and got a job."

Frank nodded. "And then you met Carl?"

"Then I met Carl, and suddenly I was loved, protected, and had money and a world of opportunities. So you see, the age difference meant nothing to me. It was just a number."

"I think I understand now," Frank said. "And I want to hear more about it, but first, may I use your bathroom?"

Rebecca smiled, waved an arm toward the house. "Just down the hall on your left," she said, then grabbed the champagne bottle and began refilling their glasses.

EIGHTY-TWO

A my screeched to a halt in front of the glass doors to the Brisbane Tower Hotel, and Joe was already at the reception desk flashing his credentials when Amy came running in.

"A young woman working for an escort company arrived here within the past hour," Joe said. "Her services were paid for by the Jacaranda Security Group, and we believe she may be in danger."

A young hotel receptionist in a dark suit and a silver nametag that said KAYLA made big eyes, then looked down at her computer and began typing. Amy drummed her fingers on the countertop. After a quick search, the woman pressed another few buttons, then turned around and grabbed a plastic card, fed it through a reader and held it out.

"Room 1410," she said. "It's one of the rooms they often use. Their guests never check in, but I did talk to a strapping girl in heels and a skirt that was short enough to qualify as a wide belt, and I told her which room to go to."

"When?" Amy said.

"Just ten minutes ago," Kayla said, then pointed to a bank of elevators. "Quickest way up is by using one of those elevators. Fourteenth floor."

Joe sprinted to an open elevator and pressed the button and Amy jumped in and the doors closed. The car began climbing rapidly. "Game plan?" Joe said.

"Armed suspect standard entry procedure," Amy said. "You cover."

"Got it," Joe said, then the elevator slowed and the door opened.

Amy scanned the signs across from the elevator, then turned right and ran down a carpeted hallway while drawing her Glock. Gentle music flowed through hidden loudspeakers, and discreet spots illuminated large paintings in wooden frames. She found the door, indicated for Joe to step across and cover the other side. Once in position, she inserted the card, retrieved it, and watched the tiny red light turn green just as the lock bleeped and clicked open.

Joe put his hand on the handle.

Amy nodded.

EIGHTY-THREE

"**P**olice! Don't move!" Amy screamed, her Glock pointed straight into the room as she moved in, passing a wardrobe on her left, while Joe cleared the bathroom on the right. Straight ahead, the small room opened up, revealing a standard hotel room layout: to the left a TV on the wall, desk and chair underneath; to the right a queen-size bed with two bedside tables. Amy kept her attention on the far side of the bed when she noticed movement from between the bed and the curtained window.

"Don't move," she repeated. Bulky arms slowly rose above a head with a gray crewcut and ears that looked too small for the skull.

With Joe right behind her, Amy walked closer to the bed until she noticed dark hair cascading out onto the carpet next to the man's knees. "Turn around slowly, then lie down on your stomach, hands behind your back."

The man did as instructed, and Amy held her gun pointed at him while Joe walked around and cuffed his hands behind his back. He then ordered him to cross his legs. Once he was immobilized, they holstered their weapons, and Amy kneeled next to a naked woman who was lying flat on her back. Her mouth was open in surprise, her lips tinged blue, and her bloodshot eyes stared vacantly up at the ceiling. Amy put a finger on the woman's neck, feeling for a pulse.

"How is she?" Joe said.

Amy stood up and shook her head in frustration. "Dead," she yelled, then turned to the man. "What's your name?"

"Lawyer," the man said.

Amy exploded. She pulled at his wrists and dragged him away from the woman and over to the desk at the end of the bed. She wrestled with the man and got him onto his knees, then she grabbed his left earlobe and yanked so hard that it split and began bleeding. She kept pulling upward, sure that it was going to detach.

"Amy!" Joe said, but she hardly registered it.

The man howled in agony and pushed himself up on his legs until he was standing upright. Amy let go, then kneed him in the balls with all her strength. The man moaned and fell back onto his knees, leaned forward and began retching.

Amy felt his pockets until she found a small flip wallet, rummaged through it and located a driver's license.

"Mr. Harrison Bussey, you're under arrest for the murder of Lin Bei. Have you got anything to say before we take you away?"

"Sure," Hank mumbled, struggling to breathe. Then he looked up at her, forced a smile, spoke two strained syllables between clenched teeth: "Fuck you!"

"Very original," Amy said, then took a step back. She pocketed the wallet, turned, swung on the ball of her left foot, and lifted her right and snap-kicked him on the side of his head as hard as she possibly could. Hank's cranium slapped sideways and bounced off his right shoulder. Something flew out of his mouth and clattered against the wall. His considerable bulk collapsed into a fetal position under the desk, his hands still cuffed behind his back.

Then Amy panicked. She'd never experienced the red mist of rage as she had just now. She fell to her knees and felt Hank's neck for a pulse. Blood was running out of his mouth. Two teeth were lying under the desk. She shifted the position of her fingers and counted. Thank God! His pulse was pounding, and he was breathing. She pushed his head back to keep his airways open, then turned to Joe, who was standing with his mouth open.

"Call it in, Joe. Now!"

EIGHTY-FOUR

U nder the guise of having to visit the bathroom, Frank silently
tiptoed into the kitchen.

The salmon fillet had been both delectable and delightful, the salad
a medley of leafy greens, the lemon mousse ambrosia. In other words,
Frank was starving.

He was fairly sure he wouldn't find any food in the fridge, yet he still
decided to take a peek. Two bottles of sparkling water on one door,
a carton of almond milk on the other. Vegetables in trays, a bowl of
apples, a lonely jar of mustard. On the top shelf, a half-empty bottle
of soy sauce lay on its side, a couple of drops staining the glass shelf.
Disaster.

He closed the fridge doors and opened the nearest overhead
cupboard, hoping to find at least a bag of nuts or dried fruit, or
anything edible which he could then take with him to the toilet and
eat before returning to the porch. Frank pushed a coffee tin aside, and
the tinny clang that sang through his hand told him the tin was empty;
only the coffee spoon was rattling around in there. He stopped, cursed
himself for not finding anything, then looked over his shoulder and
listened for Rebecca.

A flash lit up the kitchen, and Frank counted two seconds until the crack of thunder reverberated through the house. The storm was less than a half mile away.

He decided to give it a while longer and resumed his search. He spotted a bag of desiccated coconut, considered for a moment, but knew it would be a dry experience that wouldn't do much for his hunger, anyway.

Frank systematically went through other cupboards and drawers, finding china, crystal glasses, cutlery, cleaning equipment, folded tea towels, batteries; anything and everything but food. After a thorough search, he decided he had no choice but to go hungry and drink a few coffees in an attempt to suppress his raging hunger.

Only now he knew Rebecca was also out of coffee.

Frank sneaked up to the door and peeked into the wide hallway, confirming that Rebecca was still sitting out on the porch. Frank spotted the door to the bathroom farther down and across and considered whether to sneak or make a run for it; should Rebecca turn and see Frank, he wanted to make it look as though he was returning from the bathroom.

His stomach growled, but this was a different growl; familiar, but not entirely because of a lack of food.

Frank turned and scanned the kitchen one more time, once again spotted what he'd already seen, yet somehow subconsciously disregarded: the capsule coffee machine proudly placed on the marble countertop. A capsule dispenser rack towered next to it, filled to the brim with gleaming aluminum pods in various colors.

Something was missing.

Or, to be more Frank, something wasn't.

Frank's legs went heavy, his chest tightened. He shuffled back to the first cupboard he'd inspected, opened it and took down the coffee tin. His hands began shaking as he lifted the lid. Stared down. Put the lid back on. Removed it again. Stared down into the tin yet again, the butt of a large neoprene handle, the gleam of the hardened steel below, one edge smooth, the other serrated. The bottom of the tin held what looked like two tiny aluminum bottles: carbon dioxide cartridges.

"My father was an avid diver," Rebecca said from the doorway.

Frank turned, lifted his gaze from the tin. In her right hand, she was holding a Glock 22, pointed directly at Frank.

EIGHTY-FIVE

"**H**ave you completely lost it?" Joe said. He was pacing around the room.

Amy was sitting on the edge of the bed, her face buried in her hands. "He resisted arrest, attacked me, I defended myself, and together we overpowered him and got him cuffed."

"We—"

"Together, Joe! Is that clear? Be a fucking partner for once!"

Joe nodded. "Understood."

Amy stared ahead at the wall.

Joe kept pacing the room, rubbing his neck.

"Jesus!" Amy said. "I'm going to have to call Frank. I really need to talk to him."

Joe stopped pacing. "Frank? May I remind you that he no longer works here?"

"Give it a rest," Amy said, then plucked out her phone. Her left leg bounced up and down while she waited for Frank to pick up. She was about to hang up when he finally answered.

"Frank Hofmann."

"Frank, it's me, I've been thinking—"

"Thanks for calling."

"Frank, please just listen, I've—"

"I can't come to the phone right now—"

"What?"

"—but if you'd like to leave your name and number, I'll get back to you as soon as I can."

"Shit!"

"Oh, and don't forget to wait for the beep. Thanks."

Beeeep.

"Frank? It's me. Where are you? There was a woman at the party where Don was murdered, a seventh woman. An escort company—Dinner and More—sent out six girls on the night in question. Joe and I spoke to Brad Jenkins, the guy with the dog? He's sure there were seven women there, so I suspected William Forrester's alibi to be the seventh, but she's dead, and now I'm thinking about Carl, Rebecca's husband? He bought a bachelor's pad with William Forrester. Anyway, God, I'm rambling. Frank, I've got a bad—"

Beeeep.

Amy hung up.

"Shit," she said again, then walked over to the door. She checked the carpeted hallway for agents and listened for the ding of elevators, but apart from classical music, everything was empty and still. She checked her watch, put her hands on her hips and walked back into the room.

"Shit, shit, shit," she said, then looked at Joe.

"What is it?" he said.

"I have to go, Joe. I have to get to Frank, and you have to stay here, you understand?"

Joe's eyebrows shot up. "Why?"

330

"There's no time, Joe. Not now."

"But, what do I tell them when—"

"Joe, you bloody tell them what we just agreed on," Amy said, then ran to the door and turned around. "Stick to our deal, Joe. You got it?"

Amy thought she heard Joe mumble an 'aye' before she bolted down the hallway toward the elevators.

EIGHTY-SIX

"**W**hat gave me away?" Rebecca said.

"Many things," Frank said, his focus shifting from Rebecca's clear blue eyes down to her gun. Her finger was wrapped tightly around the trigger.

"This is all about seeds," Frank said, then half turned and put the coffee jar and lid on the countertop before turning back to face Rebecca.

"Seeds?"

Frank nodded. "First one was when you came to me, at Mugs & Marmalade. You told me you needed help because you thought you were being followed, and as part of your story, you said that you were having a mani-pedi at your local salon, and that you spotted a guy on a bench, pretending to read a newspaper."

Rebecca looked up at the ceiling, then back down at Frank. "Yeah. And?"

"And I said, 'pretending?'"

"Aha."

"And you replied, 'Come on Frank, who reads the newspaper these days?'"

Rebecca smiled. "Oh, yeah."

"And I told you that I do, and you said, 'Well, you're over forty, that's probably different.'"

"You have a great memory," Rebecca said. "But what's that got to do with seeds?"

"You implied that you yourself don't read the newspaper, yet you found me, and my PI ad was in the classifieds section of *The Brisbane Post.*"

Rebecca chuckled. "Plenty of people read newspapers online, Frank."

Frank nodded. "But *you* don't, because then you wouldn't have said, 'who reads the newspaper these days?'"

Rebecca waved the gun around, and Frank knew that time was short. But, like most other serial killers he'd encountered, he also knew that she enjoyed hearing how she'd been caught in the end. And right now, that was his only goal: to stall, to prolong his life.

"That's one seed, Frank. What else?"

"And every time we met, my belly growled," Frank said.

Rebecca lifted her free hand in front of her mouth, began laughing heartily. A flash lit up her moist eyes, and less than a second later, a loud snap and bang made the kitchen windows vibrate. "Your belly—" Her laugh turned hysterical, and tears once again ran down her cheeks, but this time, the drops were clear and left no trails of mascara. She gathered herself. "What are you, a cat? Do you also purr when you're in a good mood?"

Rumbles of leftover thunder ebbed into the distance.

"You always stabbed your victims from behind. Initially, it looked like professional hits, but then, with the most recent murder, it looked like someone wanted to send a message by adding messy theatrics. But, you see, big men with big muscles send messages. They cut out tongues or gouge out eyes or castrate in colorful ways. But women normally don't, because violence on that scale takes strength and dominance, something traditionally connected to gangs and their turf wars. So it occurred to me that the killer probably didn't want to send a message at all, but was simply getting bored. A serial killer evolving, someone who didn't have the big muscles, and who couldn't risk being overpowered in a potential struggle, hence the sneaky use of an injection knife. And all this made me think that the killer was a woman with her very own agenda."

"Frank, there must be over two million women in Queensland!"

Frank nodded. "But only one woman who reacted to a newspaper ad despite never reading the newspaper. And that same woman has a very strong motive, ample means and plenty of opportunity."

"Motive?"

Frank nodded. "A reason to be angry with the National Witness Protection Program, the most important seed of them all. The why."

The tip of Rebecca's right index finger turned white as she tightened the pressure on the trigger.

"What I don't understand is why seek me out?" Frank said. "Why play with fire?"

"Seeds, Frank. Stay on track. I'm intrigued."

Frank sighed. "Your husband had a health checkup three months before he died of a heart attack."

Rebecca tilted her head. "I don't think—"

"I know so," Frank said. "I can only assume that he wanted to stay fit and healthy to please his young wife, so he kept an eye on things, evidently, without telling you."

"Health checkup?"

Frank nodded. "Blood pressure, EKG, urine and blood tests for cholesterol, signs of diabetes, cancers, diseases. You get the picture."

Rebecca flinched. "You can't access a dead man's medical records."

"You can if it's a murder investigation," Frank said.

"Murder . . ." Rebecca began.

"You see, Carl's tests showed he was fit as a whistle. To add to that, there was no family history of heart issues of any kind. The chances of Carl having had a heart attack while sitting at home in his chair are next to none."

"You can't prove a thing!"

"Time will tell," Frank said, then looked at his watch. "Your husband will be lying on a metal table at Forensic Services right about now."

"What?"

"I had him exhumed."

Rebecca flinched. But then she stared at Frank, her face turning red. "He was buried five years ago. He'll be nothing but bones!"

"And if I've understood our scientists correctly, evidence of poisoning can be traced by drilling into said bones for up to twenty years after the fact."

The tip of Rebecca's nail pulsated pink as she squeezed the trigger even harder. "Your scientists? You no longer work for the AFP! What are you talking about?"

"I never told you I worked for the AFP. What are *you* talking about?"

Rebecca's big smile once again spread across her face. "Oh well, what's the use now? You're going to die anyway," she said. "You're right. I did it with a bit of natural heart-stopping poison mixed into his favorite drink, the good old Irish coffee."

Frank's bushy red eyebrows shot up. "Digitalis?"

"That's right, and do you know where you can get that?"

Frank shook his head.

"Where the beautiful Foxglove grows," she said, waving her gun in the direction of her back porch. "You know, those purple, bell-shaped flowers that grow in my backyard?"

Frank nodded.

"Are you done with your seeds, Frank?"

Frank shook his head. "Just this morning, I told you William Forrester had been arrested for murder."

"So?"

"You never asked who the victim was. Obviously, because you already knew."

Rebecca stayed silent.

"You killed Carl for money, and once he was out of the way, you had the means to do what you really wanted to do."

Frank thought he heard her giggle.

EIGHTY-SEVEN

R ain pounded down on what Frank imagined would have been highly expensive roof tiles. It sounded like a platoon of guys with hammers, all sitting up there, swinging their arms frantically. Water was streaming down the kitchen windows in a constant flow.

"Okay, Frank, it's time—"

"Like most other people, I think you started out as a normal, happy girl. Your first shock was when you were relocated from Darwin to Perth. It showed you that life was unfair, and that right didn't always equal happy."

Rebecca kept her gun trained on him.

"And then, when your parents and baby brother were gunned down, you took that as proof that law enforcement agencies couldn't be trusted to protect you, no matter what."

Rebecca cleared her throat.

"Then, paradoxically, you were put into the same witness protection program that failed to protect your family in the first place. So now, you felt at their mercy, and there was absolutely nothing you could do about it. And . . ." Frank began, then looked down at the floor.

"And?" Rebecca said.

Frank looked up. "I'm not entirely sure about the details, but I can gather that institutions and foster homes were a nightmare for you."

"Ah well," Rebecca said. "Let's just say I quickly learned about true vulnerability. Bouncing through institutions proved that no human being can be trusted. For anything. Ever."

Frank nodded.

Rebecca sighed. "While I lived with my last foster family, I was exposed to . . . shall we say, a strict, religious lifestyle that taught me two things: abuse is a privilege always found within the family, and God works in mysterious ways."

"I'm so sorry," Frank said. "But it makes sense. You were just a young girl who was taken advantage of. I imagine you must have been frightened, unloved and lonely. Carl was your ticket out of relative poverty, and once he'd fulfilled his purpose, you'd grown up. And I'm sure your thirst for revenge had grown with you, and now you had means, so you decided it was finally time to put your plan into action—to punish the system."

Rebecca slowly nodded.

"So, to prove that the National Witness Protection Program doesn't work, you set out to systematically kill everyone in it?"

"Very good, Frank," Rebecca said. "But not everyone. Only people who were in the program because they themselves had been criminals, and then turned on their own organizations in return for protection."

"But," Frank said, "what I don't understand is why not target law officials? People who actually run the program, or design it, or politicians who vote for it?"

"Because, Frank, if I were to target law officials, I would have been the victim of the biggest manhunt Australia has ever seen—one which I'm sure would have cut short my mission dramatically," she said. "By targeting low-lives who'd all been given a second chance they didn't deserve—a second chance that I never got—I could work in relative peace. Apart from you, no one's ever been close to figuring out what I'm doing."

"But, according to your theory, at least you would have been targeting the people at fault."

"No, Frank, don't you see? The only way the Australian Government will ever change the program is if they realize that it doesn't work."

"Something they probably know already," Frank said.

"Which is my point exactly," she said. "At least now, the AFP is looking into it, right?"

Frank shook his head. "I'm afraid not," he said. "I looked into it, but I got suspended for doing so because someone up high is making money on the very weaknesses that you've just pointed out."

Rebecca flinched.

"And you wouldn't have a clue who to target unless you get that information from somewhere within the AFP ranks," Frank said. "And by get, I mean buy. So, seeing how you've got the upper hand now anyway, why don't you answer that question?"

"What?" Rebecca said.

"Your opportunity," Frank said. "Who's selling you the information?"

EIGHTY-EIGHT

"I think we shall conclude this conversation, Mr. Hofmann."

Frank sighed. "I have to tell you, my colleagues know where I am. Before coming here tonight, I told them my suspicions—"

"Please, spare me. You thought you were coming here to get laid and enjoy a nice meal before heading back to your sorry excuse for an existence," Rebecca said, then chuckled. "You sounded somewhat desperate on the phone last night. Perhaps it's been a while?"

Frank shrugged. "Define a while."

"Ah, Frank, always the words with you. Your words, and your thoughts, and your seeds, and your enormous, rumbling belly. I'm afraid I'm tiring of it. You get the gist of what's going on here, and I'm happy, because it means that I'm making a difference. But now it's time for you to join the other idiots who never see it coming," Rebecca said, then moved the gun ever so slightly, pointed it at Frank's huge gut.

Frank held up his palms. "Please," he said. "Before you do anything stupid, think. Just think. You still have options."

Rebecca chuckled. "I ran out of options fourteen years ago, Frank—"

Knock, knock, knock.

Rebecca raised an index finger and held it vertically in front of her pursed lips.

Knock, knock, knock, knock.

"Police. Open the door!"

The statement was short and concise, the accent Australian. But the front door was thick and the wood dense, obscuring the voice enough to make it unrecognizable. Frank was relieved to hear they'd arrived. Amy must have figured it out and sent the cavalry.

Rebecca's eyes grew wide and without removing her gaze from Frank, still pointing her gun at him, she walked backward through the doorway, then disappeared from sight as she silently made her way up the hallway.

Frank was desperate. For a moment he considered making a run for it, heading back toward the porch, then racing through the backyard and jumping into the river, but he also knew that it was too late, that he would be too slow. There was only one thing he could do, and it was a shot in the dark, but it was all he had at his disposal. He stood still. Listened. The hallway brightened as street lighting spilled in through the front door, illuminating the walls, and then the shadows returned, and the door clicked shut again. It was unusually quiet; no conversation, no sounds of a struggle, definitely no gunshots.

"Frank!" Gregory said as he appeared in the doorway. Water was running from his wet hair down his face, the shoulders of his work jacket drenched. "So lovely to see you again," he said, just as Rebecca appeared next to him. Gregory turned his head and kissed her on the cheek. "I see you've met Rebecca. Or Hannah, depending on how you look at it."

"You—" Frank began.

"Don't look so surprised, Frank. You knew Rebecca would have to have someone on the inside. Personally, I wouldn't make a big deal out of it."

Frank's fury boiled hot, and he felt his cheeks flush, and his neck glow, and his ears tingle. "Where's Amy?"

Gregory smiled. "Oh, don't you worry, Frank. Amy's alright. For now, anyway. She's out chasing ghosts. We'll get to her later, but first, it's time for you to leave us," he said, then turned to Rebecca. "I'll go and put on some dry clothes. In the meantime, you do the honors?"

Rebecca nodded.

"Oh, and I got another one for you. Byron Bay this time, nice and close. Beautiful spot, too," Gregory said.

"How exciting!" Rebecca said. "I haven't been to New South Wales in a while, and what a perfect excuse for a road trip."

Gregory laughed, then turned and continued down the hallway in the direction of the stairs. "See you, Frank," he said, as his footsteps continued up the stairs, and Frank imagined him entering one of the bedrooms.

"Gregory move in as well?" Frank asked.

Rebecca shook her head. "He'll wear something of Carl's," she said, then smiled. "Head, heart or gut?"

In one explosive movement, Frank erupted. The fury of his wife's death, the anger of knowing that he'd inadvertently put Amy's life in danger by not reacting to the voices in his head sooner, his disappointment in himself as a fat human being; all of it culminated in an immediate, volcanic release of pent-up anger and regrets that materialized as brutal violence. He roared like a bear, and reached around his back with one arm, bent his legs, and pushed off and lunged himself straight at Rebecca. His free arm stretched out in front of him, reaching for her gun, fully aware that he'd never make it before crashing to the floor short of the target. His other arm swung around, controlling his hand that was wrapped tightly around the neoprene handle of the injection knife.

An excruciating pain radiated through his chest, and the world shifted when—mid-air—he was momentarily pushed back up before recommencing his fast descent. His brain somehow processed the falling, the pain of lead smashing into his body, as well as the muzzle flash, and then the polished floor came fast and Frank stuck out his left hand to break the fall, feeling his wrist crack and a tendon snap, yet gravity kept pulling at his large bulk and he managed to turn his head before hitting the floor, the impact cracking one of his molars. Then, and only then, did Frank's brain process the sound of the gunshot, and he heard it loud and clear, although he knew that it was already old news.

Frank closed his eyes and tried to breathe, but couldn't.

EIGHTY-NINE

F rank's lungs spasmed as he finally managed to suck in air and his nostrils burned because of the gunpowder. His brain kept replaying the sound of the gun going off. The pain was intensifying. He was lying on his belly, his left arm pinned underneath him, the fingers of his left hand pulsating with pain. Agonizing pain radiated from somewhere around his left shoulder, which was jolting through his chest like lightning strikes. Frank groaned and lifted his upper body slightly, and saw that he'd landed a foot short of Rebecca.

He looked at his own pained expression in the glossy reflection of Rebecca's black stilettos and saw her raise her gun once more. Rebecca cackled her evil laughter and fairytales of evil characters from Frank's childhood filled his head. He leaned over onto his left, grinding his teeth to suppress the agony, then crunched on something hard yet brittle. His mouth filled with blood. He managed to lift himself and turn just enough to swing his right arm with full force and bury the blade of the injection knife in Rebecca's left thigh. He felt it penetrate skin and flesh until the tip got wedged tightly inside bone. Rebecca squealed, and Frank craned his neck, looked up and found her eyes, then put his thumb on the button of the neoprene handle.

"Please—" she said, then Frank pushed the button and watched her black cocktail dress blast upward as her thigh exploded, and her smooth skin cracked in four places. A frozen bit of a fat, pink straw now dangled from a crimson hole: the femoral artery. Rebecca screamed and fell backward into the hallway, and Frank heard the gun clatter and slide just before the back of her head cracked onto the floorboards.

Frank struggled to his feet, and held his left shoulder with his right hand, staring at a pseudorealistic image of a beautiful woman lying on her back, her grotesquely deformed leg sticking out at an unnatural angle. The exposed part of her femoral artery began thawing before Frank's eyes, and the gray, frozen sheen was replaced by slowly dripping blood that turned to a quick drizzle, which gave way to a powerful spray before Frank could throw himself on his knees and, with his right hand, grab the artery and pinch it closed between his thumb and index finger. Rebecca was out, but her moving chest told him she was still alive.

Gregory came running down the stairs. He stopped three feet short of Rebecca, looking in astonishment and disgust at her body. Frank noticed the gun had landed on the opposite side of the hallway, against the wall. It was five feet away from Frank, on a sharp diagonal, and five feet from Gregory, on an opposite, equally sharp diagonal.

Gregory looked at the gun.

"You reach for that gun and I'll let go of Rebecca's artery," Frank said. "She'll bleed out in thirty seconds."

Gregory shrugged. "Well, look at her, Frank. Look at what you've done! I have no interest in keeping an ugly woman like that, so here's what happened," he said, then turned and casually strolled over toward the gun. "You came here to confront Rebecca. Things turned ugly and just as you stabbed her, she shot you," he said, then bent and picked up the weapon.

Gregory took a step forward, stopping just out of Frank's reach. He lifted the gun and pointed it at Frank's head from four feet away.

"You're too smart for your own good," Gregory said.

With Gregory's training and experience, there was no way he was going to miss from that distance. Besides, Frank was on his knees, his left arm had turned partially numb, and the fingers of his right hand were pinching Rebecca's femoral artery. He didn't stand a chance. It was game over.

"I know you're going to kill me, but please let Amy live. When I die, she won't know you're involved. Please," Frank said.

Gregory pinched his chin, lowered his gun. "You know," he said. "That's actually quite fair. I'll do that."

Blood was trickling out of Frank's shoulder wound, and he felt lightheaded. His mouth was dry, his jaw was hurting and an agonizing pain was radiating into his chest.

He'd failed miserably, the odds were stacked higher than Frank cared to think about.

"Promise?" he said. It came out almost as a whisper.

Gregory began laughing. "My dear Frank, what are you? A boy scout? Should I shake your hand? Do you want me to pinkie promise?"

"Just promise me. It's my dying wish, and you must respect that."

Gregory shook his head. "You're quite the character, Frank, very entertaining," he said, then lifted his gun again, pointed it at Frank's head. "Goodbye."

Frank began shaking. This was it. This was how it was going to end. He would finally be reunited with Caroline. He took a breath and closed his eyes and visualized her face just as the muzzle flash lit up the insides of his eyelids and a deafening blast tore through his eardrums.

NINETY

F rank saw his childhood friend and boss—Hans Richter.

Hans talked about motivation and fear and authenticity, why we do the things we do, what compels us. He talked about emotional triggers and real threats versus perceived threats, and Hans had noted one of Frank's weaknesses: that he was sensitive when it came to sounds, especially loud ones. At that moment, Hans gave Frank a piece of advice that he'd clung to ever since. It was something that completely turned his fear on its head and made him function again. Hans looked into Frank's eyes. "Remember, Frank," he said. "If you're afraid, you're alive."

The lightning was what had lit up the insides of Frank's eyelids, which meant that the deafening blast must have been thunder exploding through the house a fraction of a second later.

The windows rattled in their frames and Frank opened his eyes. The vibrations of the thunder, or perhaps it had been the surprise of the lightning strike, had moved Gregory's arm a few inches, and within another fraction of a second, Frank went through impossible calculations of risk, timing and chances. With time seemingly suspended, he felt warm all over as he remembered his talk with Amy about odds, as well as what Hans always said about distraction and theater.

"Low odds," Frank said, then let go of the artery, grabbed the knife and yanked it out.

While Gregory's gaze sought the pulsating jet of blood now cascading into the air from Rebecca's leg, Frank swung the knife around in his hand, holding the blade between thumb and forefinger.

Gregory blinked, then moved the gun back toward Frank. "What did you say—"

Frank pivoted on his left knee, threw the knife and watched it fly through the air, rotating once before burying itself in Gregory's stomach.

For the second time, he heard the gun clatter to the floor as Gregory sunk to his knees and then sat down, leaning up against the opposite wall, a look of disbelief on his face. Frank watched his expression change to regret, then calm. His eyes showed confusion, then anger, then turned unfocused and glassy. His head bopped forward, and his chin rested on his chest, his arms hanging down his sides until, at the very end, Gregory tilted sideways and lay completely still.

Frank felt his own panic spread as he once again pinched Rebecca's artery with one hand, all while stuffing his partially numb hand into her wound. The straining made Frank's own shoulder wound bleed profusely.

He rearranged his huge body and pulled Rebecca over, just a foot, just enough so that he could put his head up against the doorjamb to the kitchen and close his eyes. He kept pressure on the artery, wondering what the point of it all was. He cried out loud as he used his left hand to dig for his phone. Once it was out of his pocket, and he read the display through the well of tears, he sobbed, this time with relief.

Fourteen missed calls from Amy.

Then the screen disappeared in a watery haze, and blood dripped onto it, making it impossible for Frank to dial. He tried to wipe it on his trousers, but it just smeared and made it sticky.

Then the world tilted and blurred. The phone weighed a tonne, so he put it down. He knew he should stay awake, but his eyelids were too heavy. And he felt peaceful.

Frank was dying.

"Caroline," he said, then closed his eyes.

NINETY-ONE

The ABS reverberated through the cabin as Amy stood on the brakes through the downpour. Then the wheels blocked, and she skidded the last few yards before coming to a full stop.

She jumped out and left the car in the middle of the street. She sprinted over to the posh house, had a quick look at the security system, then climbed the wrought-iron fence, pulling herself up and over, landing in the middle of a rosebush. She was already soaked when she reached the front door, and she vaguely registered what felt like thorns in her legs and butt. She wiped water out of her eyes, then pulled her Glock 22 and used it to rap on the door. When no one answered, she stood back and shot two rounds into each of the two locks, then kicked at the heavy door and saw, to her relief, that it swung open.

She crouched and gasped as she took in the bizarre scene: to the left, sitting up against a door frame, Frank was sitting in a pool of blood, his hand between the legs of a woman in a black dress and heels, one of her legs bloated and completely deformed. Behind her, farther down the hall on the right, a figure had toppled over in another pool of blood, the bottom of his shoes facing Amy, a black handle protruding from his stomach.

Amy stood up, holding the weapon in both hands in front of her, peeking into the house. "Frank?" she said. Then louder: "Frank?"

She walked over, and with one hand, reached down and stuck two fingers under his jaw, felt for a pulse.

Nothing. No pulse.

"Amy?" Frank said, his eyes still closed.

"Frank, for God's sake! Is there anyone else in the house?"

Frank mumbled something.

"What? Frank?"

"Just Rebecca and Gregory."

"Okay," Amy said, then, "What? What do you mean, 'Gregory'?"

Frank's head moved ever so slightly and Amy was sure he'd nodded in the direction of the figure lying across the hallway.

She stood up, stepped over the woman and walked over. "Jesus Christ," she said, then holstered the gun and ran into the kitchen, finding a clean tea towel. She came back into the hallway, pressed the towel onto Frank's bullet wound, and took out her phone. She dialed a number that was answered immediately.

"I have three heavily wounded individuals," Amy said. "I need immediate assistance!"

NINETY-TWO

A my walked down a wide corridor with a gleaming linoleum floor and light ash walls. The air was stuffy and stale, and it smelled of disinfectant and disease. The cellophane crinkled as she clutched the bouquet of mixed red flowers. She looked left and right to spot room numbers until she realized Frank must be down the end on the left because Andrew Koh was sitting in a chair just outside the door.

She stopped and smiled.

"They put you on guard duty?"

Andrew shook his head. "I volunteered."

"They don't need you to help out in the dark world of cybercrime?"

"Well, okay, then. I insisted, and our new temporary commander obliged."

Amy smiled again, padded Andrew on the shoulder and entered the room.

Frank's bed was on the right. He had the room to himself, but his deep breathing seemed to have used up all the oxygen, so Amy walked over, parted the cream curtains and cracked a window. She listened to his snoring while looking out at a clear blue sky. Below that, the complicated, concrete jumble of the Inner City Bypass and the Airport Link, a mix of wide and narrow roads going up and over and under and around in smooth curves. In the distance, the large oval of the Mayne Rail Complex lay flat and barren, its dozens of tracks lined with rows and rows of dusty boxcars.

Amy found a vase, walked into the bathroom and filled it with water. She stuck in the flowers and placed them on the small table next to Frank. She reached out a hand and caressed his face, and his gentle snoring became one loud snort.

"Caroline?" Frank said, then opened his eyes.

Amy kept her hand on his face, felt the reassuring warmth of his cheek. "It's me," she said. "Amy."

"Amy," Frank said.

"Who's Caroline?"

"Someone I've never told you about," Frank said.

"Okay."

Frank cleared his throat. "But I will one day. Promise."

Amy nodded. "How are you feeling today?"

"Like I got hit by a truck."

Amy smiled. "You look better than last night. The swelling on your face has subsided a bit."

Frank grunted as he tried to sit up.

"Shh," Amy said. "Stay where you are. There's no rush."

"The pain is worse than ever," Frank said. "Did you get approval to interview Rebecca yet?"

Amy nodded. "Not only that, but the AFP has put me in charge of the case and the first thing I did this morning was to have you reinstated with immediate effect."

Frank's eyebrows shot up. "Thank you," he said. "How long have I got?"

"You're back to your original work-visa conditions, so another couple of months or so?"

"So, does that mean we can interview Rebecca today?"

"We can, but . . ."

"But what?" Frank said.

"Look, I don't want you to—"

"Just tell me," Frank said. "Please."

"Well, I don't want you to feel bad about it. You did what you had to do, you know?"

"What?" Frank said again.

Amy shrugged. "They had to amputate Rebecca's left leg, way up, so she's going to require treatment and rehabilitation for a long time."

"Oh," Frank said.

"Just thought I'd prepare you before we go in there."

"Any news with Gregory?"

Amy nodded. "Joe called me this morning from the hospital," she said. "He gave up just after six am."

"Gregory's dead?" Frank said.

"Yes," Amy said, "but don't worry. No one's pressing charges. In the eyes of the AFP, you're a hero."

Frank began nodding, then winced in pain. "I need to sit up, please. I can't believe how much it hurts."

Amy found a white remote hanging off the side of the bed, then pressed a button and Frank's backrest began moving. Amy kept her finger on the button until Frank was sitting upright. "You've been on mild painkillers since last night, that's probably why."

"Well, that's just crazy, and way too early," Frank said.

Amy shook her head. "I had no choice. If you want to interview Rebecca as an AFP agent, we need you clearheaded. Those are the conditions."

Frank began nodding again, but stopped just as quickly. "Thanks," he said, then took a sip of water from a plastic tumbler. His eyes went big as he noticed the flowers. "Are they from you?"

"You have any other girlfriends?"

Frank chuckled.

Amy thought she saw him blush.

"They're beautiful," he said, then put the tumbler down and sat back. "And how is Agent McShortbread?"

Amy laughed. "Joe's alright. I think he finally realized that values are more important than trying to impress."

"Authenticity may come back in fashion," Frank said. "You two still friends?"

Amy shook her head. "We never were, never will be."

"Good," Frank said, then grunted. "Let's pay Rebecca a visit."

"Sure," Amy said, looking Frank up and down. "Will you be wearing your hospital gown for the official police interview?"

Frank shrugged. "Does it go against regulations?"

"I don't think there's any mention of—"

"Then let's go."

NINETY-THREE

Frank's wheelchair glided down the hallway, with Amy walking right next to him. Although Frank couldn't see him, he knew that Andrew Koh was doing the pushing. Frank's right hand was on the armrest and his left in a sling.

"You seen her yet?" Frank asked.

"No," Amy said. "But the doctor in charge says she's made a remarkable recovery and is fully with it."

Frank's wheelchair stopped.

"It's here," Andrew said.

Amy opened a door, held it while Andrew pushed Frank inside.

The room was larger than Frank's, and Rebecca's bed was the only one in it. Rebecca was sitting up in bed sipping what looked like ice tea. She put the tumbler back on her nightstand when she saw them all enter.

Amy walked over on the opposite side, and Andrew positioned Frank's wheelchair at the end of the bed, facing the foot end that had a clipboard hanging from it. Frank flipped up his footplates, reached out and grabbed the bedframe, then pulled his large bulk while pushing with his legs until he was standing up. He could clearly see the shape of Rebecca's right leg under the white sheet, but the left side was as flat as a newly made bed.

Andrew walked over to the other side, stood across from Amy.

Rebecca's face was a faint shadow of how Frank remembered her. Her skin was pale and her eyes were gray and dull. It made Frank think of a fish that was no longer fresh. Her lips were narrow and dry and her recently colored hair looked dirt brown.

She looked at Frank. "Seed guy. How's your belly?"

Both Amy and Andrew turned their heads to look at Frank.

Frank looked back at the both of them. "I'll explain later," he said, then focused his attention on Rebecca. "You ready to talk?"

"What difference does it make?"

"The AFP has enough to put you away already. If you don't come clean and give us all the details, you're going to spend the rest of your life in a maximum security prison, spending all your time behind a metal door with a tiny window."

Rebecca looked at Amy and Andrew, then back at Frank. "And if I do?"

"If you do, I imagine there's a good chance we could get you into a nice psychiatric institution somewhere with a landscaped garden, Monopoly nights and all-you-can-drink apple juice."

"You don't have the power to do that," Rebecca said.

"Okay. Well, at least we tried," Frank said, then nodded to Andrew. "Let's go get something to eat."

Andrew turned to move.

"Wait!" Rebecca said.

"Our patience is up," Frank said. "My shoulder is killing me, and I've had it with you. Talk!"

Rebecca cleared her throat. "Okay, okay," she said, then took a deep breath. "I bought my information from Gregory Fordham, and he got it from a man named Walter Roscoe."

"The AFP commissioner," Frank said, then looked at Amy. "Makes sense."

Amy nodded.

Frank once again looked at Rebecca. "But why did they sell it to you?"

"I've been spending years trying to access information about new people joining the National Witness Protection Program. One day, finally, I met Gregory at a bar. We chatted, I seduced him, and Gregory become obsessed with me. He never cared about why I wanted the info, he just made sure I got it. I suppose the money and sex were enough for him."

"How did he get it from Walter Roscoe?"

"Why don't you ask him?"

"I will," Frank lied. "But for now, we'd like to start with your version."

Rebecca shrugged. "According to Gregory, Walter is a gambling addict, and he's been selling information of all sorts to the highest bidder for many years to finance his addiction."

"How does a thing like that even happen? I don't imagine Gregory going, 'Hey, can I buy you a drink? Also, would you like to buy a name of someone in witness protection?'"

Rebecca laughed. "Oh God, Frank. I purposely frequented bars where high-ranking police officials go, and it was me who asked Gregory if he had anything for sale. Believe me, I asked plenty of others before him."

"That's risky."

"Not when you offer a hundred thousand dollars. The ones who looked as though they were ready to arrest me, I just laughed at. Told them I was kidding, then showed them some cleavage. Men are so predictive."

"You paid Gregory a hundred thousand dollars for each name?"

Rebecca nodded again. "Gregory kept thirty, leaving seventy for Walter."

Frank's good arm was burning and beginning to cramp. His hand was sweating and he found it difficult to get a good grip on the slippery metal. "At least that explains Gregory's fancy shoes and exclusive watch, but Walter Roscoe? How can a police commissioner gamble that much without it becoming public knowledge?"

"Online?" Andrew said.

Frank looked at Andrew. "Walter Roscoe must be in his late fifties, early sixties."

"So?" Andrew said. "That doesn't mean he doesn't know how to use a computer."

"I just mean, a guy his age would want to smell the horses, feel the weight of actual dice as they leave his fingers and roll and bounce off of the back wall before settling back on the green felt," Frank said. "How can he do that as a public figure without the rest of Australia finding out?"

Andrew's brows shot up. "That's a good point, Frank. I sometimes forget there's an entire world outside of zeros and ones."

Rebecca took another sip of her drink and put it back. "Gregory told me Walter likes to go to Vegas."

"Of course," Frank said. "Las Vegas. How long have you been buying names of people entering the program? How far back does it all go?"

"I began shortly after my husband died."

"How many?"

Rebecca thought for a while. "Twelve."

"You've killed twelve people?"

"Well," Rebecca said. "Thirteen, if you include my husband."

"Jesus," Amy said.

Rebecca shrugged.

"Tell us how you murdered Donald Robinson," Frank said. "From the beginning. The planning. The execution."

Rebecca took a deep breath.

NINETY-FOUR

"The first time I met Carl, he was my customer."

Frank nodded. "In the upscale shop—"

"No," Rebecca said, shaking her head. "I had a gig on the side that I got through my roommate."

Frank wiped his sweaty hand on his gown, scratched his red goatee, then held onto the bed again. "Go on."

"I worked for a few months for a large brothel up in Chermside."

Amy's mouth opened. "Dinner and More?"

Rebecca turned her head, looked at Amy. "Yes," she said. "You used to work there, too?"

Frank sat down in his chair. It was high enough for him to still keep eye contact with Rebecca. "Stay on track. Keep the funny comments to a minimum."

"Fine," Rebecca said. "Yes. Dinner and More. I knew the madam there."

Amy cleared her throat. "Her name?"

"Julia Ambrose," Rebecca said. "It was like I finally had a mother again. She really got me. We stayed in touch even after I left to marry Carl. Anyway, the first night I spent with Carl, he took me to a small flat in the city. I became his regular. We fell in love, and soon after, as you already know, we got married."

"What has this got to do with the murder of Donald Robinson?" Frank asked.

"Well, after marrying Carl, I met his best friend, Bill—William Forrester. As it turned out, Carl and Bill had purchased the flat together, took their women there. Obviously Carl told Bill how we met. So, in a way, that's probably the reason why Bill thought he could treat me the way he did."

"Right," Amy said. "And on top of that, you were afraid Bill was going to tell other people that you used to work as a prostitute?"

"Bill promised to be quiet about it if I'd have sex with him a couple of times," Rebecca said, shrugging. "So I did. In the same flat."

Amy crossed her arms, looked at Rebecca. "So the pressure and the blackmail became too much, and you decided to frame Bill for the murder?"

"Yes, exactly," Rebecca said.

"That's bullshit!" Frank said.

Rebecca began fiddling with her cover, then shook her head. "Every time I was alone with Bill, he'd say he knew I killed Carl."

"Which you *did*," Amy said.

"Well, that's not the point. I don't see how he could know. There was no way. But every time he got drunk, he would call me and threaten me, telling me that he would find a way to prove I killed Carl. So—yes—I framed him. And it was easy."

"Easy?" Frank said.

Rebecca nodded. "I found another gullible guy to buy me two pairs of boots, of which I gave William a pair. You know, as a present."

"Name of Mr. Gullible?" Amy asked.

Rebecca looked at her. "Douglas Glenmore."

Amy nodded.

"And, as I predicted, Bill, the idiot, loved the attention and wore them constantly. So now, using my own pair, I could easily plant his prints at the scene."

Amy nodded. "Did you plant any other misleading evidence?"

Rebecca laughed. "I pulled hair out of his head the last time we had sex, dropped a few strands in the blood. It was a beautiful plan, don't you think?"

Frank was about to nod, then changed his mind. "How did you know that Bill wouldn't have an alibi for the night, thereby making the whole setup moot?"

"Obviously, I know the bachelor's pad, and I knew Bill still took girls there. I made an arrangement with Julia long time ago to call me and let me know every time a girl was booked for that address. Initially, I wanted to keep an eye on Carl, you see? But after he died, Julia kept informing me every time Bill went there."

"Why?" Amy said.

Rebecca shrugged. "Half of the flat was mine, so I liked knowing what was going on."

Frank stayed silent.

"Anyway, Julia called me on the evening of the sixth of February and confirmed a booking had been made for an hour. That meant Bill was out of the house, which meant I could take out Donald. I just had to make sure to not kill him during the hour Bill was with the girl."

"Thereby making sure that Donald was killed at a time when Bill didn't have an alibi?" Amy said.

Rebecca nodded.

"How did you gain access to Donald Robinson's flat?" Frank asked.

"That was the challenging part. I was just going to sit outside the building and wait until late into the night to break in, but when I arrived, I could see that the street was full of cars and there was loud music coming from the flat."

"Then what?" Frank said.

"I had to think on my feet. I called Julia from the car, asked her to send down six girls, which she did. An hour later, I intercepted them outside the block, paid them in cash and walked inside the flat together with them. To the other girls, I pretended to be a friend of one of the guests. To Donald and the gang, I was simply one of the escorts."

"You were the seventh woman," Amy said. "But, wouldn't you have to . . ."

Rebecca chuckled. "Nothing I haven't done before, and it was a small sacrifice, considering."

Frank made big eyes. "And how did you get to Donald?"

"When the other girls left, I sneaked into the kitchen and stepped into the broom closet and just stood there, waiting for the party to end and for Donald to fall asleep."

"Then what?"

"I was about to sneak out when I heard Donald talking to someone, so I stayed inside the closet until he came into the kitchen. He ended up right in front of me, his back to the closet. It was easy and quick. I think the guy he was talking to was in the bathroom throwing up when I left. In any case, I left him alone."

"How noble," Frank said. "Tell us about the murder weapon. You hinted at the fact that you got it from your dad?"

Rebecca nodded. "My dad did a lot of scuba diving in the Northern Territory. After the . . . a few weeks after my parents and little brother were killed, I was allowed back into our house and was told by the officers escorting me that I could choose three things to take with me, but . . ."

"But what?" Frank prompted.

"I couldn't stand being in the house for even a second, so I ran into our backyard where the tent was still standing. I looked inside and grabbed my Harry Potter book and my teddy. And then—for some reason—I walked into our garage and had a look around. And there, on one of his shelves, I saw my dad's knife. It reminded me so much of him, so I took it."

Amy shook her head. "And they didn't mind?"

Rebecca shrugged. "I hid it inside my teddy."

"But how did your father get a weapon like that into the country in the first place?" Amy asked.

"I think I can answer that," Frank said, then looked at Rebecca. "When your dad bought it, the weapon was still unknown in Australia, and so wasn't included in the NT Weapons Control Act until a few years after he'd purchased it."

"I believe that's right," Rebecca said, then laughed.

"What's so funny?" Frank said.

"He never used it. That knife has never killed a single animal, at least not of the marine species."

"Where did you get the carbon dioxide cartridges from?" Frank said.

"Sometimes my local home depot," Rebecca said, then smiled. "Or the supermarket. They're the same ones used in whipped cream dispensers."

Frank nodded. "Tell us how you felt so confident that you could frame William Forrester. I mean, for you to plant his hair, you must have had knowledge that his DNA was already in the database."

Rebecca took another sip of her tea.

NINETY-FIVE

"I knew Bill had a conviction on file," Rebecca said.

"Hmmm," Frank said. "The bar brawl?"

"Yes."

"I still don't get it," Frank said. "You've been flying under the radar for the past five years. Then you plan, at least in your opinion, another perfect murder, but before you execute it, you decide to make up a story about being followed and come to me with it? It makes no sense to approach me, to play with fire like that. Whose idea was that?"

"Like I said, I've been buying names from Gregory for a few years, and when you joined the AFP, Gregory said that you were beginning to join the dots between the very names that I'd purchased over the years. My kills!"

"I knew it," Frank said. "That's why Gregory had me suspended."

Rebecca shook her head. "Wrong," she said. "That was my idea, and Gregory played along. But that clearly wasn't enough to keep you away, was it? He told me you were still working the cases with Amy, so I told him I was going to play the vulnerable widow, to keep you busy with other things, and even more importantly, to get information, to keep track of you."

"Keep track of me?"

Rebecca nodded. "I wanted to keep tabs on how far you were in the investigation, you see?"

"But you *are* the murderer."

"Yes. And I was confident that you'd never find out. I was just going to derail your investigation, keep you busy with something else until you'd have to leave, but . . ."

"But?"

"Well, I clearly underestimated you," Rebecca said, then glared at Frank. "You were supposed to find William Forrester guilty, not me!"

"Jesus!" Amy said.

Frank shrugged, then cursed himself as another jolt of pain shot through his shoulder and neck. He took a moment to gather himself. "So JSG was never involved? No one followed you? They have nothing to do with the witness protection killings? Anything?"

"They were simply part of the setup to guide you toward Bill as he worked there. It was fun to watch JSG get scared to the point where they had him confess. It would have been absolutely perfect if it hadn't been for you and your fat, rumbling gut."

Amy leaned in. "Is it also fun for you to know that JSG had one of the women from Dinner and More killed?"

Rebecca opened her mouth slightly, then closed it again.

Frank sighed. Breathed in and out. Went through the last few days in his mind, then—ever so gently—nodded to himself. "I guess that's it," he said, then looked at Amy, who reached into her bag and took out a pad of paper and a pen. She handed both over to Rebecca.

Frank grabbed onto the bed, once again stood up and leaned in. "Write all the names of the people you've killed, including locations, dates and times, then sign it," he said.

Rebecca took the paper and pen and began writing.

Frank sat back down. "I'm hungry."

"You're not allowed to leave the hospital yet," Amy said.

"I'm sick of this room. I've heard enough. Think we could go down to the cafeteria?" Frank said. "My treat."

Amy chuckled. "This excursion also in your hospital gown?"

Frank looked down at himself, then winced in pain again. "Where are my clothes, anyway? My six-hundred-dollar suit!"

Amy smiled. "I binned it. It was yuck, plus your shirt and jacket had a bullet hole through them."

"Fucking deserved it, too," Rebecca said.

"Watch it!" Frank said.

Koh smiled at Amy. "I'll stay here and keep an eye on Rebecca. You two go downstairs."

"Thanks," Amy said, then walked around and grabbed the handles of Frank's wheelchair.

Ninety-Six

With his left arm in a sling, Frank used his right to fold a slice of peperoni pizza and steered half of it into his mouth. He watched strands of cheese stretch as he put the other half of the slice back on the plate, a frown growing on his forehead. "She lied to me. The whole way. From the moment she entered Mugs and Marmalade, everything that came out of her mouth was fiction."

Amy laughed. "That's cute, Frank. She lied to the whole world and killed thirteen people, and you're upset she lied to *you*?"

Frank gently shook his head. "I'm upset with myself that I bought it," he said, then put the other half in his mouth.

"Well," Amy said. "You didn't buy it all. I mean, you did get her, right?"

"I guess," Frank said, grabbing another slice. "Aren't you having any pizza?"

Amy shook her head. "On a more positive note, you saved the life of a young man in Byron Bay. There's plenty of evidence to suggest that he was next in line, and would probably have met his end very soon."

Frank touched his bandaged shoulder, nodded. "That's good to know. It's rare that we get to prevent; we usually show up after the fact, somewhere at the end," he said. "And speaking of the end, what am I supposed to do with myself for the next two months? The case is over. Shall I just make coffee and help you staple files while waiting for my return flight?"

"Well, I'm sure you still need to pack, get your car back, sell it, send some furniture and so on."

Frank shrugged, then winced in pain yet again. It was driving him insane. "I'd rather just leave a mess," he said. "Who's going to come after me in Germany?"

"Plus," Amy said, "there're also other things to consider, like invitations, flowers, candles, maybe place settings or flags or hotdogs and all the other things that come with a ceremony like that."

Frank gently rubbed his bandaged shoulder. "What ceremony?" he said.

Amy stood up, pushed her chair next to Frank's wheelchair and sat back down, taking his hand in hers. "Frank, this morning, the Minister of Home Affairs, together with the Australian Prime Minister, informed the AFP that they will grant you an honorary Australian citizenship. It's an open invitation, and you can have the ceremony as soon as you feel well enough."

"What?" Frank said. "I'm an Australian?"

Amy shook her head. "Not until you have the ceremony."

"But how?"

"I made it clear to them how you brought down a wanted serial killer all while unmasking dirty federal agents, that's how."

Tears began streaming down Frank's chubby cheeks, and he nodded enthusiastically before his brain reminded him of the bullet wound in his left shoulder, making him grunt in pain yet again. There were so many things he wanted to say, so many emotions welling up inside him. Frank felt that he'd just been handed a second chance at a fresh start, a new beginning, and he was ready to take the first step. Right there and then, he realized what he wanted to do.

Or, to be more Frank, what he needed to do.

Epilogue

F rank sat on a brand new office chair in the corner of the large
space, his legs spread, his huge gut dangling between his legs as he
leaned forward and opened his shopping bag, which was sitting on the
floor in front of him. He mumbled to himself every time he transferred
a Spoon 'N Pay bag from his shopping bag and dumped it into the
bottom drawer of his new desk.

"Cinnamon candied almonds," *plump*, "chocolate-covered raisins,"
plump, "honey roasted cashews," *plump*, "vanilla coated pecans,"
plump, "chocolate coated peanuts—"

"Move, will you?" Amy's voice came from under his desk.

Frank let go of the shopping bag and wheeled backwards. "That it?"

"It's all plugged now," Amy said, then crawled out and stood up.
"Fire it up."

Frank wheeled back to his desk and turned on the computer,
monitor and printer, and listened to it whir, waiting for it to come
to life while Amy lifted a substantial toolbox and walked over to
the entrance door. She placed the toolbox on the floor and began
rummaging around. She put a pencil behind her right ear, then took

out a hammer, a drill, a bracket with a shiny thing attached to it, a few
plugs, some screws and a screwdriver, rolled another office chair over,
placed everything on the chair and hopped up.

"What are you doing now?" Frank said.

"Putting up that shopkeeper's bell that you found in the kitchen?"

"Oh," Frank said. "When is the rest of the furniture arriving?"

Amy held up the bracket, grabbed the pencil from behind her ear
and began marking. "They wrote me they'll be here tomorrow in the
afternoon sometime."

"Hmmm."

Frank gazed around the room. The large, square office space had
once been divided in two: an insurance broker on one side; a podiatrist
on the other. Before the broker and the podiatrist, the whole place had
belonged to a hairdresser, which apparently had been the reason for
the installation of toilet and kitchenette out the back. After a decade
of haircutting, salon chairs, mirrors and sinks had all been ripped
out, and the whole place had been converted to office space, with a
thin wall erected to divide the square footage equally. Now that had
been removed, and a brand new, gray, low-pile carpet sat under cream
walls that extended up to a dropped ceiling with a mosaic of large,
yellowed panels, some with light fixtures, most without. The large
shop windows facing Vulture Street still had stickers with names of
the two previous businesses.

Behind the shopfront windows, the street disappeared as the view
was blocked by a bus stopping right outside. An elderly man boarded
the bus just as three youths hopped out the back. A moment later,
Frank heard a pneumatic hiss, watched the doors close, and then the

bus gently accelerated. Frank could once again see the Lebanese food place across the street. His belly growled.

"You hungry?" Frank said.

Amy stood on the office chair, her back to Frank, an electric drill in her hands. "No," she said, "and neither are you."

Frank grunted, then put a finger in each ear as Amy drilled.

When she was done, Amy put the drill back down, picked up a hammer and the plugs, then grunted.

"Are you making fun of me?" Frank said.

Amy laughed. "What do you think?"

"I think you are," Frank said.

Amy nodded, her back still to Frank. She hammered in a plug. "Why didn't you tell me when you first began suspecting Rebecca was involved in it all? Maybe I could have helped earlier."

Frank shrugged, well aware that Amy couldn't see it. "At first, I didn't want to believe it. Then things just suddenly happened very quickly. The night I went for dinner at her place, I decided I was going to tell you all about it the following day. I had no idea that I was going to find the knife that same night, or that they'd already planned to kill me."

"They, meaning Rebecca and Gregory?"

"Yeah. They were obviously scared that I was closing in too fast. But your question is fair, and I want you to know that I was going to tell you all about my suspicions the very next day. I just needed one last confirmation, but I guess I pushed it too far."

Amy nodded again, turned and looked at Frank. "You're not going to make that mistake again, are you?"

Frank shook his head. "Never again," he said. "From now on I'll involve you from my very first gut feeling, however faint."

Amy smiled, then turned back and hammered in another plug.

"Does it make you nervous that our newly founded PI business has high overheads and no clients?" Frank said.

Amy managed to shrug while screwing the bell in place. "We've only had the ads going for a few days."

Frank scratched his neck. "Are you sure we'll make enough money?"

"No," Amy said, turning another screw into the doorframe. "But Rebecca still owes you five grand, doesn't she?"

"Fat chance of ever seeing that," Frank said.

"And we can't even sue her."

"It's official," Frank said. "We're broke."

Amy looked at her handy-work, then hopped back down, walked over to Frank. "I'm just happy our investor isn't."

Frank nodded, looked at his watch. "Speaking of which," he said. "He should be here soon."

"Yeah."

"Sure you're not going to miss the AFP?"

"What's there to miss? Joe? Nah," Amy said.

"He's still happy in the AFP?"

Amy nodded. "I suppose."

"You said that Hank, Brian and Rebecca have all been locked up, and that the AFP is launching a major investigation into JSG and their activities. But what about Walter Roscoe?" Frank said.

"I know that his trial is imminent, and I have no doubt that he'll go down as well."

Neither of them spoke for a while, then Amy spoke again. "I believe in us, Frank."

Frank nodded, stood up and leaned up against his desk. For the first time since seeing the new place, he noticed a few buckets of paint stacked along the back wall. "What are you painting?" he said.

"I'm not."

"You're not?"

Amy shook her head. "You are."

Frank pointed at himself with his good arm. "Me? Are you sure you're willing to risk it? Don't you think we should hire someone to do that?"

"You're painting this place," Amy said.

Frank didn't have a comeback.

Amy nodded toward the kitchenette. "But first, let's have a break. Coffee?"

"You buy instant?" Frank said, then followed her out the back into a tiny hallway with two doors: an emergency exit door straight ahead and one on the left leading into the small kitchen.

Amy opened it and stood aside. Let Frank have a proper look.

Frank took one step, then did a double take. It was sitting in the middle of the narrow countertop, across from a small fridge that the podiatrist had left behind. The metal gleamed. The bean hopper was full. Below that, two group heads, a porta filter with baskets, a drip tray, buttons and dials symmetrically aligned in the space between the steam wand on the left and the hot water tap on the right. Amy had put the user manual next to the manual espresso machine.

Frank was speechless. His emotions swelled, and he could do nothing to hold them back. His dream was coming true, in more ways than one. Many more.

Amy smiled, then leaned in and gently kissed off a tear running down Frank's cheek. "You deserve it," she said. "And it wasn't that much. I got a good deal."

Frank nodded, struggled to keep the wobble out of his voice when he spoke. "Thank you," he said, then turned and put his good arm around Amy's waist. He'd never taken the time to study the shape of her eyes, the line of her nose, the curves of her lips. Her short, dark hair only just touched her slender neck, and her skin looked softer than Lubecker marzipan.

Frank took a deep breath, closed his eyes and leaned in just as the shopkeeper's bell tinkled. He pulled back and looked at Amy.

"Hello?" came a voice from the outer office. It was male. The accent Asian. "Hellooo?"

Frank recognized his voice: Andrew Koh, investor and third partner in Hofmann Investigations.

Frank held out his arm and smiled at Amy. "Shall we?"

Printed in Great Britain
by Amazon